SERIOUS CRIMES

Laurence Gough

VIKING

VIKING
Published by the Penguin Group
Penguin Books Canada Ltd, 2801 John Street, Markham, Ontario,
Canada L3R 1B4
Penguin Books Ltd, 27 Wrights Lane, London W8 5TZ, England
Viking Penguin, a division of Penguin Books USA Inc., 375 Hudson Street,
New York, New York 10014, USA
Penguin Books Australia Ltd, Ringwood, Victoria, Australia
Penguin Books (NZ) Ltd, 182–190 Wairau Road, Auckland 10,
New Zealand

Penguin Books Ltd, Registered Offices: Harmondsworth, Middlesex,
England

First published 1990

1 3 5 7 9 10 8 6 4 2

*Publisher's note: This book is a work of fiction. Names, characters,
places and incidents either are the product of the author's imagination or
are used fictitiously, and any resemblance to actual persons living or dead,
events, or locales is entirely coincidental.*

Printed in Great Britain by St Edmundsbury Press Ltd,
Bury St Edmunds, Suffolk

Canadian Cataloguing in Publication Data
Gough, Laurence.
Serious crimes
"A Willows and Parker mystery".
ISBN 0–670–83675–3
I. Title.
PS8563.08393S47 1990 C813'.54 C90–094619–9
PR9199.3.G68S47 1990

This one's for V and for B

An experiment was made
to freeze all things . . .
Leonid Martynov
Cold

I

There was a big round wooden door — a perfect circle the Chinese called a moon door — set in the wall about two feet above ground level. He got set and kicked hard. The heel of his cowboy boot slammed against the polished mahogany panels. The door buckled, but held. He braced himself and kicked again, aiming at the same spot. The screws holding the bolt shrieked and the door split down the middle, banged against the wall.

A bus sped past, lit up like a great big boat, tires whining on the frosty asphalt.

He knelt, got a grip under the corpse's arms, hauled the body over the threshold.

A taxi zipped by, as if in pursuit of the bus. He saw the roof light, thought for a panicked fraction of a second that it was the cops. It was cold, well below freezing, but the sweat was pouring off him, making his clothes cling to him like a shroud. He got the body all the way inside and let go. The close-cropped skull hit the paving stones with a meaty thud. He brought the two halves of the moon door together.

He was in an open space containing a pond and several rockeries. The outer wall loomed above him, pale gray in the darkness. There was a steep mound of rock to his left — a stylized, miniature mountain about twenty feet high. The stones were grotesque, twisted. It was mid-January but the sudden cold snap had caught the staff by surprise; the taps hadn't been turned off and a thin, silvery stream of moonlit water trickled down the slope, splashed gently on the smooth surface of the pond.

He pressed a button on his switchblade. With a jagged sawing motion, he slashed through the copper wire binding the corpse's wrists.

Except for the irregular splash of falling water, the gardens were very quiet.

He grabbed both hands and dragged the body along a tiled path towards the knee-high wall that surrounded the pond. The corpse was stiff, inflexible as a scarecrow, the limbs hard and unyielding. The man had died sitting upright in a wooden chair. His posture, in death as in life, was excellent.

He shifted his grip and pulled and pushed until he got the body half over the wall, then scooped it up in his arms, spun around three times as if he was about to throw a discus.

And let go.

The body hit the water and the surface exploded with a weird crackling sound, a burst of startlingly loud pops and explosions. An unseen bird sped screaming into the night. His heart seized up like somebody had grabbed it and squeezed hard.

He flicked a black plastic disposable lighter, leaned over the low wall and held the flame close to the water.

Ice.

The surface of the pond was covered with a thin layer of ice. He rapped the ice with the knuckles of his right hand. It felt solid as a rock. He straddled the low stone wall that surrounded the pond, stomped down hard. The ice, no more than an inch thick, shattered under the force of the blow. He leaned over, cupped his hands together and rinsed his face.

Tear-shaped beads of water hung like imperfect pearls in the jaundiced light of the moon. The ice glowed as if lit from below; a soft, radioactive luminescence. The silky black surface of the water rippled, and lay still.

Somewhere in the distance there was the faint shriek of burnt rubber. A horn blared.

Ride 'em, cowboy!

The corpse was motionless. It looked as if it was still wired to the chair.

He was suddenly very cold, shivering uncontrollably, his body trembling so hard that his vision was blurred. It was like somebody'd dropped a quarter in a special machine and the whole world was vibrating. Jesus, he'd planned everything so goddamned carefully, and just *look* what had happened.

He lit a cigarette. His hands were shaking so bad it was all he could do to bring the flame and tip of the cigarette together. He drew smoke deeply into his lungs. Be nice to snort a couple of thin white lines right about now. A little flake'd settle him right down.

Then he saw the coiled garden hose on the wall next to the outside tap, and a wonderful idea came to him, and he smiled, all his problems forgotten in the moment of inspiration.

He turned on the tap. There was a muted gurgling, and then the hose stiffened as it filled with water. The tap was insulated, or heat leaking from the building had kept it from freezing. He lifted the hose off the metal hook, shook loose the coils . . .

He walked until he found a coffee shop, sat down at the counter. The joint was empty except for a single waitress. She brought him a menu, loitered with pen and order pad in hand. She'd hennaed her hair to death and had a diamond chip earring in her left nostril. He could tell by the way she stood there, hip cocked and ready for action, that she thought she was cute as a button. She was wearing a white uniform kind of like a nurse's outfit, the name *Beverly* stitched above the breast in red thread. There was a small tattoo on the back of her right hand. A blue and red butterfly. Or maybe it was a moth. The tattoo, the earring. He rolled the menu into a tight cylinder and bounced it off the chrome top of a napkin dispenser. If she was into self-mutilation, maybe she'd think he was a drummer in a heavy metal band, it'd give her a buzz. He said, "It hurt when you sneeze?"

She gave him a look. He could see she didn't always get the picture, things often had to be explained to her, and she was used to it. He tapped his nose. The moth or whatever fluttered up to her nostril and then dropped away. She shook her head, gave him a warm smile. He knew what she was thinking. She was closing in on the end of her shift. From the look of her — kind of worn around the edges — he figured she'd been around long enough to know that when you were interested, the smart thing to do was show it.

"Know what you want, honey?"

He nodded, thinking, *not you, babe.* She was about a million years too old, for starters. And anyway, he had a meeting. He stuck the menu back in its slot behind the napkin dispenser and ordered a coffee and a slice of apple pie.

"Ice cream?"

He shook his head.

"You sure?" She hesitated. "It's on the house. My treat."

He watched her get up on her tippy-toes to fetch the pie out of the glass cabinet. Flashing her legs, which he had to admit weren't too bad at all even if she was a bit thick in the ankles. The hips moved as she sliced the pie. He said, "You mind working all alone, this time of night?"

"The boss had to go home early, kid's got the flu. Don't tell me you're gonna rob me, I couldn't stand it." She laid a napkin down on the counter in front of him, put a stainless steel fork and spoon on the napkin and poured his coffee into a thick white mug, put the coffee and pie down in front of him. He dug right in.

"How is it?"

He shrugged, poured some sugar into his coffee and stirred it in with the fork.

She said, "I got a boyfriend, but a couple weeks ago he rode his bike into the back of a truck at about eighty miles an hour. Broke both his stupid legs and he's gonna be in traction until sometime in July."

"Miss it?"

She gave him a sly smile. "What's that, honey?"

"A ride home."

"Bike's too cold, this time of year. I was thinking of ditching him anyway."

She had a nice voice, low and throaty. But probably it got that way from all the yelling she did at her dumb-ass pal in extended care. He finished off his pie, used the fork to scrap clean his plate. She offered him a refill but he turned her down.

He said, "What time you get off?"

"We close at midnight. Takes me about ten minutes to lock up."

If it'd been a good day, there might be two or three hundred bucks in the till. He wondered if she did a night deposit or just stuck the money in a brown paper bag and hid it somewhere clever.

It was twenty minutes to twelve by the big electric clock over the cash register. He said, "I got to meet a guy, but if you're interested, I can make it back by twelve thirty at the latest."

She hesitated, pretending to think it over. He saw that when she got thoughtful, she had a habit of licking her lips with the tip of her tongue. Was she trying to be sexy? After a moment she gave him another smile and said, "Yeah, okay. Sure. Why not?"

The pie was a dollar fifty, the coffee eighty cents. He stood up, got his wallet out of the back pocket of his tight black Levis, dropped three dollars on the counter. Leaning way over the counter, giving him a nice view down the front of her blouse if he wanted to take it, Beverly said, "It's on me. Who said there's no such thing as a free meal?"

"No, I couldn't do that."

"A slice of pie, who'll ever know?"

He said, "That's real nice of you," and shoved the money in the pocket of his black leather bomber jacket, crumpling the bills as if they meant nothing to him.

She walked him to the door. Jesus, what a lunatic. He opened the door and then turned and ran his hand down her back, feeling the hard bumpety bumpety of her spine under his fingers. She was shorter than she'd looked when she was standing behind the counter. Her eyes were pale green. He wondered how much the nose diamond was worth. He'd pulled a diamond ring off a woman's finger once. It was the first and absolutely the last time he'd ever mugged anybody. The ring had been on so tight he'd had to stick her finger in his mouth to lubricate it. She'd thought he was going to bite that digit right off, opened her mouth to scream and then dropped at his feet like she'd been shot. Fainted. He'd panicked, run like hell. Two blocks away, he crouched down behind a dumpster to catch his breath, and became aware of a sharp pain in the palm of his clenched right hand. He opened up and there it was, half a bluish-green carat sparkling in a pool of blood. He'd made such a tight fist that he'd cut himself.

Beverly gave him a peck on the cheek. "See you in about forty-five minutes."

He started off down the frosty sidewalk, the metal blakies on the heels of his boots scratching at the pavement.

When he'd walked into the restaurant, the first thing Beverly'd asked him was if he knew what he wanted. Yeah, sure.

Only problem was, he hadn't quite figured out how to get it.

2

It was Sunday morning, twenty minutes to ten. Willows collapsed the aluminum stepladder and put it away in the garage. He used a scrap of rag to clean and lightly oil the pruning shears and the curved blade of the saw. Rust never sleeps. He loosened the saw's wing nut, folded the blade into the wooden handle and tightened the nut.

There had been frost on the lawn, but it had melted under the faint heat of the morning sun. His black rubber boots were glossy from the wet.

He placed the tools in their proper places on the garage shelves and went back outside, into the yard.

On the far side of the yard, close up against the white picket fence, there was a small plum tree. The tree was about twenty feet high, and every summer the unpicked, overripe fruit had dropped from its spreading branches on to the neighbor's driveway. Williams had been meaning to cut the branches back for years.

Now, when it didn't matter any more, he'd finally gotten around to doing the job.

He padlocked the garage and walked across the wet grass to the base of the freshly pruned tree, pulled on his work gloves and began to arrange the cut branches in a neat pile, the butts to one end. When he'd finished piling the branches he bound them with twine and carried them out to the lane.

The lawn needed mowing, but only marginally. And in weather this cold, he'd do more harm than good. He decided to let it go.

He stepped back and looked up at the tree. Following the instructions in one of his departed wife's gardening books, he'd excised all the water sprouts and dead or broken branches, and then cut away most of the branches that were growing inwards. The tree was now about five feet shorter than it had been. Because he'd lopped off any and all growth that protruded over the fence, it had a slightly lopsided look.

Well, he was a cop, not a gardener.

He turned to look at the house, the home his parents had lived and died in. He'd hoped someday to bequeath the place to his children. Not any longer.

The house was two stories high, shingled, gray with white trim. He'd painted it himself, four years ago, and because he'd done a thorough job, the paint still looked fresh and new.

Willows climbed the steps to the back porch, kicked out of his boots and opened the door and went inside. It was twenty past ten by the electric clock over the sink.

He slipped on his shoes, tied the laces and went through the dining room and into the living room. In the front yard, where the bulk of the house kept the sun from the grass, the frost gleamed dully.

He stood by the window, lost in thought, until the real estate agent's white Mercedes pulled up. The agent, a woman named Celia Cambridge, waved at him before he could turn away. He kept his hands in his pockets. She got out of the car, juggled her keys and briefcase.

Five percent on the first hundred thousand, half that on the balance. She had suggested they list the house at three hundred and thirty thousand dollars, but advised him not to expect more than three-twenty. Willows had researched current prices in his neighborhood, but he was still shocked by the sum. Five years ago, the house had been worth a third as much. He'd worked it out on a pocket calculator, and the agent's commission at the present value would amount to ten thousand five hundred dollars. Her company would take maybe half of that, but even so, she clearly didn't have to move a hell of a lot of property to take home a bigger paycheck than a homicide cop.

Willows watched Celia Cambridge lock her car and start briskly across the boulevard towards the house. She was wearing a stylish black trenchcoat with padded shoulders, shiny black leather boots. Her hair was shoulder length, honey-colored with streaks of platinum. Willows was about ninety percent sure she wore tinted contacts and dyed her hair. Still, it was the effect that mattered. She started up the steps. He

15

went over to the front door and opened it, smiled and said hello.

She smiled brilliantly back at him, her teeth bright as track lighting, and said, "I'm a few minutes early, is that all right?"

"Fine, no problem."

She gave him another quick smile as she slipped past him, into the house. He remembered the perfume.

"Can I take your coat?"

"Yes, thank you." Under the coat she wore a plain white blouse and a solemn gray suit made of a thin, shiny material that Willows thought was probably silk.

He hung the black trenchcoat on a wooden hanger in the hall closet. There was a long blonde hair on the padded shoulder. He'd talked to several agents and he still didn't know why he'd chosen her; whether it was really because she was such a fireball, or because she was so goddamned attractive. It had been a little more than five months since Sheila had left him, taking his children, Annie and Sean, with her. He hadn't even begun to come to terms with his loss.

She said, "Shall we use the table in the dining room?"

Willows nodded. "Coffee?"

"A glass of water would be nice."

Willows led her into the dining room, pulled out a chair. She sat down, neatly tucking her skirt beneath her, and unsnapped her briefcase and pulled out the contract, six pages of documents on legal-size paper.

He went into the kitchen, ran the water until it was reasonably cold, and filled two glasses. When he came back, there were papers spread all over the table and she was nibbling at the end of a gold fountain pen, those green eyes frowning down at the close-spaced lines of type.

She glanced up, thanked him for the water and said, "The garden looks much better, now that you've cut back the tree. What was it, an apple?"

"Plum," said Willows. He was determined not to be charmed by her, angry at himself that he'd even noticed she was a woman.

She went over the terms of the contract with him, the amount and type of advertising they had agreed on, her percentage of the sale price, how soon the purchasers could take possession. A black and white photograph and brief description of the property would appear in the following Thursday's edition of the city's West Side real estate guide. She asked him about open houses.

"I hadn't thought about it."

"They're a nuisance, but necessary. I'm free a week Sunday, if that's all right. The afternoon would be best." She smiled. "Assuming we haven't made a sale by then, of course."

"Okay, let's make it Sunday afternoon."

She made a note in her calendar. "If I should get a hot prospect, how do you feel about me dropping by on the spur of the moment?"

"Yeah, sure. Fine." Willows, like all homicide detectives, was used to working long hours. He'd found that the best way to keep his mind off his domestic problems was to spend as much time as possible on the job. Lately, he was hardly home at all; the only rooms he used were the bedroom and kitchen. With only himself to clear up after, the house was easy to keep clean.

"Would you like me to phone you first?"

"You could try me here. If there's no answer, go ahead and show them around."

"You'd prefer I didn't call you at work?"

"If you can avoid it."

"Okay, that's about it." She handed him her fountain pen. It was heavy—a solid gold Sheaffer. Her hands were slim, the skin pale. A red fingernail traced across the bottom of the sales contract. "If you could just sign there . . . and there." A glossy strand of platinum-blonde hair fell across her cheek. Willows scrawled his signature. Why did he feel as if he was signing his life away?

Celia Cambridge capped her pen and put it away in her black leather briefcase. Willows stood up, stretched, and went over to the fireplace. Sheila's key was still where she'd left it, in an envelope on the mantel. He ripped the envelope in half, shook out the key and gave it to the agent.

"Thank you."

Willows helped her on with her coat. Her perfume smelled faintly of lilacs.

She paused at the door. "It isn't very professional of me to say this, but I know this can't be an easy time for you. If there's anything I can do, I hope you'll feel free to give me a call."

Willows opened the door. His breath plumed. A gust of wind chased a few dead leaves across the lawn.

"Anything at all," said the agent. She reached out and touched his arm, very lightly. "I've left one of my cards on the table. My home number's on the back."

Willows nodded, managed a smile.

Her heels clattered on the porch boards. He shut the door before she reached the bottom of the steps, worried that she might turn around, burden him with yet another dazzling smile. He leaned against the door until he heard the Mercedes start up and drive away, then walked down the hall to the kitchen. A bottle of Cutty Sark stood on the counter. He thought about having a drink, decided it was too early, and poured himself a cup of coffee.

The pot had been on the warming plate all morning long. The coffee was strong, bitter — exactly suited to his mood. He went back into the dining room and sat down at the table and stared out at the backyard. A woman in an ankle-length fur coat walked by with two samoyeds on a leash. Both dogs urinated on his pile of cuttings. The woman lit a cigarette, glanced up at the house. Willows stared at her until she looked away.

After a little while, the silence of the house began to feel claustrophobic. He became aware of the soft click of the furnace switching on, the whisper of warm air in the vents, the low hum of the refrigerator, even a tiny buzzing sound that emanated from a lightbulb that was about to go belly-up. He put his boots back on and went into the yard again.

Parker found him with a hammer in his hand and his mouth full of nails, mending a loose picket in the fence.

"Hello, Jack."

Willows drove home a nail.

"Nice job on the plum tree. Put the branches in the garage. Give them a chance to dry out. Great kindling."

Willows tilted his head, dropped the nails into his hand. "I keep my car in the garage. You want me to let my car get wet so some guy I don't even know can have a nice warm fire?"

"The real estate agent's already been here, has she?"

"How'd you know about that?"

"You told me she was coming."

"I did?" Willows frowned.

"Day before last. What're you asking?"

"Three thirty."

"A steal."

"You think so?"

"Just kidding, Jack."

Willows positioned another nail, drove it home with three quick strokes.

"Had lunch?"

"No."

"Hungry?"

"Not particularly." Willows stared at her for a moment. She was wearing faded jeans and white leather running shoes, a scuffed brown leather jacket he'd loaned her a month ago and that she obviously had no intention of returning. Her jet-black hair was pulled back in a kind of abbreviated ponytail. The crisp January air had brought color to her cheeks, a sparkle to her eyes. Not for the first time, he thought that she was far too good-looking to be a cop.

"All this fresh air, exercise. I figured you had to be hungry. What's in the cupboard, a tin of consommé soup and maybe a couple of old bones? I stopped by at a deli on the way over, bought a loaf of rye bread, some black forest ham. And I dropped in at your neighborhood 7-Eleven, picked up one of those fire logs, guaranteed to burn for three hours minimum, all the colors of the rainbow."

"Sounds enchanting. Who's gonna light it, Judy Garland?"

Parker smiled. "Finish your chores, Jack. I'll get busy in the kitchen. Just don't tell any of my feminist friends about it, that's all."

They ate on the floor in the living room, in front of the silent, nearly smokeless fire. Orange and blue flames licked at the blackened bricks. Parker had brought along a bottle of Napa Valley burgundy. Willows drained his glass and picked up a crumb off the rug. When he and Sheila had moved in, the hardwood floors had been hidden beneath beige wall-to-wall carpet. They'd left the carpet in place until the children had mastered their fine motor skills, and spilt milk was no longer a regular occurrence. Then Willows had rented a huge ungainly machine and sanded and varnished the floors, and they'd spent more money than they could afford on area carpets.

He ran his fingers lightly across the polished wood. He'd done a thorough job, three layers of varathane, the first two with a matt and the third with a glossy finish. The floor had worn well.

Outlasted the marriage.

"I wonder what kind of chemicals they use to make the flames go all those colors," said Parker.

"Carcinogenic, probably."

"More wine?"

Willows held out his glass.

"What's the magic word?"

"Gimme."

Parker poured half of what was left into his glass, helped herself to the rest of the bottle. She said, "I hear Eddy and Judith are finally going to tie the knot."

"I'll believe it when I see him wearing the ring," said Willows.

Eddy Orwell was a homicide detective. He'd had a rocky, long-term romance with a woman named Judith Lundstrom. He'd met Judith after her boyfriend had been run over by a squad car in hot pursuit of a sniper who'd shot several citizens to death. The murder investigation had terminated with the death of one of Willows' friends, a cop named George Franklin. Willows drank the Napa Valley dry.

"How'd it go with the real estate agent?"

"She seems to know what she's doing."

"I figured as much, the car she drives."

"Been snooping, have we?"

"I drove past about eleven. Couldn't help seeing the Mercedes. What's she look like?"

"The fold-out pages of *Playboy*. But sexier."

"That's a great description, Jack. You oughta be a cop."

"Sometimes I wonder."

"Or a lecher."

Willows moved a little further away from the fire. Too much heat.

"What're you going to do when she sells the house?"

"Move out."

"Sure, but where?"

"I don't know. With my half of the money, I could buy a condo in False Creek."

"Very trendy."

"Or try for a mortgage, buy a house on the East Side. Something with a couple of extra bedrooms, in case the kids drop by."

"In the summer, is that what you're thinking?"

"Yeah, I guess so. They get a week off at Easter. Maybe they could fly out then."

Parker reached out and squeezed Willows' hand. He didn't respond.

Next time, she'd bring at least two bottles of wine. And a *box* of firelogs. And maybe she should dye her hair blonde, too, while she was at it.

"What's so goddamn funny?" said Willows.

"Me," said Parker.

3

A cab rounded the corner at the far end of the block, accelerated up the street. Billy straight-armed Garret off the sidewalk and into the gutter. Garret windmilled his arms to keep his balance. The cabby jumped on the brakes, swerved towards them, took a quick look and hit the gas.

"What the fuck's wrong with *him*?" complained Garret.

"Figured we were muggers."

"Asshole."

"Yeah, but he could've been right."

"These boots are killing me."

"Everybody loves a whiner."

They'd met at midnight, both of them on time for once, a couple of blocks from the spoon with the lonely waitress. There was supposed to be a party, but neither one of them was too sure exactly where it was. They'd chased some music down a couple of streets, slipped into a Japantown warehouse converted into expensive condos and crashed a cocktail party full of weird people; fat guys with beards, anorexic women dressed all in black. A guy with no chin wanted to know was he a model? Billy asked him if there was some place they could talk quietly. The guy led him into a bedroom. Billy kicked him in his beachball belly, the stainless-steel capped toe of his cowboy boot sinking deep. He said, "How's that for model behaviour, limp-wrist?" On their way out, Garret grabbed a full bottle of Johnny Walker red from the bar. Nobody seemed to notice anything, or maybe they were into more sophisticated drugs and just didn't care.

Back on the street, they wandered around drinking the Scotch until they found a controlled intersection that was busy, but not too busy. They kept out of the wind in the doorway of a building on the corner, passed the time smoking Billy's menthol cigarettes and watching the traffic, nipping at the bottle. The lights blinked red and green and yellow and red. Pretty soon a third of the bottle was gone. Billy was seventeen and Garret a year older. They knew their beer but neither of them'd had a great deal of experience with hard liquor. The lights went red and green and yellow again, the colors blurred, bleeding into the night.

Garret said, "I think I'm pissed."

"Ghost parties," said Billy. "I hate 'em."

On the eleventh red, a cream-colored station wagon with an old man behind the wheel screeched to a stop half into the crosswalk.

"Okay," said Billy.

They bolted from the doorway, boots thudding on the concrete and then the shiny black asphalt. Garret yanked at the passenger side door. It was locked. The old man turned towards them, his face blank. Garret switched to the rear door. Locked. Billy ran around behind the car, reached for the driver's doorhandle.

The old guy finally woke up. He gunned it and the wagon shot across the intersection, leaving them standing there in a cloud of exhaust fumes.

"Asshole!" shouted Garret.

Billy sucked his thumb as he trotted back to the shelter of the doorway, shoulders hunched against the cold. He'd torn the nail. Got off easy. Another split second, he'd of had a better grip on the doorhandle and maybe broken his wrist.

Ten minutes later, while Billy and Garret were busy arguing about whether the old guy might call the cops and was it a good idea to go lurk somewhere else, a black BMW ragtop the size of a stealth bomber glided up to the red. Music in there. Loud. Some kind of jazzy sound.

The driver was a woman.

"If it's locked," said Billy, "use your boots. Kick the fuckin' door right off."

"Bet your ass," agreed Garret. The whisky had warmed him but now it was letting him down. He was so cold he'd gladly have taken cover in a refrigerator. He felt as if the marrow had been sucked from his bones and the icy wind was whistling through the holes. They scurried across the intersection. Garret yanked on the door. It swung open so easily he almost fell on his ass. Billy slid across the bench seat. Garret bundled in next to him, slammed the door. He reached across and turned the heater up full blast. The woman shouted something at them. Billy couldn't understand a word she said. He ignored her, studied the dashboard, all those lights and knobs and dials. It was a compact disc player making all the noise. He turned it off. Now the bitch was *really* wailing.

"Get out of my car! What the hell d'you want? Get out of my car!"

Billy showed her his knife. She stopped yelling. He said, "That's better. Do I *look* deaf? Times like this, I sometimes wish I was, tell you the truth."

"Gimme a drink," said Garret.

Billy handed him the bottle. The light turned green. Garret, the wimp, fastened his safety belt. Billy said, "Drive, lady."

The BMW crawled through the intersection.

"Faster," said Billy.

The woman's purse was on the seat between them. Soft black leather. He grabbed it. The clasp looked a bit tricky. Rather than risk making a fool of himself trying to figure it out, he slit it open with his knife.

"She rich?" said Garret from behind the bottle.

The purse held eighteen dollars in crumpled bills, a couple pounds of dimes and quarters.

Billy said, "How come you carry so much change, honey?"

"What?" Hardly a whisper. Garret grinned into the bottle. He'd bragged once he could smell fear on a woman the way a dog can smell piss on a fire hydrant.

"I said, how come you got so much change? Wired on the video games?"

"Parking meters."

Billy shifted in his seat so they were hip to hip. He leaned over and smelled her perfume. "Turn right at the corner." He stuffed the money in the pocket of his leather jacket, jabbed at the dashboard with the point of his knife.

She had all the credit cards in the world — VISA, Mastercard, a platinum American Express. Three different gas stations, all the major department stores. Holt Renfrew. Abercrombie & Fitch. Plastic in every color you could think of. Places and names that meant nothing to him, he'd never even heard of. No wonder she didn't have any fucking cash, she had enough cards on her to make a full deck.

Billy hunted around in the purse until he found her checkbook. The checks had a picture of the city skyline on them, and they were personalized. Her name was Nancy Crown. She lived at 3682 Point Grey Road, wherever the hell that was. Somewhere in the city. Her phone number was 734-8217. Billy ripped off a check and stuck it in his shirt pocket. He was no paper-hanger, but you never knew. A better idea, maybe he'd give her a call some time and if she wasn't home, get a truck and steal every goddamn thing she owned.

He studied her driver's licence. The light was bad and the print was small. Good picture. Better than his, which made him look like he was about ten years old. He handed the licence to Garret, who rolled down his window and threw it away without a glance.

Following Billy's directions, Nancy Crown drove down one of the winding roads that serviced the big dome that had been built to house a major league baseball team that never arrived, then over the Cambie Street bridge and up Cambie past City Hall to Twelfth Avenue, east on Twelfth to Kingsway. Billy openly admired her legs in the lights of the dashboard. He rested his arm on the back of the soft leather seat, his fingers barely touching her long blonde hair. She was tense, sitting bolt upright, her jaw tight, eyes staring straight ahead. But she was a pretty good driver, he had to give her that. Kept to the speed limit, stayed in her lane.

At Kingsway, Billy told her to make a right. The street was wide, a main artery feeding commuter traffic into the city; three lanes going each way, separated by a low concrete divider. Not too many parks, in this part of the city. There were lots of dingy shops, though, and used car lots, burger joints. No surprises for Billy and Garret — they'd travelled this route a thousand times before.

Billy pointed at the white and blue neon of a BC Tel booth at the far corner of the next block. "Pull over by the phone."

"Why, what do you want?"

"Pull over, Nancy."

The car rolled to a stop. Garret got out of the car and went over to the phone. He knew how Billy's mind worked. If there was a pay phone right where they were, there wouldn't be another one for miles. Billy used the BMW's dashboard lighter to fire up a cigarette, offered the pack to Nancy. "Smoke?"

"No, thank you."

"Hey," said Billy, "you're welcome."

The neon washed all the color out of Garret's face, cast his eyes in dark shadow. He stuck his finger in the coin return slot, poking around for a stray quarter. Nancy Crown gave Billy a sideways glance, caught his eye and quickly looked away. He felt himself flush with embarrassment. Garret yanked at the receiver, grabbed it with both hands and ripped it right out of the box.

Billy said, "A bad thing has happened to you, but it's your lucky night, Nance."

She stared at him, her eyes dark. He ran his fingers through her hair, stroked the back of her long slim neck.

Billy said, "Know why?" His voice was soft. Nancy Crown watched the point of his switchblade punch raggedy little holes in the black leather dashboard. Tyler was going to have a fit.

She took a deep breath, and said, "Why?"

"Because you got to meet me, of course. For probably the first time in years something *interesting* happened to you." Billy grinned. "Now will you *please* get the fuck outta my new car."

Nancy Crown's eyes were wide with shock. Billy gave her a push, shoved her away from him. She fumbled with the door handle. He reached across and gave her a hand. Chivalry. But she didn't bother saying thank you this time, had forgotten all about being polite. He watched her run down the sidewalk, not looking back, those long, slim legs jackrabbiting her along. Garret climbed back into the car. He slammed shut the door and Billy burned rubber away from the curb. Nancy had already made half a block when they shot past. She heard the car coming but didn't look back. Billy leaned on the horn and flashed his lights. They drove a few more blocks down Kingsway and turned right on Miller.

"Miller time!" shouted Garret, and thumped his heels on the dashboard.

Billy ignored him. He was already thinking that he was a fool, that he should've kept her for awhile, made her do things to him. The fact was, she was probably in her late twenties. He could've shut his eyes, pretended she was Kim Bassinger or maybe Farah Fawcett.

"How much you get?" said Garret.

"Just enough to cover all my cigarettes you smoked, dummy."

"You got a fuckin' fistful of charge cards. Gimme the VISA and keep the rest."

"Eaton's. You can have the Eaton's. Buy yourself a Polaroid camera and take dirty pictures of your mother."

Garret stared out the window, his jaw working. "One of these days, Billy, you're gonna go too far."

"Fuck you, Garret."

They glared at each other for a long moment, and then Garret turned away. Billy thought he was such a tough dude. Well, fine. Let him keep on believing it.

Garret said, "What're we gonna do now, call it a night?"

"Wanna steal some radios?"

"Not really."

"Me neither." Billy lit a cigarette. "What kinda radio we got in our new car?"

"I dunno, can't see a brand name."

"Turn it on. Punch some buttons."

The Stones. Some violin shit. Billy Joel. That weird black kid carved himself up or whatever. Slept in bed with a human skeleton, he'd heard. Barbara fucking Streisand. Yuck. Paul McCartney sounding like he was about a thousand years old.

"Rip it out," said Billy.

"Now, while we're drivin'? Shit, I could get myself electrocuted!"

"The way we're headed, it's probably gonna happen sooner or later anyway."

"What're you talking about, man?"

"Kidnapping. Unlawful confinement. Grand theft auto or whatever they call it. You rip off some dude's Chevy, nobody gives a shit. But hey, try stealing some bitch's BMW, that's another thing. *Especially* if she's in it at the time." Billy punched Garret on the shoulder. "They get us now, it's the chair for sure."

Garret thought it over for a while, frowning, and then said, "This is Canada, man. You could slaughter a whole fuckin' kindergarten, all they can give you is life."

"Bust that radio out of there," said Billy. "Be a good boy and do what you're told."

Garret didn't usually carry a knife but he always had a big screwdriver on him. The way he figured it, if the cops ever busted them, they'd pat Billy down, find his blade and charge him with carrying a concealed weapon. Then frisk Garret, find the screwdriver and figure he was an electrician or something, let him go. He chopped at the console, slashing at the leather, trying to gouge the radio free. Whack whack whack. McCartney made a sound like he'd swallowed a five-cell flashlight. Bits of leather and chunks of high-impact plastic sprayed across the seat. Whack whack. Garret grabbed and twisted, using his arms and the strength in his wrists. The radio came free, trailing half a dozen red and blue umbilical cords. Garret tossed it in the backseat. "Do I fuckin' pass, teach?"

"Wanna rob a store?"

"What's open, this time of night?"

"There's a Mac's about a half a mile away."

Garret shook his head. "I'm tired, let's go home."

"Chickenshit."

"It's been a long night, Billy." Garret slumped back in his seat. Just to keep his hands busy, he popped open the glove compartment. Porsche sunglasses, registration papers. A baggie containing about a quarter of an ounce of marijuana and some loose cigarette papers.

"Hey, look what I found."

"Roll it up. Whatsa matter, you stupid?"

Garret rolled a joint, fired up and sucked smoke deep into his lungs.

Billy said, "Hey, what about me?"

Garret tried to pass Billy the joint. Billy knocked it away.

"Roll me one of my own," he said.

"Sure," said Garret. Billy had a real strong thing about sharing. He just hated it.

Billy dropped Garret off at his front door, burnt rubber all the way down the street. He parked Nancy Crown's black BMW in an alley six long blocks from his mother's house, grabbed the radio out of the backseat, got out of the car and started to walk away. The sky was clear. There was a skinny fingernail moon down low on the horizon. Billy swore, tossed the radio in somebody's backyard and climbed back into the car.

He found Nancy Crown two blocks from where he'd left her, walking rapidly down the sidewalk in her long black dress and high heels. He pulled the BMW up against the curb and stepped out on the sidewalk. She stared at him, her face pale. Billy stared back. She was taller than he'd thought, nice figure. Cold, shivering. He handed her the keys. She didn't thank him. Well, what the hell did he expect. He said, "Nice meeting you, Nancy," and turned and walked away.

Twenty minutes later, Billy slipped his key into the lock and opened the door and was safe at home. All the lights were on, but the house was empty. His father had died when he was eleven. Cancer. His mother was out, as usual, probably playing bingo and having a high old time. Billy had a six-pack of beer he'd bought from a drunk at twice the legal price. He'd meant to stick a few cans in the fridge, but had forgotten. If there was one thing he hated more than no beer, it was warm beer. There was no ice in the freezer. As usual, his mother had used it all and not bothered to refill the tray.

He went into the living room and flopped down on a threadbare sofa stained by a thousand spilled drinks and scarred by a hundred forgotten cigarettes. He picked up the phone and dialled Garret's number. Garret's old man was a lush, never heard the phone ring and even if he did wouldn't bother to answer it. His mother worked nights, so she was no problem.

Garret picked up. Billy said, "Hey, you gonna be okay?"

"About what?"

"That little ride we took tonight. Think, Garret. Use your fuckin' brain."

"Yeah, sure. I'm fine."

"You got a problem, gimme a call."

"I will, Billy."

"Don't talk about it to nobody else."

"I won't."

"You sure as shit better not. Understand what I'm sayin'? Keep your mouth shut."

"Sure, Billy."

"I'm ruthless."

"I know it."

"And I want those sunglasses, you fuckin' thief!"

"No way," said Garret.

"I'm gonna wait until you fall asleep and then come get 'em," said Billy. "Sweet dreams, sucker." He slammed down the phone, went over to the big Sony television and turned it on. The screen flickered. He cranked up the sound and went back to the sofa, shoved an overflowing ashtray out of the way with the toe of his boot and put his feet up on the coffee table, making himself comfortable. He'd picked up the TV the same way he got most of his stuff. Find an upscale neighborhood, cruise the lanes and alleys on garbage collection day. People bought a new TV or stereo or whatever, they almost always tossed the cardboard box it came in. When Billy saw a box waiting to be picked up, he'd slow down, take a look. If it was electronics, he'd case the house. Most of the time, in an expensive area, both the husband and wife worked. He'd park in the alley, in the carport or garage if there was one, then go around to the front door and knock real loud. If nobody answered and everything else looked good, he'd do a break and enter. Snatch whatever he was after and anything else that caught his eye. He always took the box, too, because it added to the resale value.

He flicked his cigarette at the ashtray and turned his attention to the Sony. It was that gap-toothed guy from New York, didn't like animals. Letterman. Billy cranked the sound up a notch. He lit a cigarette, then turned the disposable lighter up as high as it would go, so it was like a miniature blowtorch, and ran the flame back and forth across his forearm, burning away the hair.

The talk-show host was reading postcards from his fans, making wise-ass remarks and tossing the postcards through the phoney window behind him, the pre-recorded tape of breaking glass playing over and over. Real fuckin' witty. Billy blew a smoke ring at the TV screen. The band blew a few notes. Two short guys in three-piece suits came out from behind the curtain, one of them leading the other by the arm. The guy who was being led kind of shuffled his feet. He stared straight ahead, and when his buddy let go of his arm, he stopped dead in his tracks with his arm suspended in mid-air, didn't move an inch.

The short guy Letterman was talking to took something out of his pocket. A black plastic box with some knobs on it, and a chrome rod sticking up. He grabbed the rod and pulled, extending it. An antenna. Billy finally got it. The guy had a remote control device. He stepped back from his buddy and twisted a knob. The guy stepped briskly forward. Another twist and he turned sharply left. Gave the camera the finger. Letterman said, "Is that it?" and mugged the camera, obviously unimpressed. The guy with the controls looked mad. He twisted a dial and his pal turned, jerked sharply towards the talk-show host, grabbed at him and missed and veered towards the bandstand and took a swing at the sax player.

Letterman ducked behind his desk, smiled his goofy, gaptoothed smile at the camera. Billy pushed himself off the sofa and switched off the TV. He went into the bathroom, urinated noisily into the toilet, missing a little. Dope and booze, a deadly combo. He flossed and brushed his teeth, splashed cold water on his face, smiled into the mirror as he combed his hair. A handsome dude. He left the light on, so his mother, who was more often than not a little disoriented when she rolled in, could see where she was going. Assuming she got home at all.

Billy's bedroom was at the back of the house. He shut the door and bolted it, turned on the overhead light and went over to the window, slowly undressed. When he was down to his jockey shorts, he took the weight of his genitals in his hand and idly scratched himself. Then he stripped off the shorts and stretched, lifting his arms high above his head. He turned in a full circle, like a model on display. Maybe she was watching, and maybe she wasn't. He began to stroke himself. After a couple of minutes a light came on in an upstairs room of the house next door.

Billy and his neighbor's daughter stood there looking at each other, both of them naked. She turned slightly away from him and began to brush her hair. When Billy'd seen enough, he pulled the curtains and turned off the light and went to bed. Her name was Wendy and she worked at a bank downtown. She was in her early twenties but as far as Billy knew, she'd always lived at home. Probably always would, a girl who looked like that.

By three o'clock in the morning, the sheets were soaking wet, twisted around his body like a shroud. He couldn't sleep. He got out of bed and pulled on his jeans, unbolted his door and went into the living room. His mother was stretched out on the sofa, her mouth wide open, snoring softly. Billy crept past her, grabbed his cigarettes and lighter. He padded down the hall and into the kitchen. The phone was on the table, a squat black shape waiting for him on yellow Formica. He ironed the crumpled check flat with the palm of his hand, and dialled Nancy Crown's number.

The telephone rang three times, was picked up by a male with a deep, throaty voice.

Billy said, "Lemme speak to Nance."

"Who is this?"

"She had a bad experience. Maybe you heard about it. I just wanted to make sure she was okay."

"Who am I speaking to?" The voice was stronger now; angry and cold.

"Wake her up, man. Don't be an asshole. She wants to talk to me, just ask her."

"What's your name?"

"She tell you what I did to her? I bet she didn't. Probably won't even admit it happened. But you wanna know something? She's gonna remember it for the rest of her life."

The phone crashed down in Billy's ear. He cradled the receiver and went over to the sink, ran cold water over his cigarette and dropped the sodden butt in the garbage.

His bed had grown cold. He lay under the blankets, shivering, clutching himself. The girl next door hadn't done a thing for him. It was Nancy he couldn't get out of his mind, stop thinking of. Her face in profile. The way she'd glanced at him out of the corner of her eye. The smell of her perfume. Her hair, silky and smooth.

He lit another cigarette. Was he in love? Is that what had happened, he'd fallen in love? No fucking way. He scratched his shoulder, the inside of his thigh. He itched all over. His heart pounded. He was cold and then he was suddenly hot, feverish. His face felt sticky and wet. He wiped sweat from his eyes with the back of his hand, rolled over on his back, tossed the sheets aside and lit another cigarette and used the glowing tip to trace her name in the darkness.

Was the guy on the phone her husband? Jesus, he'd sounded old enough to be Billy's father. Mean enough, too.

Billy squeezed his eyes shut and tried to imagine what the guy looked like. His mind formed a composite of all the half-remembered, nasty, dominating husbands he'd seen on television or at the movies; and came up with a man who was grossly overweight, jowly, in need of a shave, balding . . .

A goddamn animal. Possessive, domineering, brutally selfish.

Billy fell asleep punching the sonofabitch's lights out, giving him exactly what he deserved.

4

The phone call came at 6:47. Willows picked up on the third ring.

"Jack?"

"Yeah, who is it?" Willows' voice was thick with sleep.

"Eddy Orwell."

Willows fumbled for the lamp. He switched it on, and there was a burst of white light and then a soft tinkling sound as the filaments inside the bulb fragmented. He yanked open the curtains, flooding the bedroom in a soft gray light.

"Guy that owns the *Chinese Times*, went missing a couple of weeks ago?"

"Kenny Lee."

"Yeah. Well, we just found him."

"Tell me about it, Eddy."

"He's in the Sun Yat-Sen Gardens, playing with the fishes."

"You call Parker?"

"She's on her way."

"So am I," said Willows, and hung up.

The coffee machine had an automatic timer, set for seven o'clock. Willows switched it to manual. It made a virulent hissing noise. He went into the bathroom and turned on the shower.

By the time he'd finished dressing, the coffee pot was full. He rinsed a stainless steel Thermos with hot water, poured in the coffee, added milk and screwed the lid on tight.

There was a light dusting of frost on the windshield of his '43 Oldsmobile. He unlocked the car, climbed in and started the engine, the heater. He turned on the wipers, but they didn't seem to have much effect, so he turned them off again. He drank coffee while steadily warming air blew across the windshield, slowly clearing the glass.

It was ten minutes past seven when he pulled away from the

curb. It was a weekday, Monday morning, but traffic heading into the downtown core was still light. He arrived at the gardens at twenty-two minutes to eight, parked in a metered space on the street next to the Starlite Films building.

The uniformed cop patrolling the sidewalk in front of the gardens recognized Willows. They exchanged greetings as Willows walked briskly towards the main gate.

The Sun Yat-Sen Classical Chinese Gardens were set well back from the street, surrounded by a twelve-foot-high wall of smooth white stucco. The entrance was to the left. Willows walked down a narrow pathway of flat white paving stones, past the gift shop and into a small, open courtyard. There was a booth where tickets could be purchased, and next to the booth a rack on the wall that held free brochures in English, Cantonese and Japanese.

Willows helped himself to an English language copy, stuck it in his pocket.

There was another uniform lounging in the entrance to the gardens proper. Willows didn't know him. He flashed his shield. The cop stifled a yawn as Willows walked past.

There was a building to his left, high-ceilinged and spacious, the wall made of heavy wooden lattice and sheets of plate glass. Willows took a look inside. The room was bare except for a portable tape deck plugged into an outlet in the far wall. He unfolded the brochure and studied the map, orienting himself. The room was called the Main Hall.

He continued along a paved corridor, past a column of tortured white rock. Parker was standing at the pond's edge, talking to an elderly Chinese man in a white shirt, dark blue suit and highly polished black shoes.

The body, Willows realized with a shock, was still on the ice. The late Kenny Lee was sitting in a full lotus position, legs crossed and back erect, his hands in his lap.

Parker said, "Morning, Jack. Doctor Yang, this is Detective Jack Willows."

Willows said hello. Yang's hand was cold and soft, his grip fleeting.

Parker said, "Doctor Yang manages the gardens. He discovered the body."

Yang was about five foot six, with smooth, unlined features. He was very thin. Willows guessed that he was in his late fifties. He said, "Could you tell me what time you found the body, Doctor?"

"As I told the young woman, it was six thirty this morning, perhaps a few minutes after."

"Do you always arrive so early, Doctor?"

Yang gave him a sharp look, as if he resented being questioned so directly. "Am I a suspect?"

Willows smiled. "No, of course not." He waited patiently.

"Is this your first visit to the gardens, Detective?"

Willows nodded.

"In the gift shop you will find a very reasonably priced and informative souvenir album."

"The gift shop is closed, Doctor."

"If you read the album, you would learn that the purpose of these gardens is to provide an oasis of calm in this busy city. A refreshment for the heart, as they say in China."

Yang turned to look at the body. "At times I feel a need to refresh my heart, Detective Willows. Perhaps it should not be so, but I find the gardens most healing when I am the sole occupant."

"When did you phone the police?"

"Immediately I saw Mr Lee's body."

"You recognized him, then?"

"I've known him for many years. But we were not friends."

"Did you identify him right away?" Lee's face was glazed with a thin coating of ice and frost. Willows waited for the answer.

"No. After I made the call. Even though I initially only took a quick look, the face was vaguely familiar to me . . . " Yang shrugged.

"Where do you live, Doctor?"

"The Kerrisdale district. Do you know it?"

"Yes, of course." Kerrisdale was on the south side of the city. There were views of the Fraser River Delta, the airport. It was an expensive neighborhood, large lots and big houses full of doctors and lawyers and their well-dressed wives, Filipino nannies and kids that wore dark blue uniforms and hardly knew a public school system existed.

Yang watched Parker fill the pages of her notebook. His face was devoid of expression. Willows noticed that he hardly ever blinked.

Willows said, "Could we have your address, please?"

Yang slipped a pale yellow leather billfold from the breast pocket of his suit, flipped it open and handed Parker a business card.

"What time did you leave home this morning, Doctor Yang?"

"At a few minutes before six o'clock."

"Are you married?"

"Yes, certainly."

"Was your wife awake when you left the house?"

"She drank tea with me." Yang frowned. "Have you begun to suspect me after all, Detective Willows?"

Willows had a job to do, but he had to be careful. He had no doubt that Yang was very well connected. He smiled and said, "At this point, we still don't know for certain that a crime has been committed. When there is no crime, how can there be a suspect? The more questions I ask now, the fewer I'll need to ask later. In any case, my only wish is to trouble you as little as possible."

"I am greatly troubled already. The serenity of my beautiful gardens has been disrupted." Yang indicated the macabre corpse with a wave of his hand. "This will be in the newspapers, on the radio and television . . ."

"We'll do our best to keep the media on the other side of the wall," said Willows.

"That would be very much appreciated. And now, if there are no further questions . . ."

"Not right now, no. Thank you for your time, Doctor Yang."

Yang gave Willows an almost imperceptible bow, as if it was a reflex action that he was not entirely able to control. He turned and walked down the path towards his office. His back was rigid and the movement of his arms and legs was stiff, mechanical.

"What d'you think?" said Parker.

"I think he's a little nervous. But I can't say I blame him." Willows turned to look at the body. "Know what else I think?"

"No, what?"

"That it's too early in the morning to have to deal with something like that. C'mon, let's go talk to Eddy."

Orwell and a couple of uniforms and the ME waited where the gracefully curving shoreline of the pond was closest to the body. A cop named Mel Dutton stood a few feet away from them, inserting a fresh roll of 400 ASA color film into his Nikon.

"Get some good ones, Mel?"

"Two-hundred-mil telephoto." Dutton snapped the back of the camera shut, advanced the film. He handed the Nikon to Willows. "Here, take a look." Willows squinted through the viewfinder. From head to toe, Lee's body was encased in varying thicknesses of ice.

Willows handed the camera back to Dutton. "Why hasn't he been moved?"

"Because that ice is less than two inches thick and the water underneath it is about four feet deep and so cold it'd freeze your balls off." He grinned at Parker. "If you had any, that is."

Orwell was watching them, but keeping his distance. Willows caught his eye. "You call the fire department, Eddy?"

"They're on the way," said Orwell, strolling over. He had his hands in the pockets of his black leather trenchcoat. His blond hair was combed straight back and it looked soaking wet, but wasn't. Willows could smell the gel.

"How'd he get inside?"

"There's a door over there." Orwell took his hand, sheathed in a skintight black leather glove, out of his pocket. He pointed. "Behind that column."

"Nice coat," said Willows. "Nice gloves, too."

"Thanks," said Eddy, warily. He slipped his hand back in his pocket.

"I heard a rumor you asked the Chief if you could trade in your Smith for a Luger. True?"

"Very funny, Jack." The look Orwell gave Willows was intended to be sardonic, but came across as merely wounded. He turned and marched back to where Willows truly believed he belonged — with the uniformed cops.

"Sometimes," said Parker, "the telephone rings and I'm in such a hurry to answer it that I get out the wrong side of the bed. And then I'm grumpy all day long. That what happened to you, Jack?"

"Never. Was it Yang who dialled nine-eleven?"

Parker nodded.

Willows began to walk in the direction Orwell had pointed out. The switchboard operator would have logged and taped Yang's call. He'd listen to it later that day.

The winter sun, low on the horizon, was a pale, shimmering ball of light. The smooth surface of the pond glittered coldly. Lee's milky-white corpse sat hunched in the middle of the expanse of ice, solid and unmoving, as if it had been there forever.

Parker said, "We're going to have to drain the pond, we hope to find anything."

"And probably all we'll find is that we wasted our time."

"Eliminating possibilities is never a waste of time, Jack," said Parker sweetly.

The moon door, two dark, polished half-circles of mahogany, stood out in stark contrast to the gardens' white-painted wall. The wood was shattered in the area of the lock. Willows studied the deep indentations in the polished surface. It looked like the door had been kicked in by a horse. He said, "Dutton take any shots of this?"

"Not yet."

"All that ice . . . Yang must have pretty sharp eyes."

"The face is clear enough."

"Yeah, I guess so." Willows wondered if he was due for a trip to the optometrist. He turned and whistled shrilly. Dutton glanced up. Willows waved him over.

During the past year, Dutton had put on twenty or maybe twenty-five pounds. His heavy coat and the cameras slung around his neck gave him added bulk. His chin shook as he waddled down the walkway towards them. His eyes were watering and his bald head was pink from the cold.

"Take a few shots of the door, Mel. See the heel marks?"

Dutton nodded. The sun wasn't bright enough to cast shadows. He'd have to use the flash.

Willows crouched, studied the grass in the area of the door. They'd have to sweep the whole area, probably end up with a garbage bag full of litter. He fumbled in his jacket pocket for his tape measure, pulled six inches and held the tape up against the door next to the heel marks while Dutton shot half a roll of film. When Dutton was finished, Willows measured the distance from the ground to a cluster of overlapping heel marks on the door.

Thirty-nine inches. What did that tell him? The group of heel marks was located about three inches below the lock. He balanced on his left leg and brought his own leg up. The heel of his shoe made contact with the door two inches above the dents in the wood. He was a six-footer. That would make the killer about five foot ten. One thing for sure, he wasn't a midget.

"That it?" said Dutton.

"For now. I want the boulevard searched. You might find some footprints in the grass."

The fire truck had arrived. Willows and Parker went back to the pond. There were four firemen. They had a wooden ladder about thirty feet long. Two of them slid the ladder across the ice, past the body. The smallest of them started to climb over the rock ledge surrounding the pond.

"Hold it!" yelled Willows.

"You don't want us to go get him?"

"I'll do it."

The fireman pulled off a bulky yellow rubber glove and stroked his walrus moustache. He didn't say anything, but he didn't try to hide his disappointment, either. Willows swung over the ledge and stepped gingerly on the first rung of the ladder. The ice groaned and crackled. To avoid crashing through the ice, he was going to have to distribute his weight as widely as possible. On his hands and knees, he began to crawl along the ladder.

"Smile, Jack!" yelled Dutton. Willows heard the firemen laughing. Orwell, too. His knees ached from contact with the rungs. The ice moaned again, as if it was in pain.

Willows got close enough to reach out and touch the hunched figure of Kenny Lee, and stopped.

Lee was naked. His entire body was covered in an encrustation of ice. In his lap, the ice was perhaps three or four inches thick. Icicles hung from his nose, the lobes of his ears. Dribbles of ice ran like veins across the smooth ice that coated his arms. His feet were sheathed in ice. Fat drops of ice lay like huge warts across his ice-encased shoulders. Stalactites of ice fell from his bent legs to the surface of the pond. He was burdened with a back-pack of ice. His mouth was wide open, as if he'd died screaming. A frozen waterfall poured out from between his lips and down his chest. He wore a tight skull-cap of ice. Everywhere Willows looked, there was ice.

Lee's face was thin and bony. His features were softened by the layer of ice that covered him, and in the pale, bleached light of early winter, his eyes looked like two frosty balls of frozen slush.

Willows crept along the ladder, so he could take a look at Lee from a different angle. He could see the outline of Lee's spine through the ice. The man was extremely thin, almost emaciated. There were no visible wounds, but under the circumstances, that didn't mean a thing.

Willows called out to the firemen for an axe.

It took him almost half an hour to chop the corpse free of the ice, hack a circle all the way around the body. By the time he'd finished he was soaking wet and trembling from the cold, his knuckles were scraped raw and his face stung from splinters of ice.

He managed to get his arms around Lee's body, tried to pull the corpse up on to solid ice.

"You want a hand?" yelled Orwell.

Willows ignored him. He used the axe to smash a larger hole in the ice, took a deep breath and jumped into the water. *Christ*! Naked, Lee weighed maybe a hundred and thirty pounds. Dressed in his suit of ice, he was twice as heavy. Willows tipped the corpse at an angle, managed to get the flat base of ice over the lip of the hole. He pushed hard, and Lee slid several feet across the surface. There was a ragged cheer from the crowd of cops and firemen. Willows dragged the ladder over the hole. He climbed up on it and moved closer to the corpse, reached out with both hands and shoved hard. Kenny Lee, still sitting bolt upright with his legs crossed and his hands in his lap, rocketed across the ice and bumped up against the stone wall surrounding the pond.

Willows crawled slowly back down the ladder, climbed stiffly over the stone retaining wall. His hands were numb. His body was so cold he couldn't shop shaking, he was out of control.

"Nice work," said Orwell. "Dutton must've taken about a thousand pictures. Here, have a souvenir." Grinning, he handed Willows a Polaroid.

Parker drove Willows back to 312 Main, dropped him off at the back entrance and wheeled the unmarked patrol car into the underground garage. Willows took the elevator down to the basement. There was a spare change of clothes in his locker, but his hands were trembling so badly he couldn't work the combination lock, and had to ask a passing cop to do it for him. He stripped off his clothes, grabbed a towel and headed for the showers.

When he walked into the squadroom, half an hour later, there was a six-inch-tall stuffed penguin standing in the middle of his desk, in a small puddle of water. He glanced around, but only Parker would meet his eye. The half-dozen other detectives in the room didn't seem to have noticed his arrival. He slid open his desk drawer and pulled out a letter-opener, used the blade to viciously disembowel the penguin and then tore its head off and tossed the gutted and decapitated bird into Eddy Orwell's wastebasket.

"Nice throw," said Parker. "How you feeling, a bit hungry?"

"Yeah, maybe a little."

"Nothing like a good swim to sharpen the appetite."

Willows said, "How would you know?"

Parker smiled. "Let's go grab something to eat."

She took him to the Ovaltine Cafe, on Hastings, just around the corner from 312 Main. They found a booth near the back. The waitress was about sixty years old and balding. She looked at Parker and said, "Pot of tea, and a blueberry muffin." Parker smiled and nodded. Willows ordered a full breakfast — eggs over easy, sausages and hash browns, toast.

"Coffee?"

Willows nodded.

"Be right back." As a rule, cops were a tight-fisted bunch. But the waitress knew that this one, when he was with his partner, sometimes left a generous tip.

Parker said, "Yang didn't seem too pleased when you told him we'd have to drain the pond."

"He didn't seem too pleased about anything."

"The *Chinese Times* guy. Kenny Lee. How long had he been missing?"

Willows shrugged. "A couple of weeks. Nobody was all that worried about it. I forget who told me, but apparently Lee disappeared once before, about a year ago. He was gone about a week and then his wife got a phone call from Reno. Lee'd gambled away all his cash, run his plastic to the limit, sold his return ticket and couldn't even cover his hotel bill. I called Tommy Wilcox but he was out."

Parker nodded. Wilcox was Missing Persons. The food arrived. The blueberry muffin had come with two pats of butter. She sighed, and put the butter off to one side, where it couldn't do any harm.

Willows said, "You worried about your weight again?"

"None of your business."

Willows wiped his fork on a paper napkin, sprinkled pepper on his eggs. A quartet of uniforms strolled past, all four men covertly eyeing Parker.

Willows shovelled a forkful of egg into his mouth, chewed and swallowed.

Parker said, "Did Lee have any children?"

Willows shrugged. Plucked a fresh napkin from the dispenser, wiped his mouth.

Parker said, "There were no threats, demands for money? Somebody snatched him, held him a couple of weeks and then killed him. That's it, end of story?"

"We don't know how he died. Maybe it was suicide."

"Yeah, sure."

"We don't know how long he's been dead, either. Yang said the gardens had been closed all weekend. And for all we know, Lee's been in cold storage since the day he disappeared."

"That's not the point, Jack." Parker checked the pot, fished out the teabag.

Willows said, "Pass the ketchup."

"The guy gets kidnapped. He's a businessman, owns a newspaper. Anything there that might have landed him in trouble?"

"I don't read Cantonese. Or Mandarin."

Parker watched him douse the sausages with ketchup.

Willows glanced up, caught her eye. He said, "I know what you're thinking, and you're right. But it tastes good."

Parker ate some muffin. It was stale. She stared at the pats of butter. "We need some help on this. Maybe Fred Lam."

Willows nodded. Lam was one of four Chinese-Canadian constables on the force. He wiped his plate with his last slice of toast.

Parker said, "We can get Tommy to pull the file. See what's there. Know what I think?"

"I think you're going to short tip the waitress because you just realized she forgot to bring the lemon for your tea."

Parker smiled. "That, too."

"What else?"

"I'll bet you the price of breakfast whoever killed Lee was in contact with the family. I've got a gut feeling we're looking at a failed extortion attempt."

Willows shrugged. "Maybe. And then again, maybe not. Lee ran a newspaper. He was owner and editor, and he was bound to make enemies. Plus, he was a part-time, out-of-control gambler. Could've been a hundred people wanted him dead."

"They dumped the body where it would be found right away, be sure to cause a stir in the community. Soften things up for their next shot at it."

Willows' beeper shrieked.

"Got a quarter?" Parker gave him a look, fished around in her purse and gave him two dimes and a nickel. There was a payphone at the front of the restaurant, near the cash register. Willows dialled, spoke briefly, hung up and made his way back to the table.

"That was Tommy." Standing, Willows finished his coffee.

Parker said, "You want the rest of this muffin?"

"Next time, ask *before* you pick all the blueberries out."

Tommy Wilcox offered Willows a chair, went over to the big gray legal-size filing cabinet next to his desk and pulled the Missing Persons Report, numbered 90-027, on Kenny Lee. Wilcox wore a white shirt, plain blue tie, brown tweed jacket and dark brown pants. He had sad, pouchy brown eyes and looked as if he'd seen it all before and expected to see it all again. Wilcox worked alone, and he was a very busy man. In the City of Vancouver, three to three and a half thousand missing person reports are filed every year, and Wilcox handled every single one of them. He sat down, adjusted his jacket, flipped open the file.

"Okay, the initial call was fielded on the first of January, twenty-two hundred hours, by the Communications Centre. The non-emergency nine-eleven number. Mrs Lee was worried because her husband was late getting home from work. Communications suggested it was too early to be concerned, told her to call back in the morning."

Willows nodded. Standard procedure.

"Okay, she called back at seven hundred hours. An early bird. Distraught. We took Lee's description and broadcast it to all units. A copy of my report went to Communications." Wilcox's shirt collar was too tight. He scratched his neck, adjusted the knot of his tie. "Mid-afternoon, she called us again. None of his friends or business acquaintances had seen him. He'd missed an important meeting. I put the info on CPIC."

"When?" said Willows.

"Soon as I hung up."

CPIC was the Canadian Police Information Centre, a computerized data-base shared by police forces across the country. Wilcox hadn't wasted any time.

"While she was on the phone," Wilcox continued, "I asked her would she mind coming down to the station. She showed up a little before five, right at the end of my shift."

Willows glanced out the window. It looked cold out there. Low, heavy dark clouds. He wondered if it was going to snow again, if the winter would ever end.

Wilcox took a disposable lighter out of his pocket, turned it over and over in his hands. He hadn't had a cigarette in almost three full days, and he was just about ready to explode. "Mrs Lee had everything I asked for," he said. "The usual background info, a pretty good head and shoulders shot — recent and decent. I checked the sudden death reports with the coroner's liaison. Phoned the hospitals, looking for John Does that fitted his description. No joy. Next couple of days, I got on the phone and talked to the people who'd seen him last. People who worked for him, his friends, the neighbors. Nobody had any ideas. I got some copies of the picture out to the media, and went to work on my backlog."

Wilcox put the lighter back in his pocket. There was a pack of nicotine-substitute gum on his desk. He helped himself to a stick. Yeah, better. He pulled out the lighter again, stroked it fondly.

"Three days later, he's still missing. But the guy pulled a disappearing act a few years ago. Turned out it was a trip to Vegas. His wife says it doesn't happen any more. Okay, fine. The guy doesn't drink. There's no problems with other women. His business was doing good. I phone the Vegas cops. They don't know what I'm talking about. Okay, I ask Mrs Lee for permission to talk to his doctor. Doc tells me Lee was healthy as a horse. No sign of depression. I get his blood type, checked the availability of X-rays. What else . . . Phoned his dentist and asked for a copy of his dental chart."

Wilcox flicked his lighter, sparking long tongues of flame. "By now, a week's gone by and I got the guy figured for a homicide. Maybe somebody'll stumble across the body, and maybe he's buried so deep we'll never find him in a million years." Wilcox glanced out the window. It was still January. He sighed. "A couple days later, I think it was the tenth, it's in the file, I get a call from the grieving widow. She says her husband's safe at home, we can call off the dogs."

"Any explanation?"

"Nope."

"You confirmed it was really Mrs Lee that called?"

Wilcox chewed furiously on his nicotine substitute, which was suddenly doing him no good at all. "It was her voice, Jack. No doubt about it. Also, she knew the case number."

"Just asking, Tommy. Do the Lees have any kids?"

"A son and a daughter. The girl's thirteen, attends a local high school. The son's twenty-two years old, for the past three years he's been living in Boston."

"Doing what?"

"Business admin at Harvard."

"And that's it, you never heard from Mrs Lee again?"

"Nothing, not a word. I figured the guy'd taken another trip to Vegas, got cleaned out. Was wandering around in the desert in a barrel. Or maybe got himself mixed up with a showgirl, something along those lines."

"I want the names of the people you talked to, his friends and neighbors, everybody."

"You got it," said Wilcox.

"I mean now, Tommy."

"Right after lunch."

"You'll work faster on an empty stomach."

Wilcox sighed. He unwrapped another stick of gum and stuck

46

it between his jaws, clamped down hard. Homicide dicks were always in such a goddamn hurry. The people they worked for were *dead*, for God's sake, and they were gonna stay that way forever. So why the big rush?

Willows stood up. He started to walk away and then stopped and turned and looked Wilcox straight in the eye. "Half an hour, Tommy?"

"Yeah, sure. Think we should synchronize our watches?"

"What time you got?"

Wilcox glanced down at his wrist. It was twelve, no, thirteen minutes past ten. He looked up, ready to share this information.

But Willows was gone.

5

Christy Kirkpatrick had enjoyed a long and varied professional life, and believed that during his career as a forensic pathologist he had been privileged to see and do things that other men rarely even dreamed of.

But this was weird. This was, in fact, weirdness beyond weird.

The city morgue is situated in an old orange brick and mullioned-window building located on Cordova Street, just around the corner from 312 Main. The operating theatre is located on the top floor of the building, in a large, square, brightly-lit room. The floor and two of the four walls are covered with small, glossy blue tiles. The remaining walls are lined with lockable refrigerated stainless-steel drawers that are just the right size for storing a body. There is a massive cast-iron and frosted glass skylight in the ceiling. If you look closely, you can see where repairs were made to the skylight in the spring of 1947, when a cop named Wilbur Cartwright fell through the glass while moonlighting for a sleazy tabloid that wanted candid shots of the autopsy of a notoriously fickle B-movie star who'd asphyxiated in the arms of her blind lover.

Directly beneath the skylight stood two zinc tables. Each table is seven feet long and three feet wide, and stands exactly forty-two inches above the tile floor. A constant stream of cold water flows along a shallow groove that runs down the middle of each table, from the slightly elevated top end all the way down to the bottom, where a chrome drainage pipe vanishes into a hole in the tiles.

Kenny Lee's corpse, still in a classic full-lotus position, sat proudly erect in the middle of the table closest to the door.

Kirkpatrick was trying to melt him down with a 1000-watt Philips *Vanite* blow dryer. He'd been wielding the blow dryer for the better part of two hours. His wrist ached, and the whine of the machine's tiny electric motor was driving him crazy.

As he'd plugged the Philips into the extension cord, he'd worked out a simple strategy. He'd start at Lee's head and work his way to his feet. His theory was that the warm, melted water that dripped down the body would help speed the thawing process.

It had started well enough. The ice that covered Lee's face was less than an inch thick. Kirkpatrick found that he could hold the nozzle of the hair dryer as close as two inches away from the surface of the ice, but no closer, because the melt had a tendency to spray back at him, and he didn't care to risk electrocution.

After almost two hours, he was just clearing the last traces of ice from Lee's face, directing the flow of hot air upwards at Lee's snub nose to loosen the two plugs of ice that filled his nostrils.

He switched the hair dryer to his left hand, flexed his aching wrist and aimed the dryer so the blast of hot air was directed at the bridge of Lee's nose. He had a small bet going with himself — which nostril the ice plug would fall out of first.

He'd also given some thought to working out how long it was going to take to thaw out the whole body, from head to foot. What he had failed to consider when he'd started was the fact that Lee wasn't simply sheathed in ice, his entire body — even the marrow in his bones — was frozen through and through.

Kirkpatrick wondered if there was a mathematical formula for calculating the time required to thaw a given number of cubic feet of frozen human flesh. He couldn't recall studying such a formula at med school, but then, there was an awful lot about med school that he couldn't remember.

Thank God.

The telephone rang. Kirkpatrick switched off the dryer. He could hear fat drops of melted water hitting the puddle that had collected on the tile floor. It was slippery down there. He'd have to watch his step. He went over to the telephone and picked up.

Willows said, "What've you got, Christy?"

"Nothing much, Jack. I'm still trying to melt the ice off him."

"I thought you'd be finished by now." There was an edge to Willows' voice. "How long is it going to take?"

"In some places, Jack, Lee's covered in a layer of ice that's as much as six inches thick. But the main problem is that his body's frozen solid, too. If you think about it, the water falling on him couldn't have frozen unless the entire corpse was thirty-two degrees or less." Kirkpatrick paused, and then said, "You see what I'm getting at?"

"Over the weekend," Willows said, "the temperature in the city dropped to a maximum low of twenty-one degrees. The Sun Yat-Sen Gardens were closed to the public from six o'clock Friday evening until Monday morning. Was there enough time, during that period, for the body temperature to drop from ninety-eight point six to the freezing point?"

"I don't know," said Kirkpatrick. "It depends how much the guy weighed, and I can't find that out because he's still covered in ice."

"Parker and I worked out roughly how long the hose had been running by the volume of the flow and the amount of water sprayed on the corpse and surrounding ice," said Willows. "Our guess is between six and eight hours."

"What time was it Yang discovered the body?"

"Approximately six thirty."

"So the hose was turned on, say, between ten and midnight?"

"Somewhere in there."

"Then my guess is Lee was killed at least twenty-four hours before he was dumped in the pond. And that the body was frozen solid at the time he was dumped."

"So it's fair to say the body was stored outside, or in an unheated building for twenty-four hours or more before somebody turned him into an ice sculpture?"

"Right."

"How long before he thaws, doc?"

"I'd say at least two days."

Willows sighed, and hung up.

Kirkpatrick cradled the receiver and went back to the zinc table. He studied Lee's face. The skin had a faint greenish tinge. Lee had combed his hair straight back, and that's the way it was now, except for a bit sticking out over his left ear. Kirkpatrick resisted the urge to use his comb. Lee's eyes were wide open. He was staring straight ahead, into distances so vast they were immeasurable. But then, that's what you were supposed to do when you meditated, wasn't it? Lose focus. Slip outside yourself. Kirkpatrick reached out and gently pinched Lee's nose. The plugs of ice shot out of Lee's nostrils and into the palm of his hand.

Lee sat perfectly still — about what you'd expect from a man who was colder than a freshly-mixed margarita.

Kirkpatrick took a quick pass with the dryer. A single tiny crystalline bead of water hung trembling from Lee's eyelash. He remembered a late-night movie he'd seen on TV a few weeks ago, about a group of explorers who'd stumbled across a frozen stiff locked into an iceberg somewhere in the arctic. A Neanderthal type, who'd been in a state of suspended animation for several thousand years. The explorers had made the mistake of thawing him out, and he'd turned on them and . . . *eaten them.*

Well, after a fast that lasted two or three thousand years, they should have expected the poor guy to have an appetite.

Tentatively, Kirkpatrick reached out and touched the droplet of crystal-clear water that hung trembling from Lee's eyelash. There was, of course, an explanation for the movement. Passing traffic would cause the building to vibrate. Although the vibrations were usually too minute to notice, they were always there. The whole city was constantly shaking, if you thought about it.

One thing for sure, Lee sure as hell wasn't *alive.*

But just to make sure, Kirkpatrick reached out and pressed the tip of his index finger gently against the dead man's eyeball. The orb was cold and unyielding. Lee's eye, like his brain and all his thought processes, was frozen solid, hard as a bowling ball.

The telephone rang again, startling him badly enough to make him scream and drop the hair dryer, which fell into the puddle of melted icewater. A bright orange bolt of electricity arced from the dryer to the zinc table. The air filled with the stench of melting plastic, and then a circuit-breaker somewhere deep inside the bowels of the old building automatically turned over and all the lights went out.

There was a moment's silence, and then a chunk of ice shattered on the tile floor.

Christy Kirkpatrick's overworked heart did a backflip, raced out of control. He screamed again, but much louder this time, as if his life depended on it.

Then the battery-powered emergency backup lighting system clicked in, and he managed to get himself under control. My God, what a terrifying experience! He went over to the sink, splashed cold water on his face. His chest ached where his heart had thumped against the bones and flesh. He silently vowed that *no one* would *ever* learn about the day all the horror movies he'd ever seen sprang to life and nearly did him in.

6

It was cold. Garret could feel the chill in his bones. His knee joints, as he scuttled down the alley, were stiff and tight.

"C'mon," whispered Billy. "Move it! Haul ass!"

Garret turned to look back down the alley. Billy's rusted-out Pinto was parked under a mountain ash. The cold snap had pinched the last dead leaves from the tree; the branches were bare except for clusters of shrivelled red berries. What was left of the Pinto's chrome trim gleamed beneath a streetlight. Piece of shit. Garret drove a '65 Mustang powered by a 289-cubic-inch V-8. Black on black. He spent every spare dime he made on the car, and he loved it the way he'd never loved his mother. They were using the Pinto because the Mustang was in the garage, waiting for a new fuel pump Garret couldn't quite afford.

The car they were going to break into was a green Volkswagen Golf. It was three years old and worth maybe eight thousand dollars. Whoever owned the car had spent another three grand on the stereo system. The dashboard was crammed with a Blaupunkt tape deck, state-of-the-art Alpine CD shuttle, Alpine speakers and a sub-woofer, the whole system powered by a 200-watt Sony amplifier. The Golf was parked in a paved lot behind a bakery. The owner started work at two in the morning and didn't finish his shift until noon. By then, Billy and Garret would be long gone and so would the stereo.

Garret stood in the distorted diamond-pattern shadow cast by a chain-link fence, keeping watch, as Billy approached the car from the driver's side. There was a thin burst of white light from his flash. He barked like a dog, a whispered howl of triumph.

Garret rubbed his hands together, breathed little puffs of smoke.

"Clear?" whispered Billy from the darkness.

"Yeah, yeah. Hurry up!"

Billy raised the ball-peen hammer and hit the side window just above the door lock. The window exploded. Billy reached inside, unlocked the door and swung it open.

The Golf's interior light came on.

Billy stuck the flashlight in the back pocket of his jeans and attacked the dashboard with the hammer. He had the Blaupunkt out in fifteen seconds flat. The CD shuttle was a little trickier. Delicate electronics, he couldn't nuke it with the hammer, had to go easy. Cut some wires. Thirty seconds. He could hear Garret pacing back and forth in the lane, heels clicking on the asphalt. Billy had to watch himself — there were loose wires and chunks of shattered plastic and glass all over the front seat. He went to work on the amplifier. He needed a medium-size Philips screwdriver and he didn't have one. Fuck. He yanked on the Sony's support bracket, pressing his shoulder up against the steering wheel for leverage, using brute strength to do the job. The bracket tore free without warning and he hit his head against the rearview mirror.

The Golf shifted on its springs. Hail on the roof. No, Garret's knuckles.

"What the fuck's taking so long, man?"

"Fuck off!" hissed Billy.

He popped open the glove compartment. A road map of the city, registration papers. Kleenex. He passed the radio and CD player and Sony amp to Garret, climbed out of the car and eased shut the door. The Golf's interior light went out. They hurried down the alley.

Billy slipped behind the Pinto's wheel. He paused to light a cigarette, knowing the delay would drive Garret crazy, and then turned the key in the ignition. The Pinto's dinky four-cylinder engine coughed twice and then caught, spewing a cloud of burnt oil at the mountain ash. Billy put the car in gear and drove to the end of the block and hung a right, turned on the headlights.

Garret, starting to relax, leaned back in his seat and rested his boots on the Pinto's scaly dashboard.

Billy ran a stop sign, not even bothering to check for oncoming traffic. He felt flat, depressed. Let-down. He could remember when busting into a car gave him a nice little buzz, really got him pumped up. But he'd done it too many times. It was like playing the same record over and over and over again. Or spending too much time with the same girl. Didn't matter how crazy about her you were when you got started, after a while nothing much was happening. You were bored. He blew a lungful of smoke at Garret's surly profile.

"Fuck off," said Garret.

Billy laughed.

It was Tuesday, three o'clock in the morning. The graveyard shift. They'd been doing business since a little past midnight, scoring Porsches and Golfs and the odd Mercedes. The way they worked, their *modus operandi*, Billy would pick a neighborhood and then cruise around in the Pinto, looking for cars parked in unlighted driveways or unlocked garages. He had a little penlight he used to make sure the car had a decent radio. He was quiet, but not too quiet. If the car owner was an insomniac or it turned out there was a couple of pit bulls tucked away on the back porch, forget it. Billy kept a baseball bat in the car, but it was only for self-defense, in case some asshole pushed him too hard.

If there was no problem, everything looked good, Billy wrote down the address on a piece of paper. When he had maybe a dozen cars lined up, he arranged the addresses in order so they could go from one place to another as efficiently as possible. The radios, as they bagged them, went into a cardboard box in the trunk of the car. Usually, they'd hit seven or eight cars out of twelve. The other cars wouldn't be there or something about the situation wouldn't be quite right.

It wasn't a bad way to make a buck. A bit on the risky side, but they'd usually come away, in the space of two or three hours, with anywhere from two to four grands' worth of electronics.

From the fences, of course, they'd be lucky to get twenty cents on the dollar. Still, it was a lot easier than shovelling hamburgers at McDonalds. And there was always the chance of catching a bonus. One warm summer night in July, Billy had busted a Porsche and walked away with a hundred grams of coke. Garret had wanted to deal it but Billy said no. His argument was they didn't know shit about dealers or dealing, might put somebody's nose out of joint without even realizing it. End up in some back alley garbage can with a couple broken legs. "Let's don't fuck with luck," was the way Billy put it. So they had a couple of girls over and got all bright-eyed and snuffly. Had a pretty good time, all in all.

Garret said, "You hungry, wanna grab something to eat?"

Billy shook his head. He sucked on the cigarette, flicked ash at Garret's lap.

"Steal some more radios? I know where there's a Jag, guy keeps it . . ."

"I ripped my fuckin' hand wide open. Look at that, for fuck's sake."

Billy thrust out his hand. They passed under a streetlight, and in the sickly blue glow Garret saw the cut, a raggedy slash that ran the length of Billy's thumb.

"How'd you do that?"

"Fucking dashboard. Pulling the Blaupunkt." Billy sucked at the gaping wound, rolled down his window and spat blood, rolled the window back up again.

"Wanna smoke some dope?"

Billy didn't answer. Garret took that for a maybe. Encouraged, he said, "I got a six-pack of Coors. We could . . ."

"Where'd you get it?"

"The dope?"

"No, stupid. The booze."

"Off a guy outside that liquor store in the mall, on Broadway by Kingsway."

"What'd you pay him?"

"Ten bucks."

"Plus the beer."

"Yeah, right."

"Ten bucks for a six-pack. Whyn't you get him to buy you a case?"

"Too heavy. I got no wheels, remember?"

Billy flicked his cigarette. The butt hit Garret square in the chest, a shower of orange sparks on black leather.

"Jesus, Billy!"

They were about three blocks from Garret's apartment. Close enough. Billy pulled over to the curb, turned off the lights.

"Beat it."

"Huh?" said Garret.

"Read my lips," said Billy. "Fuck off."

"You expect me to *walk* home? In this cold? C'mon, I'm gonna freeze my ass off."

Billy leaned across the seat, opened Garret's door and gave him a push. Garret sat there for a minute, his head down. Billy could see he was working out his options — climb out of the car or get his head kicked in. Even for a dummy like Garret, it wasn't all that tough a choice. He got out of the car. His lungs puffed small clouds into the night. "See you tomorrow?"

"Shut the door," said Billy. "And don't slam it."

"Asshole."

"Everybody's got one." Billy's thumb had stopped bleeding. He tilted his head, sniffed the cold night air. Night lights lit up the peak of Grouse Mountain. Lots of snow up there, cold and white and pure. Pastel ski bunnies shifting ass as they cruised the powder.

Garret eased shut the Pinto's door and turned his back on Billy and started walking down the street. The sky was dark, stuffed with heavy black cloud. An icy wind seeped through his jacket and began to gnaw at him. He shoved his hands deeper into his pockets. It was so damn cold his eyes were watering. He glanced over his shoulder, wondering where in hell Billy was going, this time of night.

Billy and he had been together a long time, but there were parts of Billy's life that Garret knew nothing of. Fair enough. Garret had plenty of secrets himself. His baddest secret was that Billy didn't scare him one little bit. Billy thought he was in charge. In many small ways, he ran roughshod over Garret, and Garret let him do it. There was a reason for this. Garret was fast approaching the time when somebody dangerous and dumb and disposable would be exactly what he needed.

Billy was headed for the West Side of the city, an address on Point Grey Road. He didn't know exactly why he'd decided to make the trip, and it troubled him.

Garret's idea of a fun time was cruising up and down Kingsway or maybe Hastings Street, cutting in and out of traffic, leaning out the window and yelling at people, spitting at pedestrians. Billy was just the opposite. He didn't like to waste time. Everything he did, he did with a purpose. As far as he was concerned, wasting time was a waste of time. So what did he think he was up to, driving halfway across the city for no reason that made sense?

Truth was, he didn't know.

He crossed Main Street at Twenty-fifth, running a yellow. Now he was an East Side kid on the West Side of the city. Unknown territory, where there were a lot more parks and the parks had trees. What else? People owned poodles instead of dobermans. The girls were prettier. Better dressed, anyhow. He'd heard about West Side girls. That they'd put out for anybody, but didn't much enjoy it.

At Oak Street, he stopped for a red and pulled out Nancy Crown's checkbook. He squinted at the address in the glare of passing headlights. Point Grey Road. What the fuck kind of address was that? Thirty-six-hundred block. He was still miles away. He revved the engine, waiting for the green. A police car pulled up beside him. Billy leaned back in his seat, looked straight ahead, letting the engine idle. Be calm, look calm, act calm. So what if they pulled him over, took a peek in the trunk and saw he could tune in a dozen different stations at once? At his age, there wasn't a whole lot they could do to him — he'd be in and out of jail faster than an egg in a frying pan.

The light turned green. The cop punched it and the patrol car cut in front of Billy, turned sharply right, made him hit the brakes to avoid a collision, the blue and white flashing past in front of him and accelerating down Oak. Cowboys. Like Garret, cops were always in a hurry and never going anywhere. Billy lit a cigarette. Probably they had a hot date with a jelly donut.

At Broadway and Arbutus, Billy stopped at an all-night Chevron station, pumped ten dollars worth of gas into the Pinto and cleaned the windshield. The kid guarding the cash register had long black hair combed straight back, a rash of pimples across his chin and down his neck. He was too big to rob. Billy asked him for directions. By the time the kid finished talking to him Billy was still lost but at least now he didn't have any doubt about it. He bought a city map for a dollar and a quarter.

3682 Point Grey Road was easy to find, because the address was written over the green-tinted glass roof of the garage in hot pink neon.

A glass garage. What the fuck kind of mess had he gotten himself into? Jesus.

Billy parked the Pinto on a side street about half a block away. It was half past three, dark as it was going to get. He checked to make sure he had his knife and flashlight, took a quick look up and down the street, locked the Pinto and ambled along the sidewalk towards the house.

The house was set well back from the street, behind an evergreen hedge that screened a sound-deflecting six-foot-high wall of textured concrete blocks. Billy forced his way through the hedge, got a hand on top of the wall and levered himself up in one easy, fluid motion. He sat there for a moment, orienting himself.

The garage was at the front, to the left of the house. The walls were textured concrete blocks painted dove-gray, and the sloped roof of huge sheets of green-tinted safety glass was supported by green-painted metal joists. The garage doors were also made of big sheets of green glass. The interior of the garage was brightly lit by a dozen or more twenty-foot lengths of neon suspended on wires from metal tubes. The outwash of neon lit up the whole front yard, stained everything pale green, made it look as if it was under water. Billy had never seen anything like it. He felt as if he'd just come off the farm, and it made him angry.

There were two cars inside the garage: a bronze Mercedes and Nancy's shiny black BMW cabriolet. The Mercedes had a vanity licence plate that read, HIS TOY. A third car, another bronze Merc, same year and model, was parked at a careless angle in the driveway. The plate read, HER TOY.

The forecourt — what Billy thought of as the front yard — was paved with interlocking pink brick. There were a number of small trees and shrubs in oversized clay pots, each plant individually lit by a cleverly sited spotlight.

The house was low, very modern. Stained wood siding and small aluminum windows. Billy thought it must be pretty dark in there, and that it was weird they had so few windows in the house when the whole damn garage was glass. As if the cars had a need to look outside but the people didn't. Or, taking a minute to think about it . . . The people who owned the cars wanted to show them off but didn't want anybody to know who owned them . . . Then what was the fucking point? Billy shrugged, giving it up.

The front door was sunk deeply into the house, in a kind of alcove about fifteen feet wide. A fancy double iron gate prevented anyone from getting to the door. The wattage put out by the security floods was bright enough to read a goddamn comic book, had Billy thought to bring one along.

Billy stepped up to a small window on the right-hand side of the house. The blinds were drawn. All he could see was a faint reflection of his own face.

He followed a concrete path around the side of the house. No windows, not even one. Security spots placed under the eaves laid overlapping pools of light on the pathway. But the neighboring house had no side windows either. It was crazy. He was right out there in the open but there was no way anyone could see him because of the lack of windows and the fact that the hedge and concrete wall hid him from the street.

The path sloped steeply downhill. The house loomed above him. It was a hell of a lot bigger than it looked from the front. He placed the palm of his hand, fingers splayed wide, against the wooden siding. He felt, or at least thought he felt, a barely perceptible vibration — as if the house was a huge sleeping beast.

He continued down the path, found himself in the backyard. There was a weird effect down at the far end. Steven Spielberg stuff. Pale mist, a soft, curling vapor. Lights dancing in the air. He paused, giving his eyes a few moments to adjust to the gloom. It was a swimming pool. A goddamn heated swimming pool and the dancing lights were the subterranean lights of the pool reflected in a fence made of glass panels.

Billy raised his eyes, looked beyond the pool. There was nothing out there. No more houses. Just a huge inky black expanse of nothingness and then, miles and miles away, a sweep of tiny glittering lights. He realized the blackness he was staring at was the ocean. Nancy Crown lived right on the water. Jesus! Billy's mind raced. He tried to calculate how much money it would cost to own a great big slab-sided house on the water. To own *waterfront*. And a glass garage and a matched pair of Mercedes Benzes and a fat black BMW ragtop. And Christ knows what else. Millions, probably. And he'd dinged her for eighteen bucks and a handful of loose change. With his back to the house, he hunched his shoulders and lit a cigarette. Then he moved past the steaming pool, across thirty feet of electrically-heated slate flagstones to the wind-break of glass at the far end of the yard. The lights of the city, bright and glittering, were off to his right. He pulled hard on the cigarette, sucked smoke deep into his lungs, exhaled slowly. And then glanced down.

His stomach lurched. The ocean was forty or maybe fifty feet below him, and it was a sheer drop.

Billy had a thing about heights. Turned his legs to jello. He moved away from the glass wall, squatted down on his haunches and fought to get his breathing under control.

The house was three stories high, each level set back from the one below it. There were balconies on all three levels, and through the rising mist from the pool Billy could see matching sets of ghostly white patio furniture on each balcony. Except for the concrete posts and beams that supported the structure, the back of the house was made entirely of huge sheets of plate glass.

No curtains had been pulled. It looked to Billy as if every light in the joint was burning. The house had an open floor plan, to take advantage of the view. From where he was sitting at the back of the yard, Billy could see most of the ground floor, about half of the second floor and a little bit of the top floor. There was no sign of life anywhere inside the house. No movement and not a sound.

Despite the three cars parked out front, he had a hunch nobody was home. He tilted his watch towards the house, studied the luminous dials. Almost four o'clock in the morning, all the fucking lights blazing away ... Maybe something went wrong with the gas stove and she was in there lying on the kitchen floor, half-dead, dying ...

Billy pictured himself doing a B&E. Picking up one of the wrought-iron chairs over by the pool and tossing it through a window. Finding her lying there with her skirt up around her hips ... Yeah, sure. He flicked the cigarette butt over the glass wall and into the ocean. A car sped past on the road out front, tires whining on the asphalt. Billy tried to imagine the view on a sunny day. Like something out of a magazine.

Maybe she was alone, maybe there was no one else in the house. Her husband had to be a pretty heavy guy, to afford a place like that. Probably had to do a lot of travelling. He could be anywhere. Toronto or New York or Hong Kong. That'd explain the lights. Nancy was nervous, frightened of being alone. Billy stood up. He walked around the pool and sat down in one of the webbed deck chairs. The metal frame was bitterly cold, but the chair was more comfortable than it looked, and the night air was warmed by the steaming water. He lit another cigarette, stretched out his legs, thought about what he should do.

Assume the house had a security system.

Not outside, because down here by the beach they'd get all sorts of birds, raccoons . . . The alarm'd be going off every ten seconds. But inside, there'd be something real sophisticated. Expensive stuff, top of the line. Motion detectors. Infrared. Maybe a direct line to a security company. Shit Billy knew existed, from talking to a guy he knew who did a little burgling, and also from watching TV. Stuff he'd have to watch out for, if he went inside, but, really, he had no idea how to handle.

Sitting there by the pool, the steam falling on his jacket and turning to frost, Billy smoked the cigarette down to his fingers and then flipped the butt into the pool.

Case the joint, that's what he'd have to do. Case the joint. Figure a way in and a way out.

The top floor was where he wanted to go. Because that's where the bedrooms would be.

Billy imagined Nancy Crown lying on her back on white silk sheets, mirrors all around, her naked body reflected from a thousand different angles.

He wondered what her husband was like, what kind of guy he'd be. A what, stockbroker? Some fat, sweaty jerk who was always shooting off his mouth, always needed a clean shirt and a shave.

Billy lit a fresh cigarette.

An accountant. Accountants handled other people's money and some of it stuck to their fingers. They knew how to make money make money. He pictured a skinny guy with wire-frame glasses, pink cheeks.

But what if he was, say, a crook? Not corporate, white-collar crime, either. Maybe a big dope dealer or somebody who was into gambling. Heavy. Well connected. The kind of guy who'd have Billy killed and the next morning not even remember doing it?

Nah, that was bullshit.

But the point was, Nancy Crown's husband could be anybody. A gun nut, packed a .45 around the house and was just itching to blow somebody away.

All Billy knew for sure was that to own a house like that, you had to be rich. And if you were rich, chances were pretty good that the money you owned had belonged to a whole lot of other people, and you had taken it away from them, one way or the other.

So he was probably in over his head and he oughta get out of there. Right now, right this minute. Before the rich, powerful, ruthless son of a bitch who was Nancy Crown's husband hauled his ass out of bed to take a whiz and happened to look out the window.

Billy pushed himself out of the metal chair. He went over to the lip of the pool and knelt down and trailed his fingers across the surface of the water. So warm, so soft.

What he needed to do was distance himself. Clear his head so he could think straight, work out all the angles, possibilities.

He stared at the house and thought about how she might look. Baby-doll pajamas? Or was she naked between the sheets? He imagined her lying on her side, the curve of her hip, the sweeter curve of her ass. Mist rose from the pool and vanished in the freezing night air and Billy let his mind focus on Nancy Crown, imagined her this way and that way, in all the poses he could remember from all the magazines he had ever read.

He smoked the last of his cigarettes down to the filter and tossed the butt into the pool. Then he stood up and stared out across the harbor, miles and miles of cold black water.

She was almost close enough to touch. There was nothing between them but half a dozen quick strides and a thin panel of glass.

It drove him crazy, just thinking about it.

7

A few flakes of snow — or maybe it was ash from a distant chimney — drifted down from a slate-gray sky.

Inspector Homer Bradley leaned back in his dark green leather chair. He put his feet up on his desk, used the toe of a polished black loafer to nudge aside the carved cedar box in which he kept his expensive Cuban cigars. The three silver crowns on his right shoulder gleamed in the light from the fluorescents.

He waved the Kenny Lee file at Willows. "Not a lot here, Jack. What else have you got?"

"Not much," said Willows. He glanced at Parker but she was looking out the window, peering over the top of the adjoining building, watching the snow fall into the harbor. Due to the influence of the ocean, the city's climate was fairly mild. It rarely snowed more than two or three times during a winter, but this year the mountains on the North Shore were glistening and white.

"You talked to Lee's wife?" Bradley corrected himself, "I mean, his widow?"

Willows nodded. "She couldn't tell us a thing."

Bradley picked up the file, flipped it open and read briefly. "He disappeared when?"

"January first," said Parker. "Didn't come home from work."

Bradley studied the top photograph in the open folder that lay on his desk. Lee had a narrow, unlined face. He was fifty-seven years old. Bradley would have guessed his age at about forty-five. He glanced out the window. The snow, if that's what it was, was much thicker now, big fat raggedy flakes drifting straight down out of the sky. It deadened the sounds of traffic. The office was warm, the only sound a faint hissing from the overhead lights.

Willows said, "It would help if we had someone on the case who spoke Cantonese."

"Andy Wah's working traffic. I've asked for a reassignment." Bradley swung his feet off the desk. He flipped open the lid of the carved cedar box and selected a cigar. He used a pair of tiny gold-plated clippers to delicately chop the end off the cigar and said, "You come up with a cause of death yet?"

"Maybe this time tomorrow. Kirkpatrick's having a little trouble thawing out the body."

"But it was murder, you're sure about that?"

Parker said, "We found an eighteen-inch length of copper wire outside the gardens, on the boulevard. The wire had been tied in a figure-eight pattern. The knots were still intact — it had been cut. There was some blood. O positive. Lee's type. We checked with his doctor."

"You did, huh." Bradley fired up a big wooden kitchen match, waited until the flame had settled and then lit his cigar. He dropped the burning match in a used coffee cup, blew a stream of smoke towards the ceiling, sighed contentedly.

Parker continued. "Now that the ice is beginning to melt, it's obvious that Lee has massive bruises and lacerations on his wrists and ankles that are consistent with his being tightly bound for an extended period of time."

"It's almost certain," said Willows, "that he was kidnapped. It could be the kidnappers communicated with his family. Even ordered Mrs Lee to tell Tommy Wilcox he'd come back home, was okay. The reason we didn't get much out of her is because she has a heart condition and had been heavily sedated by the family doctor."

"Wonderful."

"Kirkpatrick thinks Lee was dead at least twenty-four hours before his body was dumped in the pond. But so far, there's no way of knowing how soon he died after he was snatched."

Bradley studied the texture and density of the ash on the end of his cigar. "You interviewed the people Lee worked with?"

"Some of them."

"Did he have any business partners?"

"He was the paper's sole owner. His father started the business in nineteen-thirteen."

"Father still alive?"

Willows shook his head. "He died five years ago. But according to the staff, Lee was running things long before then."

"Who inherits?"

"The wife, his son and daughter."

"Figure any of them might've bumped him off?"

Parker said, "I doubt it."

"Why?"

"The daughter's thirteen years old. The son's at Harvard. Now that his father's dead, he'll probably have to come home."

Bradley said, "And the grieving widow'd probably have a heart attack if she tried to waste him, so the whole damn family's in the clear." He tipped ash into the coffee cup. "Did Lee have any pressing gambling debts?"

"Not that we know of."

"The kid in Boston, he might know something."

Willows nodded. "He's flying out for the funeral. We'll talk to him."

"Be nice to get this one solved, Jack. You touch base with the Asian Crimes Squad?"

"Claire talked to Sergeant Montecino."

"And?"

Parker said, "Except for that case about five years ago, the gangs have stayed away from kidnapping. Nobody knows why. Extortion, yes. But body-snatching, no."

Bradley tipped about a dollar's worth of cigar ash into his ashtray. There were four men of Chinese descent on the Vancouver police force. None of them had worked undercover. The Chinese community was too tightly-knit, and the work too dangerous. The Asian gangs were hitting the front pages at least once a week. Worried parents were sending their kids across town to West Side schools to stop the gangs from recruiting their children. Bradley had several unsolved gang-related murders on his hands, one of them almost two years old. Community relations, never good, were rapidly deteriorating. Another dead-end case and the chief would be after his ass.

"Know what this cigar cost?"

"No idea," said Parker.

"Jack?"

66

"A nickel?"

Bradley snorted, spewing smoke. "Seven dollars. Can you believe it! I first started smoking the things five, maybe six years ago. At the time, you could buy 'em in that cigar store down in Gastown for two bucks apiece, six for ten dollars. I was a staff sergeant, married and supporting a family. In the course of a day, I'd smoke three of the suckers, never even think about it. And I'd *enjoy* them, because I could *afford* them. Now the cigars are three times as expensive, but I can still afford them because I got promoted and I make more money." He waved the cigar in the air, making thin donuts of smoke. "But I'm not enjoying this particular cigar one little bit. Know why?"

"Why?" said Parker.

"Because there's a killer out there, some wise-ass with a garden hose who thinks he's real cute. And I'm not going to enjoy anything very much until we nail his ass to the courthouse wall." Bradley gave them a hard look. "Got it?"

"We're motivated as hell, Inspector."

"Good."

"What'd you think of Bradley's pep talk?" Parker said as she and Willows hurried across the alley behind 312 Main, picked their way through rutted, grease-streaked slush and into the reverberating depths of the police parking lot.

"I've heard better."

Willows had pulled an unmarked Ford Fairlane from the motor pool. The car was parked two floors beneath ground level. They walked side by side down the concrete ramp. A patrol car squealed around the corner behind them. The car swung wide, and the uniformed cop behind the wheel leaned on the horn. Willows grabbed Parker by the elbow and pulled her out of the way. The cop winked at them as the car shot past. It was a game, like it or not, that everybody played.

The Fairlane was parked at the far end of the third level. Willows unlocked Parker's door and then walked around to the far side of the car, climbed in. Parker fastened her safety belt as Willows turned the key. The engine kicked over and the exhaust vented blue smoke.

Vice busted drug dealers and confiscated their shiny new

Porsches, BMWs and Corvettes, but the city in its wisdom auctioned the cars off, instead of letting the department keep the vehicles for its own use. Sometimes Willows contemplated a move to Miami Beach, where it never snowed and hardly ever rained, and homicide dicks wore thousand-dollar silk suits and rode in style.

He put the Ford in gear and started up the concrete incline towards ground level.

"Where we headed, Jack?"

"Starlite Films." Willows braked at the alley. He checked to make sure there was no oncoming traffic and made a left turn. "With your looks, haven't you ever thought about being a movie star?"

Parker rolled down her window. A blast of cold wet air rushed through the car.

"Hey, what're you doing!"

"Getting a breath of fresh air, Jack."

Starlite Films was located in a squat brick building directly across the street from the Sun Yat-Sen Gardens. There was metered parking on the street, a parking lot next to the building. There were seven spaces but only three of them were occupied. Willows parked the Ford next to a shiny black Jeep Wagoneer, flipped down the sun visor so the plasticized white and black card reading POLICE VEHICLE was clearly visible. He and Parker got out of the car, locked it, and walked across the lot and into the building. There was no elevator. Stairs led to a receptionist's desk on the second floor.

The receptionist was in her early twenties, a slim redhead with bright green eyes, maybe just a bit too much makeup. She was wearing a pleated black skirt, white blouse. Her lipstick was dark red, and matched her nail polish. Her nails were very long.

There was a matt-black Olivetti on her desk. Parker had a hard time imagining her risking those nails on the typewriter keys.

Willows introduced himself and Parker, gave her a quick look at his shield.

She said, "I'm Cynthia Woodward. I take it you're here to enquire about the body that was found in the pond yesterday morning?"

Willows nodded.

"Well, what can I do for you?" The woman spoke to Willows, ignored Parker.

"We think the body was put in the pond late Sunday night, or maybe early Monday morning . . . "

"Why?"

The question caught Willows by surprise. He hesitated, and then said, "There are indications the body had been on the ice about six to eight hours before it was discovered."

"We were open Saturday until four o'clock. Four in the afternoon. I was the last one out of the building, I locked up."

"So, from four o'clock on, there was no one here?"

"I'm afraid not."

"You don't employ a night watchman?"

"No, we never have."

"What about the janitorial service?"

"They do a weekly clean-up. On Sundays. I believe they start at ten in the morning."

Willows went over to the window and looked out. Even from the second floor, he could see over the wall of the gardens. The pond, or at least most of it, was clearly visible.

"The top two floors. What's up there?"

"Mr McGuinn and Mr Sandlack have offices directly above us. The fourth floor is used as a storage area."

"I'd like to talk to them. Would you mind letting them know we're here, please."

"Mr McGuinn is in Los Angeles."

"How long has he been gone?"

"Since Wednesday."

"And Mr Sandlack?"

Cynthia Woodward picked up a telephone, delicately tapped a button. The diamond on the third finger of her left hand flashed in the light. She said, "I'm sorry to disturb you, Mr Sandlack, but there's a policeman here who'd like to talk to you." A pause. "About the body that was found in the gardens." She listened for a moment, nodded. "Yes, sir. I'll send them right up."

Willows started towards the stairs. The secretary frowned after him.

Parker said, "That's a lovely perfume you're wearing. Would you mind telling me what it is?"

"Fabergé." The woman smiled. "Mr Sandlack's office is the first door on your left."

All five foot six inches and one hundred and twenty pounds of Eugene Sandlack was waiting for them in the corridor. He was wearing a gray silk suit, an off-white shirt and a dark gray silk tie, shiny black slip-ons. Sandlack expertly shot his cuff as he offered his hand, flashing a gold Rolex and half a pound of eighteen-karat gold chain. No wonder Cynthia Woodward hadn't seemed too impressed when Willows showed her his tin. Sandlack's teeth were very white. His short, curly hair was gelled and glistening, with a sprinkling of silvery-gray at the temples. He had a Palm Springs tan and there were pouches under his dark brown eyes. He shook hands with Willows first, and then Parker.

"What can I do for you, Officers?"

"We're enquiring about the body that was found in the pond across the street on Monday morning."

"Kenny Lee, wasn't it?"

"You knew him?"

"Never met the guy. Heard about it on the radio as I was driving to work. And, of course, when I arrived at the office, I couldn't help noticing that there were cops all over the place. Lucky thing I heard the report on the news. Otherwise, I'd have figured some bastard was shooting a movie in my backyard, and I already got enough problems with my ulcer." Sandlack indicated the open door leading to his office. "Come on in, make yourself at home."

The office was airy and spacious. A computer rested on a large mahogany desk by the window. There were oak filing cabinets ranged along the far wall. A small bar occupied the opposite wall. Sandlack leaned a slim hip on the edge of an oak desk that was big enough to land a small airplane.

"Can I get you a drink? Coffee . . . "

"Nothing, thanks."

"I presume you're here because our building overlooks the gardens."

"We were hoping you, or one of your employees, might have seen something unusual."

"Sorry, can't help you. Cynthia and I talked about it. She probably already told you, the two of us were the only ones here on Saturday, and we were both gone by four. So the place was empty from then until eight o'clock Monday morning — and by then you guys were already on the job."

"Does Miss Woodward usually work on weekends?"

"*Mrs* Woodward," said Sandlack.

Willows nodded. "Right. Does she usually work on weekends?"

Sandlack's tan turned a shade darker. "No, certainly not. I've been working on a pilot for a new series, and I had a deadline."

Willows said, "I understand there's a janitorial service?"

"Sundays, from about ten. You want their number?"

"Please."

"Cynthia'll give it to you, she's got it on the Rolodex." Sandlack waggled a manicured finger at Parker. "I been trying to work out where I saw you before. You had a bit part in a *Wise Guy* episode a few years ago, am I right?"

"Not me," said Parker, smiling back.

"Something else?" Sandlack frowned. "Help me out, refresh my memory."

"I used to work traffic. Maybe I handed you a ticket."

"Jesus, that's sure as hell a possibility. A silver Rolls, you remember the car?"

"Not really."

"So you've never done any acting, huh. Interested?"

"I don't think so."

"Tom Cruise, the name ring a bell?" Sandlack's Rolex had slipped sideways on his wrist, but in his excitement he didn't notice. "Tom's ninety percent signed to do a flick called *Ultimatum*. Ten million budget. He plays an oceanographer. But Tom's also, and the twist is that the greedy bastards who pay his salary don't know this, a very committed ecologist. What happens, there's an oil spill, see, and . . . " Sandlack grinned. "We could run a screen test, fit you in somewhere . . . "

"Thanks, anyway."

"Think about it, okay?" Sandlack went around behind his desk, opened a drawer, scribbled a number on the back of a rectangle of stiff cardboard. "My private number. You change your mind, just give me a call. In a six-week shoot, you'd make more money than a cop earns in a year." He smiled. "And if anybody shoots at you, it's blanks."

Parker slipped the card into her purse.

"If you think of anything . . . " said Willows. He gave Sandlack one of *his* cards. It wasn't made of expensive white bond, but it did have nice gold and blue lettering on it.

Sandlack slipped the card in the breast pocket of his shiny gray silk suit without bothering to look at it. He made a complicated, expansive gesture with his manicured hands. As if he had something else to say but didn't know how to put it. Or maybe he just wanted to show off the Rolex and the thick gold chain on his left wrist. He said, "If I think of anything, I'll have Cynthia call you right away. We can shmooze, take a lunch." He grinned. "In the meantime, am I free to leave town?"

"Of course," said Willows. Thinking, *just do me a favor and don't come back.*

On the way out, they stopped at Cynthia Woodward's desk and were given the number of the janitorial service that had the contract to clean the building.

Willows said, "We're going across the street for a few minutes. Okay if we leave our car in your lot?"

"No problem," said Cynthia. "I mean, why spend money on the meter when you can stay with us for free?"

On the way across the street, Parker said, "I liked his jewelry."

"You did, huh?"

"His chains," said Parker. "I've always had a thing about men in chains."

"Put him in a pair of cuffs, he'd be perfect."

"Solid gold, of course."

The fire department had put several pumps to work, and the water level had fallen drastically, resulting in the collapse of large areas of ice. Willows estimated it would be another couple of hours before the pond was pumped dry.

He and Parker visited Dr Yang in his office. The doctor was not in a good mood.

"The closure of the gardens for a day or two is tolerable," he said from behind his desk. "But all this negative publicity. My telephone never stops ringing! The world is full of ghouls!" Yang removed his glasses and angrily polished them with a paisley-patterned handkerchief. "This world is unique — the only classical Chinese gardens outside mainland China. I have a sacred trust! And do you know, I suspect Mr Lee's body was put in the pond because racist elements wish to damage our reputation!"

"I'd advise you not to share those thoughts with the media," said Willows.

"It won't last," said Parker. "Reporters have a short attention span. Give it a day or two, they'll be gnawing on some other bone."

"Yes, well. I certainly hope so."

There was a *bonsai* — an artfully clipped miniature pine tree — in a carved stone pot on Yang's desk. Yang reached out and touched a branch with the tips of his fingers. It was a strange gesture, delicate and somehow vaguely erotic.

"You have finished questioning my staff?"

Willows nodded.

"Were they of any assistance?"

"No, I'm afraid not."

"I thought as much." Yang's telephone rang shrilly. He flinched. The telephone rang again. He took a moment to compose himself, then scooped it up and said in a very quiet voice, "Dr Yang speaking."

He listened carefully for a moment and then said, "Yes, certainly. I'll see you then," and hung up.

"My wife. She called to remind me that I am to pick up a bottle of white wine on the way home tonight." He smiled at Parker. "We are having guests for dinner. Life goes on."

At a few minutes past five, the pumps sucked the last of the water out of the pond. Darkness had fallen, and a ring of lights had been set up around the perimeter. Willows borrowed a pair of knee-high rubber boots and joined the search team. Three hours later, all they'd come up with was an empty beer bottle, a number of candy-bar wrappers and other debris, several coins and a soggy five-dollar bill.

Just as they decided to call it a night, a fireman poking around in the area of the drainage vent stumbled across a brass key frozen in a hunk of ice. The key and beer bottle and money and candy-bar wrappers went into separate evidence envelopes. The search team took off their rubber boots and dispersed.

It was still snowing as Willows and Parker walked across the street to the unmarked Ford parked in the Starlite Films lot.

The snow was fresh and clean as it fell from the sky, but turned to slush as soon as it touched the pavement. Willows wondered what the weather was like in Toronto. Cold. He thought about phoning the kids when he got home, and then remembered the three-hour time difference. It was past eleven in Toronto. Annie and Sean would be in bed, sound asleep, dreaming.

"What're you looking so serious about?" said Parker.

"I was just thinking that it's about time you got a decent job, met a guy and settled down."

"You want me to take Sandlack up on his offer, is that it? Marry Tom Cruise?"

"Sure, why not?"

"You know what I think?"

"What?"

"I think it's been a long day, and we could both use a hot meal."

"And a stiff drink."

"That, too," said Parker, smiling.

8

Billy and Garret's favorite fence was a skinny bald guy they'd nicknamed Crayon. He was tall and thin and wore skin-tight clothes, but they called him Crayon mainly because his skin was kind of sticky-looking, waxy. Crayon's real name — or at least the one Billy knew him by — was Dennis. Dennis the Menace.

The fence lived in a crumbling stucco house on East Seventeenth, directly across the street from a BC Hydro sub-station. No matter what time of the day or night you dropped by, he always seemed to be home.

Billy parked his Pinto, got out and slammed shut the door. The chain-link fence protecting the sub-station was about ten feet high, topped with three strands of barbed wire. There were metal signs all over the place: WARNING! HIGH VOLTAGE! DANGER! KEEP OUT!

Or fry, and die, thought Billy. He listened to the faint buzz and crackle of electricity. The power station looked and sounded like a set from an old horror movie. He was reminded of Ted Bundy, the serial killer who'd got the electric chair in Texas. Snap crackle pop! So long, Ted. Billy'd read everything he could about the guy. Now, as he walked around to the back of the Pinto, he tried to imagine what it must feel like to have several thousand volts tossed through your body. The horror of *being there*. Did it hurt, that ultimate jolt? Or was the sensation of pain so huge that it drowned out the pain itself, and there was only a kind of vast numbness, as your hair burnt and your eyes popped out of your head . . . ?

Billy shivered, and it wasn't the cold that had given him goosebumps. That was the great thing about Canada. No death penalty. You could wipe out half a city, they'd give you a life sentence but they couldn't take your life away.

He unlocked the Pinto's trunk and pulled out a battered cardboard box full of stolen radios and related electronic equipment. He slammed the trunk shut and, the box held tightly to his chest, jogged across the street and down a narrow, slimy concrete pathway that led around to the side of Dennis' rotting, neglected house.

At the back, there was a wide wooden door. Billy bent a knee to take the weight of the box, knocked twice.

His knuckles stung — the door was the only solid part of the house, and it was unyielding as a rock. He waited. Nothing. His arms ached. The box was getting heavy. He swore imaginatively, pounded on thick wood with the meaty side of his fist.

Without warning, the door swung open roughly the width of a human eye.

The bright beam of a flashlight played across his face, blinding him.

"Billy."

"Yeah, right."

"You're supposed to be here at seven."

Billy held up his left hand. He tapped the crystal of his watch, a Seiko he'd boosted, brand-new and still in the gift box, out of the backseat of an Audi. The beam of the flashlight settled on his wrist. He said, "That's what time it is, Dennis. On the nose."

"Just hold on a minute, okay. I got somebody with me, I'm runnin' late."

The door slammed shut.

"Fuck you," said Billy, but not too loud. He put the box down on the damp sidewalk and pulled out a crumpled pack of Viceroys. In the brief flare of the match, his face was all bone and shadow. He flicked the dead match over the fence into the neighbor's yard, stuck his hands in his pockets and leaned against the house. It was the coldest winter of his short life. He wondered if it was going to snow again. His mind drifted back to Ted Bundy. In Texas, you murdered somebody, there was a good chance you'd go to the chair. But at least it was warm all year round, you wouldn't freeze your ass off. Billy had never been to Texas, but he knew about the state's weather from watching *Dallas* on his mother's television. A guy could learn a hell of a lot, sitting on the couch with a cold beer, watching TV.

He held his left wrist up close to his face and sucked hard on his cigarette. In the quick orange glow of the burning end, he saw that it was almost ten past seven.

Jesus Christ but Dennis was an asshole. The way he operated, it was amazing he managed to stay in business. About the only place in the whole world Billy could think of where the service was worse was at the chain take-out chicken joint down the block from his mom's.

The door swung open.

"Sorry about that," said Dennis.

Billy twitched guiltily. It was as if Dennis had been reading his mind. "Hey," he said, "no problem."

Dennis stepped aside and Billy went through the open door and into the basement. The fence slammed the door shut, secured it with an inch-thick steel deadbolt and a pair of metal bars as thick as Billy's wrist. The first time he'd done business with Dennis, Billy'd figured all the steel was to keep the cops out. Dennis had thought that was pretty goddamn funny. He'd explained that when your customers were thieves, you had to worry about securing the premises against theft. As for cops, well, cops were like roaches — if they wanted in, there was no fuckin' way you were gonna keep them out.

Dennis pointed at the cigarette. "No smoking down here, kid. You know that."

Billy dropped the Viceroy on the concrete floor, ground it to a pulp under his heel.

"Whatcha got for me?"

Billy slid the box on to a heavy wooden counter just inside the door.

"Five Blaupunkts, a couple Alpines including a CD player, and an MEI deck with a set of Pioneer speakers. Also a real good Sony power amp."

"MEI?" Dennis used the tips of his fingers to play a little tune on his scalp. It was as if he was trying to access information, get at the brain that lay beneath the surface of taut, shiny pink skin. He said, "Never heard of it."

"Mobile Audio Systems. It's a shuttle deck. Real nice piece of equipment. Dolby, Music Search. Retail, cost you five, six hundred bucks."

"Retail," said Dennis. "What the fuck is that? I never heard of it." He went over to a bookshelf by the wall, looked through his catalogues, shook his head.

Billy pulled the radios out of the box, lined them up on the counter. A shuttle deck was designed so the radio slid in and out of a compartment mounted in or under a car's dashboard. The owner could remove it in seconds, take it with him or lock it away in the trunk. On the other hand, if the guy left it in the car . . . No wires to cut, just push a button and pop it out. Shuttle decks were a lazy thief's dream.

Dennis came back to the counter thumbing through his Blaupunkt and Alpine catalogues. He started to look up the prices.

Billy stuck a Viceroy in his mouth, then remembered the no smoking rule. He dropped his lighter back in his jacket pocket.

"Still working with that red-haired pal of yours, Garry?"

"Garret."

Dennis shrugged. "Whatever." He licked his thumb and turned a page. Billy had a fast mouth, was always knocking his pal, putting him down. He saw himself as a tough guy, but somehow Garret worked it so Billy was the one who played delivery boy, took the risks. And Garret always gave Dennis a call later, to see how much he'd paid . . . Keeping tabs on Billy without letting him know about it. Garret had the brains, no doubt about it. Probably Billy's IQ was about the same as his shoe size.

Billy leaned a blue-jeaned hip against the counter, glanced casually around the basement. Dennis' main thing was fencing stolen property, but he also bootlegged beer and hard liquor after hours at a hundred percent mark-up. Not that out of line. Restaurants had the same profit margin. Dennis preferred cash but would barter if he had to. One end of the basement was like a clothing store — long wooden racks stuffed with jackets, most of them leather. Billy tried to imagine being hard up enough for a drink to sell the shirt off his back. He couldn't picture it.

"Forty each for the Alpines," said Dennis. "Except this one, I'll go fifty. For the Blaupunkts, I'll go sixty apiece. Twenty for the MEI shuttle. I don't like the look of all those little buttons. Hit 'em hard enough, they might fall off and then where would I be?"

"No fuckin' way," said Billy.

"Add it up, kid. Six hundred and fifty bucks. Not bad wages for kicking the shit out of a few car windows. Something you'd probably do for nothing, anyhow."

"I don't do nothin' for nothin'," said Billy.

Grinning, Dennis started to put the radios back in the box.

"I'll do it," said Billy. "You might drop one, and then where would I be." He took a Blaupunkt from Dennis and put it in the box.

Dennis rubbed his jaw. He needed a shave, and in the quiet of the basement, Billy could hear the dry, scratchy whisper of the bristles under his palm. He shrugged and said, "Okay, let's make it seven hundred."

"Eight," said Billy.

Dennis dug around in his back pocket and hauled out a wad of fifties, folded in half. He counted off fourteen bills, slapped the money down on the counter so each bill partially overlapped the one that had gone before it.

"Seven. Take it or leave it."

Billy grabbed the MEI and stuck it under his leather jacket. The money went into his jeans.

Dennis stared at him for a moment, then nodded and said, "You got a bad attitude, kid. I like it. You're gonna go far, you don't get nailed."

Billy laughed. "How the hell's anybody ever gonna catch me, when I can hardly keep up with myself?"

But driving home in the Pinto, scrubbing at the windshield because the heater didn't work and the glass kept misting up, Billy was so angry he wanted to smash something, or burst into tears.

Seven hundred bucks for a whole goddamn week spent skulking around back alleys, parking lots, rich people's garages. And he owed Garret half which left him with a lousy three-fifty. Billy added it up. Three hundred and fifty times four was . . . one thousand four hundred dollars a month. Times twelve . . . The numbers got all scrambled around in his brain. It was hard to think and drive all at the same time . . . Something like sixteen or seventeen grand a year. Wowie.

He flicked the butt of the Viceroy out the window, lit another. Sixteen grand a year. Fuckin' cigarette money. And he'd already, though Dennis didn't know it, gone down twice, spent time at the

Willingdon detention centre. Couple more months he'd be eighteen years old. No more juvie heaven, with his record. Dennis had given him something to think about — getting caught. Next time it'd be adult court. Two years less a day in Oakalla, that pig-pen. Big time. Hard time.

And all for what? Three-fifty a week, barely enough to stay afloat. He couldn't live with his goddamn mother forever, could he?

For a long time now, Billy had been thinking that he had to get into another line of work. Something riskier, and better paying. Not banks. The average take was less than a grand and he'd heard the cops' clearance rate was seventy percent. Real bad odds. He had to figure out a better way. Some way of making a lot of money without hanging his ass too far out into the wind.

What kind of success could Dennis ever hope to be, when he didn't even know his own product line? Fucking dummy. Billy rolled down his window and chucked the MEI shuttle deck on to the road. The radio cartwheeled across the pavement, hit the curb and disintegrated. A waste. But the thing was, he'd wanted to make a point. Dennis had to be made to understand the way things were.

It was Billy who ripped people off. Not the other way around.

9

Mrs Lee lived in the Oakridge district, two blocks from the children's hospital. Parker drove south on Oak to Thirty-third, turned right. It was a solid, middle-class neighborhood; the houses were large and in good repair, the gardens spacious and well-tended.

"What was the address again?" said Parker.

"Eighteen twenty-seven."

The house was a sprawling rancher with a shake roof and dark-stained cedar siding. It was on the north side of the street, near the end of the block. The snow had been shovelled from the pink-colored concrete sidewalk that wound from the street up to the house.

Parker pulled the Ford in tight against the curb and turned off the engine.

"How're we going to handle this?"

Willows shrugged. "I guess the main thing is, let's try not to give her a heart attack."

"Good thinking, Jack."

"I'll ask her a few questions. We'll see how she reacts. If it doesn't seem to be going very well, I'll back off and you can take over."

"And in the meantime, don't steal the silverware, right?"

"Or grab all the cookies on the plate, or slurp your tea."

There was a doorbell. Willows punched the button. Chimes sounded inside the house.

The door swung open immediately, as if the girl on the other side had been waiting for the knock.

Willows introduced himself, and Parker.

"Come in, please." The child extended her hand in a curiously formal gesture. "I am Melinda Lee."

Melinda Lee was thirteen years old, with the slim, compact body of a ballerina. She had a tiny face; her delicate bone structure set off by large brown eyes. Her thick black hair was cut very short. She wore a white blouse and a dark blue pleated skirt, shiny black patent-leather pumps. She offered Willows her hand, and after a moment's hesitation, he took it. Melinda Lee's palm was cold and damp. She turned to Parker, nodded and said, "My mother is waiting in the living room. Please come this way." She offered a tentative smile. "Because her English is not very good, I will stay and translate, if you like."

"Please," said Parker.

The living room was to the right of the entrance hall. Mrs Lee was sitting in a reproduction antique oak rocking chair in front of the fireplace. She wore a thick, bulky black sweater, and her lower body and legs were covered by a fringed black shawl. A photograph of Kenny Lee stood on the mantel. Parker noticed that everything in the house looked new — the carpets and furniture, even the paint on the walls. Mrs Lee's eyes were closed — she might have been sleeping. Her daughter spoke softly to her, and she raised her head and gave the two detectives a little bow.

"Sit down, please."

Parker chose an ornately carved wooden chair by a writing desk near the window. No draft — double glazing. Willows sat in a wingback chair on the opposite side of the fireplace from the widow Lee.

Willows took out his notebook. "We're sorry to have to bother you at a time like this, to intrude on your grief. Hopefully, this won't take long."

"The main thing is to find the murderer," Melinda whispered dramatically. A bad actress delivering a bad line. Parker stared at her, and she blushed.

"Our main problem," said Willows, diving right in, "is that we don't have a motive. Was . . . Did your husband keep large quantities of cash in the bank?"

Mrs Lee hesitated. Melinda spoke softly to her in Cantonese. She shook her head, and Melinda said, "We have discussed this. Except for the money required to run the household, all the profits went back into the newspaper."

"We understand your father gambled, is that right?"

"Mah-jong," said Melinda promptly.

Mrs Lee burst into tears and buried her face in a linen handkerchief.

Melinda ignored her. "He belonged to a society, and he was an excellent player. I have seen him play. He won far more often than he lost. Otherwise he would not have enjoyed the game. But in any case, the stakes were not large."

"Could you be a little more specific, please?"

"He told me that during an entire evening, it was not possible to lose more than five or ten dollars."

"How often did he play?"

"Once a week. Wednesday nights."

"And that was the extent of his gambling? Did he, for example, frequent the track?"

A look of confusion fluttered across Melinda's face.

"Play the horses," explained Parker.

"No, never. Of course not. Except for the mah-jong, father was not a gambler. Neither did he smoke, or drink alcohol. The newspaper took all his energy. He was a very hard-working man."

Mrs Lee had stopped crying. Willows glanced at Parker. There was something going on between Melinda and her mother — he had a sense of unresolved conflict. He wanted to separate them. Parker, catching Willows' eye, immediately realized what he wanted.

"Melinda, would you mind showing me the kitchen? I'd like a glass of water."

Melinda stared at her. After a moment she said, "Yes, of course." As she led Parker out of the room, she spoke briefly to her mother in Cantonese. Willows saw the old woman's eyes narrow. He wondered what Melinda had said — a warning of some kind?

Willows moved the wingback chair a little closer to the rocker.

"The problem is motive," said Willows bluntly. Mrs Lee watched him, her eyes bright. He said, "If someone killed your husband, it was done for a reason. A large gambling debt he couldn't pay or refused to pay. Or something to do with his business . . . A partnership offer he turned down, an article he printed . . . Do you know what extortion is?"

Mrs Lee burst into tears, the sound of her anguish filling the living room.

Willows sat there, waiting.

Mrs Lee stood up. The black shawl puddled on the pale green carpet. She walked slowly and silently across the room to the writing desk by the window, eased open the top drawer and withdrew a plain white envelope. In a voice fragile as a paper flower, Mrs Lee said, "There was one telephone call. It came on Sunday, the tenth. My husband was on the line. He sounded as if he was in pain. He told me he'd been kidnapped, and that the people who held him wanted two hundred and fifty thousand dollars."

Mrs Lee slid shut the drawer. She made her way slowly back to the rocking chair. Willows handed her the shawl. His eyes were on the envelope, but he didn't let his impatience show.

"My husband spoke in a monotone, almost as if he had been drugged, and he spoke only for a few brief moments. He ignored my questions, and he forbade me to call the police. Then he told me I was to pay nothing, not one penny."

She handed Willows the envelope. He held it by the edges, between his thumb and index finger.

"As he told me not to pay, there was a cry of pain, and the line went dead." Mrs Lee stared at the envelope in Willows' hand. "He did not want me to involve the police, but I had already done so. And that is why I telephoned Detective Wilcox and told him my husband was safe."

Willows made a gesture of sympathy. "You didn't hear from him again?"

"There were no more telephone calls. But two days later, in the morning, I found that someone had slipped that envelope through the mailbox."

"What does the envelope contain?"

"As you would expect. A demand for the money. But for one hundred thousand dollars, this time."

"Could you have afforded to pay?"

"Eventually, perhaps. At the bank there is a joint account but it never contains more than a few thousand dollars. There are other accounts, but I know nothing of them, other than that they exist. My husband was a very secretive man. He did not think there was any need for me to have access to the accounts."

"Would you have paid, had you been able to?"

"Yes," said Mrs Lee firmly.

"Given more time, could you have raised the money from outside sources? Friends, relatives . . . "

"Perhaps."

"Would the kidnappers be aware of this?"

"It is impossible to say."

"Were there any further attempts at communication?"

"No."

The fireplace was gas-fed. The flames danced across the ceramic logs, radiating heat.

Willows said, "You did what you could. All that matters now is catching the man who killed your husband."

Another burst of tears.

Parker and Melinda came back into the room. The girl sat down on the carpet next to her mother.

"The phone call," said Willows. "When your husband was on the line, did you hear any other voices, someone in the background?"

"Yes, yes." She stared at Willows. "How did you know of this?"

"What kind of voice was it?"

"A woman's. Young."

"Was she talking to your husband, or to someone else?"

"Not to my husband."

"Could she have been Chinese? Did you notice an accent of any kind?"

"No."

"Was it a local call?"

A look of confusion crossed Mrs Lee's face.

"Could it have been long distance?" said Parker. "Did you hear the jingle of coins, an operator's voice?"

"No, nothing like that."

"Was there any background noise? Traffic, some kind of machinery, music . . . "

"Yes, there was the woman's voice and then there was music."

"What kind?"

Mrs Lee turned to her daughter, spoke rapidly in Cantonese.

"Country and western," said Melinda. "Very loud. The woman's voice my mother mentioned? It was the voice of a radio disc-jockey."

Willows had several more questions. He asked them one by one, and the answers he received were detailed and totally uninformative. Half an hour later, he gave Mrs Lee his card. "If you think of anything else . . . "

"We'll call you," said Melinda.

"Right away," said Willows. "I can be reached any time during the day or night."

"Yes, thank you."

"Your brother, Peter, will be coming home for the funeral?"

"Of course."

"When he arrives, would you mind asking him to give me a call?"

"Why, what do you wish to speak to him about?"

Willows smiled. "Nothing in particular. Just a few routine questions."

Outside, a skim of frost had collected on the Ford's windshield. Willows turned the heater on full, and then the wipers. The ice slowly turned to slush.

"Any thoughts?" said Parker.

"The girl kept butting in."

"Protecting her mother, that's all."

"And Peter. You see the look on her face when I said I wanted to talk to him?"

Parker said, "She's just a kid. Scared, doing her best to cope. Peter's in Boston. Her mother spends all day in her rocking chair. So she's stuck with the job of trying to be head of the family."

"Acting a role she's too young to play."

"You got it."

"You're probably right," said Willows.

The windshield had cleared. He turned off the wipers and put the Ford in gear.

They took the white envelope containing the ransom note down to CLEU, the Coordinated Law Enforcement Unit facilities on East Eighth that were shared by the City and neighboring municipalities. A technician named Albert Witte pulled on a pair of disposable latex gloves and shook the letter out of the envelope

86

and on to his desk. Witte was about five foot ten, thin. His hair was combed straight back and he had pale blue, washed-out eyes. He wore a white lab coat over wide-wale green corduroy pants and a matching vest.

"Very unusual," he said. "Very creative."

The ransom note consisted of words and phrases that had been cut out of magazines and newspapers and then glued to a sheet of stiff cardboard. The note was short and to the point.

Witte said, "This is the newspaper guy, body turned up in that pond in Chinatown?"

Willows nodded.

"First thing we'll do is dust for prints. Use the laser if we can't pick anything up. Also, we should be able to figure out what newspapers and magazines were used. The brand of glue, you want it." Witte studied the envelope. He said, "It'll take us a while, but we can determine who manufactured the envelopes. From the envelope flap, we might be able to figure out a blood type. Got a suspect?"

"Not yet."

"There's a rush on this, naturally."

"Naturally."

"I'll get at it first thing in the morning."

"Why not right now?"

"Because I go home in five minutes."

"Put in some overtime."

"For what, so I can pay higher taxes?"

Willows said. "What do I have to do, make a phone call?"

"It's your quarter," said Witte, smiling. "Do what you want with it. I got to tell you, though, it'd be less of a waste if you stuffed it up your ass."

Back in the Ford, Willows stared moodily out the windshield at the gray slush, hunched pedestrians. He said, "When I was a kid, we had one of those old wringer washing machines, but no dryer. In the winter, mom hung our clothes out on the line on the back porch to dry. When it was really cold, below freezing, she'd bring in the laundry and everything would be stiff as a board. Sometimes I'd grab one of the towels and pretend it was a magic carpet. Sit a doll on one and run around the house . . . "

"You had a doll?"

"My sister had dolls. I'd borrow 'em."

Parker smiled. "I just can't picture a tough guy like you playing with dolls, Jack."

Willows nodded his understanding. "Yeah, neither can I, sometimes. Childhood. Time steals it away, along with every other goddamn thing you ever thought you owned. I don't know why it is, but after a while it all seems as if it happened to somebody else."

"You're thinking about Melinda Lee."

"Acting the adult. Trying to protect her mother from something."

"From us, maybe?"

"Maybe," said Willows. "You get anything out of her while you were in the kitchen?"

"Only that the fridge's automatic defroster wasn't working."

Willows waited for a break in the traffic and then turned right on Oak, towards the city.

"Most of my sister's dolls were blondes or redheads, but my favorite had brown eyes and short black hair."

"Just like me," said Parker.

"No," said Willows, grinning. "Just like my mother."

10

There was a pool hall on East Hastings that Billy liked to go to —
it had a brass button on the door you had to push and if the guy
inside didn't object to the way you looked, he'd hit another
button and a buzzer would sound and you could go inside. The
first time Billy'd gone there he'd spent a couple of hours hanging
out on the sidewalk in front of the place, leaning on a parking
meter and smoking. Watching the citizens go by. He'd been broke
and had nothing better to do, figured he'd see what kind of people
were turned away, before he took his chances.

Nobody was turned away. Nobody. Even a couple of beat cops
got let in, and they didn't even bother to push the button, just
banged on the door with a nightstick.

But, Billy noticed, the cops were kept waiting long enough to
give the paying customers time to flush their stash down the toilet,
drop a blade on the floor where it could be anybody's . . .

"You do it," said Billy. It was cold, and he didn't want to take
his hands out of his pockets.

Garret tweaked the brass button with his thumb and index
finger, like it was a nipple. Here he was doing Billy's chores again.

"Quit fuckin' around, will you?"

Garret got a grip on his temper, pushed the button. The buzzer
rasped. Billy shoved the door open with the pointed, metal-
capped toe of his cowboy boot, swaggered inside.

The pool hall was a favorite hangout of the Red Eagles, a
Chinese youth gang. There were eight full-size tables in two rows
down the length of the room. To the left of the door there was a
wooden counter with a glass top, the cash register. Beyond the
counter stood a rack for cues, a Coke machine and several video
machines. The owner was a short, fat Chinese guy named Mike,
who was maybe fifty years old and never looked at you but

always seemed to know exactly where you were. Mike carried a sawed-off pool cue tucked in the back pocket of his baggy pants, and he was the only Chinese Billy'd ever met who always needed a shave.

Mike ignored Garret, nodded to Billy. "How's it hangin', white boy?"

"Ask your girlfriend," said Billy, grinning, as he sauntered past Mike, through the blue haze of smoke and soft murmur of conversation and brittle clatter of the balls, towards an empty table at the far end of the room.

"Eight ball," said Garret. There were about a dozen Chinese kids and their girls playing pool or the video games, or just standing around looking tough. Garret was careful not to catch anybody's eye.

Mike reached under the counter and came up with a plastic tray containing the balls. There was a rumor Mike also kept a double-barrelled twelve-gauge under the counter. Garret believed the rumor was based on fact. There was something about Mike, a kind of vacant look in his eye. As if he didn't give a shit about anything and was just waiting for a chance to prove it.

"Table number two."

There were three vacant tables in the pool hall. Number two was up front. Billy was chalking up a cue at the table closest to the toilets, way at the back.

"How about six?" Garret pointed at Billy. "He's got a problem with his bladder, might have to make a run for it."

"Special favor," said Mike.

"Just don't give us no special rate."

Mike flicked a switch, and a double row of frosted neon tubing over the table snapped on, making the green felt come alive.

Garret wandered over to the rack of cues, gleaming lengths of polished maple. It cost ten dollars a month, but Billy kept his own personal cue on the premises, in the common rack but under lock and key. Garret didn't have that much interest in the game; he'd rather spend the money on his Mustang. He chose a sixteen-ounce cue, rolled it across an empty table to make sure it was reasonably straight, then dug around in the pocket of his Levis until he found three quarters, which he dropped in the Coke machine.

"You shoulda took a bent one," said Billy, pointing at Garret's cue as he approached the table. "With your eye, it'd help you shoot straighter."

"Fuck you," said Garret.

Billy grabbed Garret's Coke, drank deeply, wiped his mouth with the back of his hand. "Rack 'em."

Garret dumped the balls on the table, gathered them close together with his arms and then arranged them in a wooden triangle. He lifted the triangle carefully, to avoid disturbing the set of the balls, and dropped the rack under the table.

Billy flipped a dime. The coin flashed under the lights. "Call it."

"Heads."

The dime hit the green felt, bounced once and rolled into the middle of the table and fell over on its side.

Billy bent to peer at the coin. "Your lucky day, Garret."

Garret picked up the off-white cue ball and walked down to the far end of the table, positioned the ball and crouched over his cue.

Billy finished chalking up. He drank some more of Garret's Coke.

A video game went *bonk boing bonk.*

Garret's shoulder dipped as he made his shot. The cue ball shot down the length of the table and hit the racked balls with a sound like a small bone breaking. The balls scattered across the table, bounced off the rubber. The six ball dropped into a corner pocket.

Billy lit a cigarette.

Garret tried a bank into the near side pocket, missed by an inch.

Billy blew smoke out of his nostrils and lined up his shot.

One of the Chinese kids sauntered over, a gang member who called himself Pony. He leaned against the table. Pony wore his hair short; it was about an inch long except for a long tail at the back which he kept gathered together with a red rubber band. Billy figured that was why they called him Pony, because of the ponytail. Billy blew twin streams of smoke out of his nostrils and nodded at him. The kid nodded back. Double cool. Smoke rolled across the table like a little fogbank. Billy made a difficult shot into the far corner pocket, and tried to look as if he did it every day of his life.

"Nice shot," said Pony. "How you doin', man?"

Billy shrugged. "Gettin' by."

"Got a car?"

"I got a car," said Billy, "but I don't got a sign on the roof that says taxi."

Pony smiled. He had nice teeth. He said, "Maybe you wanna buy a radio."

Billy sank the thirteen in the far side pocket. Ash from his cigarette fell on the table. He glanced up the room at Mike, but Mike was busy making change. Garret drained his Coke and crushed the can. Pony grinned at him. Billy wiped the ash into the felt with the palm of his hand, leaving a pale gray smear. He chalked his cue and lined up his next shot.

"It's a Pioneer," said Pony. "High-power. Forty watts. Hundred bucks, and for an extra twenty I can throw in a nice pair of Alpine speakers, still in the box."

"I didn't come here for a radio," said Billy. "I already got one, unless somebody just stole it."

"Then what *are* you doing here?"

"Playing pool," said Billy, "or didn't you notice?" But he and Pony were playing another little game, a kind of verbal tag. Billy was there to buy himself a piece. Pony was there to sell it to him. The question was, who was going to make the first move?

"Your shot," said Garret.

Billy, feeling reckless and lucky, called a double bank into the side pocket and missed by six inches.

Pony wandered over to another table. He put his arm around a girl Billy figured was maybe fifteen years old and weighed eighty pounds — ninety if you counted her eye shadow and lipstick.

The video game went *bonk bonk bonk*.

Garret kissed the four ball off the eight into the end pocket and made a similar noise.

"You call that?" said Billy.

"Yeah, sure," said Garret, grinning. "Four ball off the eight and into the end pocket."

"Fuckin' fluke."

"You'd take it — why shouldn't I?"

"Anybody ever tell you that you were a first class asshole, Garret?"

"Anybody ever tell you, Billy, that you *weren't* a first class asshole?"

Sniggering over his little joke, Garret lost his concentration and missed an easy shot. Billy truly believed that was the root of all Garret's problems — that he had a sense of humor. He lit another cigarette, ran his fingers through his hair. Pony was staring at him from across the room, and so was his little chipmunk of a girlfriend, her cheeks puffy with bubblegum. Or maybe it was a cud she was chewing on, and that explained the vague, faraway look in her big brown eyes. Billy said something to Garret, giving himself a chance to look away. He turned back to Pony and the dude was still staring at him. Billy had a moment of uneasiness, but there was no belligerence in Pony's eyes. It was as if he was trying to see deep inside Billy, figure him out.

Garret sank the fourteen and twelve balls, then ran out of luck and missed, but accidentally left the cue ball tight up against the rail so Billy couldn't get a decent shot.

Billy sank a ball anyhow, the seven. He dropped the five and the one. Garret was starting to look worried. Billy missed. Garret made that snickering sound again, his confidence instantly restored. What he didn't know and would never in a million years figure out was that Billy was toying with him, leading him on.

Garret sank the ten cleanly. He went over to the counter, got Mike to make change and then bought himself another Coke. Billy waited until Garret popped the tab, then sank his last three balls and dropped the eight on a tricky three banks in the side shot, giving the ball just the right weight, so it rolled slowly up to the pocket and seemed to hang there for a tantalizing second or two, before dropping with a thud.

Game over.

Garret, that clown, spewed a mouthful of Coke foam into the neon lights and made them sizzle. Mike glanced up from his paper. He frowned but didn't say anything, because he wasn't sure what had happened and didn't care to risk making a fool of himself.

"Rack 'em," said Billy.

They were halfway through their second game when Pony finally wandered back to the table. He moved in so close that Billy could count his eyelashes. "So, I hear you're looking for a piece."

"A piece of what, cherry pie?"

"No, a large calibre handgun. You know what it is, thing that

93

you point and pull the trigger and it makes a real loud sound. Like, bang!"

"Then what?"

Pony shrugged. "The neighbor's dog don't bother you no more. Whatever."

Garret was down at the far end of the table, studying the possibilities offered by the lie of the cue ball. He showed no interest in the conversation, which was fine with Billy.

"What've you got for me?"

"A Colt Python," said Pony. "You like that name, Python? Powerful fucker, three fifty-seven Magnum. New out of the box, never been fired. Short barrel, about the size of your dick. Easy to conceal."

"How much?"

"Three hundred and fifty-seven dollars," said Pony, straight-faced.

Billy let his eyes go cold. The price they'd talked about on the phone was three hundred. The whimsical surcharge was Pony's payback; what he needed to regain the face he'd lost by bringing the subject up in the first place. Billy said, "Want to shoot a game, double or nothing?"

Pony shook his head. "I seen you play, Billy. It's the one thing in the world you do better than me."

"Three hundred and fifty-seven bucks. That's real cute, Pony."

"Includes a box of bullets and a big color poster of Clint Eastwood, get you in the right mood."

Billy gave a little jerk of his head. "Let's have a look."

"Linda's got it."

"Who?"

Pony jerked his thumb at the eighty-pounder wearing too much makeup and a fringed black leather jacket, faded blue jeans with little silver studs down the outer seams.

"Okay, fine. You want to introduce us?"

"Show me some money."

Billy flashed his wad, stuck it back down inside his boot.

"Don't go away," said Pony, and made his way back through the tables towards the girl.

"What?" said Garret from the far side of the table.

94

Billy ignored him. He watched Pony say a few words to Linda and then reach around behind her and slap her on her skinny little ass, make her jump.

"Ouch," said Garret.

Billy lit a cigarette. The girl gave him a long, slow look, her dark eyes cutting through the haze of smoke, and then turned her back on him and disappeared into the women's washroom. Billy looked at Pony, and Pony nodded. Billy glanced around the room. Nobody was paying any attention to them. He leaned his cue against the table. "I'll be back in a minute. Don't even think about moving any of those balls."

Garret said, "Sure thing, Billy." There was no law against playing eight ball. But they caught you carrying an unregistered handgun, that was entirely another set of circumstances. So if Billy wanted to act like a fucking cowboy and take all the risks, Garret was happy to oblige. No problem whatsoever.

"Anybody follows me into the can," said Billy, "you jump in real quick."

"Yeah, okay."

"I mean it, Garret."

"Count on me. No problem."

Feeling kind of weird, Billy yanked open the door and went into the washroom. There were two cubicles. Pony's lightweight squeeze was in the one at the rear. She was sitting sideways on the toilet seat with her back against the plywood wall.

Billy looked down at her, his hands on his hips.

She said, "Come on in, Billy."

Billy squeezed inside the cubicle. He said, "How'd you know my name?"

"I asked Pony. He told me."

Billy shut the door and shot the bolt.

Linda said, "I asked him what your name is because I think you're kind of cute." She lowered her eyes, licked her lips. "Would you like me to do something for you?"

"Yeah," said Billy.

She pushed away from the wall, rotated on the toilet seat so she was facing him. "Just tell me what."

"Show me the gun," said Billy.

The gun was in a plastic bag. It was a Colt, all right. A .357

Magnum stainless with walnut grips. The metal was cold and oily and felt very dense. Billy cocked the hammer. The gun made a crisp clicking noise and the cylinder rotated clockwise.

"Gimme the bullets."

"Pay me."

Billy lifted a leg, rested the heel of his boot on her blue-jeaned thigh. He retrieved his wad of twenties and counted out three hundred and sixty dollars. "Keep the change, honey. Buy yourself a couple more pounds of eye-liner."

Linda folded the bills in half and shoved them in the back pocket of her skin-tight jeans. Billy was amazed — he wouldn't have figured you could slide a dime in there, the denim was so snug.

"Okay, now gimme the bullets."

"Pony's got them."

"Stand up," said Billy. He turned her around so she was facing the knife-scarred, cigarette-burnt wall of the cubicle.

He frisked her carefully, ran his hands slowly over her body, cupped her small, soft breasts. He felt her nipples stiffen, and laughed.

"Pony care if I do this?"

"I don't know."

"What d'you *think*, baby?"

The girl shrugged. Billy pressed up against her. He kissed the back of her neck. "You gonna tell him?"

"Not unless you want me to." She bit her lower lip, staining her teeth red with lipstick.

Billy dropped the Magnum back in the plastic bag. He stuck the gun under his belt in the small of his back and said, "Go get me the bullets. A whole box, your fag boyfriend said." He squeezed her thigh, applying enough pressure to make her gasp in pain. But she didn't move, made no attempt to get away. A tough cookie, he had to hand it to her.

He said, "I'll wait right here, okay?" She nodded, and he unlocked the door and pulled it open and pushed her out of the cubicle.

He heard the heels of her cheap imitation cowboy boots on the tiles, the faint hiss of the pneumatic door opener. He dropped his cigarette in the toilet and lit another one.

A gun. A Colt .357 Magnum. Why had he arranged to make the buy? What did he have in mind, for Chrissakes? He didn't really know. But the fact was, he'd always wanted to own a gun, and now he did.

Billy told Garret to drive the Pinto. He wanted both hands free to hold the Colt. My, but it felt nice. The weight of it, and the knowledge of what it could do. He rolled down his window and threw away the plastic bag, rolled the window back up and lit a cigarette. Cradling the revolver in his lap, he stared malevolently out the car window at the pedestrians slip-sliding through the slush.

Garret kept bitching about the Pinto's brakes, which were so bad he had to pump them when he wanted to stop.

"You ever get in an accident, Billy, it's negligent homicide. Cops'll toss you in the slammer for the rest of your fuckin' life."

"Yeah," said Billy. He pulled back the hammer, took a bead on a woman in a white plastic raincoat tip-toeing her way through a puddle by the curb.

"You got to drive defensively. Know what a car is? A ton of metal goes about twenty times faster than most people can even think."

Billy squeezed the trigger. The hammer dropped and Billy said, "Pow! Gotcha, baby!"

"Hey, put that thing away."

"Shut up and drive, Garret."

Billy tore open the box of wadcutters Pony had sold him, loaded the Colt's cylinder with six fat bullets.

"You should leave one chamber empty," said Garret.

"Why?"

"The one the hammer is on, it should be empty. So the fuckin' thing don't go off by accident."

"What if I want to shoot six people, I'm supposed to ask the last guy to wait a minute while I reload? Or what if I wanna shoot one person but he's a big mother and it takes six hits to put him down?"

"With a cannon like that," said Garret, "the guy we're talking about would have to be an elephant."

"Fuckin' expert," said Billy scornfully. He stuck the muzzle of the gun in Garret's ribs.

"Jesus, Billy!"

"I got to tell you, Pony saw the way you were lookin' at his midget girlfriend, and he didn't much like it. Fact is, he was so pissed off he paid me a hundred bucks to splash your guts all over the fuckin' road."

"What?"

Billy ran the blade front sight across Garret's ribs. "Next side street, turn right."

"A hundred bucks?"

"Yeah, I know. I even asked him, what happened, you win a fuckin' lottery? Told him fifty's plenty. More than enough." Billy reached up and gently tapped Garret on the head with the barrel of the gun. "Hey, I'm just kidding. Relax."

Garret's shoulders sagged. "What the hell you want a gun for, anyhow?"

"Funny thing is, I didn't know when I bought it. I mean, I wanted it, but I didn't know why."

"But now you do?"

"Yeah, I think so."

"What's that supposed to mean?"

"Beats me. Maybe that sometimes you know what you want before you know why you want it."

Loaded, the Colt seemed about twice as heavy as it did empty. Billy aimed through the windshield at a big yellow McDonald's sign about a block away.

"I'm hungry. Let's grab a burger."

"What'd you want a fucking gun for, Billy?"

"Big Mac and fries, a chocolate shake. That sound just about right?"

Garret made his face go all twisted and tight, so he looked scared to death. But inside, he was laughing. He'd been working on Billy for months, setting him up. Priming him for the jump from petty theft to something a lot bigger. Now, finally, it looked as if all his work was about to pay off.

"My treat," said Billy. He unzipped his jacket and dropped the Colt into the inside pocket, zipped back up. The gun was sort of like Linda — small but deadly. There was no way anybody could tell he was packing. He popped open the glove compartment, tucked the box with its remaining bullets under a Shell road map.

Vancouver City Council had recently voted not to give Shell any of its business because of the company's commercial dealings with South Africa. Ever since then, it was the only place Billy bought gas.

He glanced at Garret, who was hunched over the wheel, staring straight ahead.

"Better get into the curb lane," said Billy.

"I'm not hungry."

Billy leaned over and grabbed the wheel. The Pinto swerved sharply. Behind them, a horn blared. Billy gave the offended driver the finger, not even bothering to look at him. Garret swore as he braked hard, fighting to bring the Pinto under control. They turned into the McDonald's parking lot. Garret found an empty slot. He parked the car and turned off the engine.

"My treat," said Billy.

"I already told you, I'm not fuckin' hungry."

"You will be, when you belly up to the counter and smell the fat." Billy leaned over, yanked open Garret's door and gave him a playful shove.

"You aren't gonna bust the place, I hope."

"Don't worry about it." Billy slid across the seat, out of the car. He gave the door a kick, slamming it shut. It went *thunk*, but it sure as hell didn't sound like a Mercedes.

As they ambled across the asphalt parking lot towards the tinted sheet glass and tasteful, pastel-painted steel columns of the restaurant, Billy explained that he was tired of breaking into parked cars, the money was lousy and the work didn't give him that fine adrenaline rush any more. He told Garret it was about time they moved up in the world, his thoughts when he'd sold Crayon the last batch of radios, how when you figured it out on an hourly basis, they were working for peanuts.

"I still don't know what the fuck you're getting at," said Garret, watching the McDonald girl's ass move as she industriously shook the fat from a wire basket full of french fries.

"If we're gonna make some serious money," Billy said, "we got no choice but to commit some serious crimes."

"Serious crimes, huh. What the fuck does that mean, exactly?"

"Gimme six ketchups," Billy said to the girl behind the counter. He turned to Garret. "I hate this goddamn place. They never give you nothin', unless you remember to ask for it."

"Well . . ." said Garret.

But Billy had spotted a table by the window and was already walking away. The hamburger and fries sat on the counter. What did Billy expect, that Garret was gonna scoop it up and trot after him like some kind of personal fucking *valet*, or something?

He turned back to the girl behind the counter, who was standing there with a blank expression on her face, like Garret had asked her for a date, or more likely a roll of toilet paper. "What're you looking at?" Garret rapped the counter with his knuckles. "He asked you for six ketchups, and you gimme five. What's the matter, you ain't learned to count on both hands?"

Sitting in the booth by the window, his mouth full of ground beef and sesame-seed bun and dill pickle, Billy told Garret all about his brand-new wonderful idea.

They were going to pull an armed robbery, shoot people if they had to, do whatever it took to walk off with maybe a couple million bucks.

Garret choked on a Chicken Mcnugget.

Billy thought he was laughing and lost his temper and kicked at him under the table, lashed out and caught him on the kneecap.

"Fuck off!" yelled Garret, rubbing his leg.

People were staring at them. Mothers and little kids with shocked faces and hands full of dripping food.

Billy stared right back at them.

At home, late at night in the bathroom, his cold eye on the toothpaste-specked mirror, he'd practised the look he was giving them and the message was — leave me alone or I'll shoot you dead.

Mothers whispered to their children and the jaws went back to chewing.

Billy turned his rage on Garret. "Know what your big problem is? You got no fuckin' ambition."

Garret gobbled into his chicken.

Something inside Billy's brain twitched and he found himself thinking about Nancy Crown. He smiled at Garret and said, "Wanna play ketchup roulette?"

Garret nodded. His mouth full of meat made a curious whuffing sound.

"I'll go first." Billy tossed an individual-size, one-ounce plastic bag of ketchup in the middle of the table and flicked it with his finger. The bag of ketchup spun around twice and stopped. Billy's fist came down hard. The bag burst and a red jet shot across the table and splattered over the pastel fabric of the bench seat.

"Missed me."

"Your turn," said Billy.

Garret spun the ketchup, slammed his fist down hard enough to make his hamburger jump.

A stream of ketchup jetted up at a sharp angle and slammed into Billy's chest, made a bright red smear right over his heart.

"Jesus, look at my shirt! My mom's gonna kill me, you dink!"

11

Christy Kirkpatrick rinsed the last of the antiseptic soap from his large, freckled hands, yanked a paper towel from the dispenser and dried himself off. He offered his hand to Mrs Kenny Lee.

Mrs Lee stared at the hand, but didn't touch it. He understood her reaction. She was thinking that the hand he wanted her to shake was the same hand that had sliced into her husband, pried him open, discovered secrets her hands had never known . . .

Kirkpatrick went over to the far wall. He slid open a stainless steel drawer, gave Parker a quick look. She discreetly nodded. Kirkpatrick pulled back the pale blue rubberized sheet that covered Kenny Lee's mortal remains.

Mrs Lee gasped. Her knees buckled. Parker caught her, took her weight. She was very thin, with the bone structure of a child. Holding tight, Parker said, "Is that your husband, Mrs Lee?"

A whispered response. Too faint to hear, but good enough.

"Thanks, Christy."

The pale blue shroud billowed and then, with a faint rustling sound, like a distant wind rustling brittle dead leaves, collapsed across Kenny Lee's puffy, sightless face.

The drawer hissed shut.

Parker felt something wet on the back of her hand. She looked down and saw that Mrs Lee was silently crying, the grief spilling out of her. Parker wondered if she should call car 66, the police unit that assisted with sudden death notification, victim trauma.

Mrs Lee had already indicated she didn't want any professional assistance, but Parker didn't think she was in any shape to make that kind of decision.

She'd give her time to calm down. Drive her home and then mention the trauma unit again.

It wouldn't be the first time she'd played chauffeur to a grieving husband, wife, or lover.

And, she knew, it wouldn't be the last.

12

Nancy came dripping out of the shower, grabbed a fluffy pink towel from the heated rack and wound it around her hair and walked naked into the bedroom. Through the plate glass she could see the harbor, the water dull as lead, a lone sailboat tacking into the wind.

Down the hall, in her husband's study, she heard the soft twittering of the goddamn fax machine. Tyler had three push-button telephones lined up in there on his desk; all of them red. He also had an IBM computer and a couple of printers, something called a modem. A Canon color copier. Plus the Sony TV and video recorder he used to tape business-related programs from the Knowledge Network, but never had time to watch.

Tyler's *study*. His *business machines*. Well, maybe he fooled the income-tax people, but Nancy knew better. The machines were toys for adults who'd grown up too fast and couldn't make the adjustment, that's all. She hated the den. Tyler never remembered to shut the door and it seemed to her that something in there was always clicking or buzzing or clanging, making some kind of irritating *noise*.

Nancy scrubbed at her hair with the towel, tossed the towel on the bed. She stood in front of the mirrored doors of the walk-in closet and tried to be objective about her body.

Not bad. Not bad at all, even if she was the only one in the family who noticed. She ran her fingers through her pubic hair, fuzzing it up, and then clasped her hands behind her head, striking a centrefold pose.

Not bad at all, really.

The telephone on the chrome and glass nighttable next to the big kingsize bed rang twice and then the answering machine kicked in and a woman named Sheila that Nancy sometimes worked out with at Ron Zalko's wanted to know if she was free for lunch — maybe a wildflower salad and glass of white wine and one of those trendy vegetarian designer pizzas and if so call back by eleven.

Fat chance, thought Nancy.

She crossed the silvery carpet to the sliding glass door, opened the door and stepped out on to the balcony. The cold hit her, and she almost cried out; it was like being slapped all over at once. Her skin felt tight as a drum. Down at the far end of the pool, the elderly maintenance man in his crisp white coveralls and blue baseball cap with a dolphin on it had his back to her as he scooped at the water with a long aluminum pole with a net on the end.

God, but it was cold! Lotusland, they called the city, because of its temperate climate. Well, it wasn't lotus weather today. The maintenance man extended the aluminum pole. The calm, mist-shrouded surface of the water rippled briefly and was calm.

The pool was fifty feet long and twenty feet wide, and in the winter it cost almost six hundred dollars a month to keep the water at a steady seventy degrees. It wasn't like Tyler to invest that kind of money unless there was a guaranteed payback. It had taken her a long time to realize that in this particular case the payback was ostentatious consumption — a chance for Tyler to impress his business colleagues and friends.

Nancy folded her arms across her chest, covering her breasts. The odd way the maintenance man was holding his pole, it was as if he was fishing. But for what? There were no leaves in the water and she doubted there'd be any drowned bugs in there, not at this time of year. She watched him bring the pole in, hand over hand, reach into the mesh and pull something out and stick it in a green plastic garbage bag.

Up here. Nancy giggled softly, like a schoolgirl. *C'mon, big boy. Take a look.* God, what was the matter with her?

The maintenance man swished the net into the water again, resuming his hunt. He walked around to the far side of the pool. He was thirty feet below her and less than a hundred feet away; close enough so she could see he needed a shave, and that he was concentrating so hard on his simple task that he was biting his lower lip.

Nancy hugged herself a little tighter. Her body was covered with goosebumps. She was shivering so hard she thought she might vibrate right off the balcony. She tilted her head to one side, shook a few drops of water from her hair and went back into the house and shut the door hard enough to make the glass rattle in the frame.

She lay down on the bed's rumpled silk sheets. It was Wednesday, just past noon. Just over two days since she'd seen him.

The telephone rang again. The answering machine picked up. She watched the spool of tape turn around and around and listened to herself tell whoever was on the other end that she couldn't come to the phone right now but if they'd leave a message she'd . . .

The sound of the caller slamming down the phone made her jump.

Some people! Could it have been Tyler? No, he never lost his temper. He'd simply have left a message, told her to phone back, whatever. And anyway, he'd have had his secretary place the call.

It could have been anyone. She'd been thinking about him . . .

Sunday night. When she finally got home, Tyler was sound asleep and, judging by the amount of noise he was making, sawing down whole forests of trees. She was in a strange mood, terrified and sexy. She'd taken a quick shower and slipped into bed, whispered his name.

Another tree dropped. She pinched shut his nostrils and the snoring stopped. She kissed him and he grunted and rolled over on his side. She told herself he worked his butt off so she could have a million-dollar house on the water and a kitchen full of top-of-the-line brand name appliances, and he had every right to be tired.

So what if the honeymoon had lasted about as long as a barrel ride over Niagara Falls? Nobody was perfect.

She eased out of bed and slipped into a terrycloth bathrobe and left Tyler to his clear-cutting.

Downstairs, she went into the living room and poured herself a double Ne Plus Ultra, turned on the fireplace and curled up on the sofa.

She shouldn't have let that good-looking kid walk off with her checkbook. But what was she supposed to do, get him in an armlock and take his knife away from him?

The clatter of metal against concrete brought Nancy back to the present. It was impossible, to be kidnapped and robbed and then a few days later casually accept an invitation to lunch on flowers and pizza. It had been what the Argentinian bartender at her golf club liked to call a *seminal experience*. A very sexy word, seminal. She wasn't exactly sure what it meant. She kept meaning to look it up, forgetting.

What she did know was that her joyride with the two kids had changed her, somehow.

But she wasn't exactly sure how. Not yet, anyway.

At three in the morning Tyler had come downstairs and awakened her and told her about the semi-obscene phone call he'd just received, and what in hell did it *mean*?

Nancy had told him.

Tyler said, "I thought you were at the Arts Club with Madeleine."

"After the play, we went back to her apartment for a drink. On the way home, I stopped for a red light and a couple of kids jumped in the car and made me give them a ride up Kingsway."

Tyler blinked twice.

Nancy said, "God, that's an ugly street. I tried to tell you all about it when I got home, but you refused to wake up."

Tyler flushed. "It wasn't a conscious decision, for Christ's sake. I took a sleeping pill."

"One of them threatened me with a knife."

"Did . . ."

"No. In fact they didn't even try."

Her loving husband nodded, as if that was perfectly understandable. He said, "Did they rob you?"

"Of course they robbed me! It'd be pretty unusual, wouldn't it, if they weren't interested in sex *or* money."

Tyler said, "Sorry, honey. I'm a little distraught. Did they take your credit cards?"

"Yes, and my checkbook."

"With your phone number and address on it."

"*Our* address, Tyler."

"Right, right. *Our* address."

Nancy said, "I'm tired. I'm going to go to bed."

"You can't do that. We have to phone the police."

"Why?"

"Because you've been kidnapped."

"Nothing happened, Tyler. And I'm too upset to be interrogated by the police."

Tyler opened his mouth to argue.

Nancy said, "And I've had a lot to drink. In fact, I wouldn't be surprised if I were drunk."

Tyler studied the level of whisky in the bottle, and sighed.

In the morning, they ate breakfast in silence. Tyler finished his second cup of coffee and went over to the cordless phone on the wall mount by the kitchen counter and punched a three-digit number.

Nancy said, "I wish you wouldn't do that. I really do."

Tyler, studying his watch, said, "Yes, this is an emergency." There was a pause and then he gave his name and Nancy's name, their address. After another pause, he gave a brief description of the previous night's events. He was remarkably concise. When he hung up, he turned to Nancy and said, "They'll be here sometime this morning." He smiled. "Got a very dicey meeting with the Mitsubishi people, or I'd stay and help out. You know how it is. I miss this one, I'm dead meat."

Nancy said she understood. She was an understanding woman, right? What else was new?

The cops arrived in an unmarked car. There were two of them. They were both wearing dark blue trenchcoats and they were very polite, softspoken. They explained right away that they were homicide cops and that they'd taken the call because there'd been a murder in Chinatown over the weekend, not far from where Nancy had run into trouble, and they were following up all possible leads. They didn't seem very pleased about it. One of them, he said his name was Eddy Orwell, reminded Nancy of the famous actor Arnold Schwarzenegger. Tyler was no film buff but when he was working late she often rented a video and made popcorn in the microwave, had a fun time.

Orwell wasn't as tall as the actor but he was built the same way, like an upside down pyramid, and he had Arnold's excruciatingly slow way of talking — as if every word he uttered cost him a little bit of pain. The first question he asked Nancy was where her husband was. She told him Tyler could be reached at the office, but that he had a meeting scheduled with some very serious people from Tokyo, and would prefer not to be interrupted.

Orwell's partner's name was Farley Spears. Nancy didn't think much of him. He hadn't bothered to wipe his feet when he came into the house, and he wore a mud-brown fedora which he clearly had no intention of removing. As if this wasn't more than enough, he kept glancing around the living room as if he was trying to decide what Nancy owned that would fit into his pockets.

Neither detective seemed to think very much of her little adventure. Orwell did most of the talking. He asked her what time of night she'd been accosted, where she'd been earlier that evening, who she'd been with. Nancy had given him Madeleine's full name and address and telephone number. Then Orwell had asked for a detailed description of the men and she'd answered about a million questions, told the cop what they'd looked like and what they'd said . . . She was surprised at how clearly she remembered things.

Orwell occasionally made soft grunting sounds as he labored to get it all down in his notebook.

When Nancy told him about the stolen checkbook, he suggested she notify the bank.

"Yes, I've already done that. My husband suggested it would be a good idea."

"Oh. Well then . . . " Orwell looked faintly annoyed, as if he thought everything had already been taken care of and she was wasting his time.

Nancy said, "I'm worried about them coming to the house."

"Yeah?" Frowning, Orwell tugged at his ear. Almost as if trying to fine-tune it because what he was hearing didn't make a great deal of sense to him.

Nancy blushed.

"Have there been any obscene phone calls?" Spears asked.

"No, none." A *semi-obscene* phone call, Tyler had said. Close enough. Why was she keeping it a secret?

Spears said, "Does the fireplace work?"

"Yes, certainly."

"It's a little chilly in here. You mind turning it on?"

Nancy switched on the gas.

"Is that as high as it goes?"

"Yes."

Spears nodded doubtfully. He stepped closer to the flames and pulled off his black leather gloves with the rabbit fur lining, held his hands out to the warmth. His eyes were bright and his skin had a glossy sheen. Was he ill? If so, Nancy hoped he wasn't contagious.

Orwell had several more questions, but it seemed to Nancy that none of them were very much to the point. One of the last things he asked her about was what kind of footwear the men had worn. She didn't remember. Cowboy boots? Nancy shrugged. She really had no idea.

She asked him if he wanted her to go downtown and look through the mugbooks, or whatever they were called.

"Yeah, sure." He didn't sound very enthusiastic. "That's probably a good idea." He shot his cuff, studied his watch. "Tomorrow afternoon, probably. We'll give you a call."

Monday night, Tyler came home a little after seven. Nancy'd cooked fresh string beans and a baked potato and pork ribs with lemon. He asked her how it had gone with the detectives. Nancy surprised herself by breaking into hysterical laughter, which quickly dissolved into a flood of tears.

Yesterday, Orwell had phoned and invited her down to 312 Main to look over the mugbooks. He'd even offered to send a car. Nancy turned him down. The BMW was being repaired at the dealer's, but she'd driven the Mercedes, with its repulsive HER TOY licence plate.

She'd spent almost three hours looking at the kind of faces you'd never expect to see commemorated on a postage stamp. None of the rapists or murderers or kidnappers or break-and-enter specialists or child-molesters had looked even remotely familiar.

Orwell had walked her back to her car, which was parked almost two blocks away, in an uncovered lot on Pender. He'd looked at the vanity plate and frowned, but hadn't said anything. As she'd unlocked the door he'd given her his card and said, "Lemme know right away if you get a phone call, okay?"

"Promise," said Nancy. Orwell was holding the door open, half leaning into the car. His blond hair was cut very short and his scalp was pink from the cold. She had turned the key and the Mercedes' engine had caught and made a nasty, snarling sound.

Orwell had smiled, and eased shut the door.

Nancy had weaved her way through the crowded lot towards the ticket booth. The tab was four dollars and fifty cents. She'd kept the receipt because she knew Tyler would ask her for it. His accountants seemed to find a way to write off just about every penny she spent.

The detective, Orwell, had asked her if threats had been made or if there had been any sexual . . . overtures.

No, she'd said. Had there been a hint, just a tiny little itty bitty bit of regret in her voice? Orwell had looked down at his notebook. Maybe he'd thought she was making a move on him. Wrong. It was the kid she'd been thinking about, not him.

Sick. Sick, sick, sick.

Driving home, she'd wondered if she'd have recognized Tyler, her husband, if she'd stumbled across his face in the mugbook.

Down the hall, in the *study*, Tyler's fax machine twittered briefly.

And she knew damn well what the maintenance man was fishing out of the pool because she'd taken a stroll in the yard after breakfast to replenish the bird feeders.

Cigarette filters. White ones. Like the kind the kid with the green eyes and thick black hair smoked.

And one of the lawn chairs had been moved so it faced the bedroom; she could see the scrape marks in the snow. And there'd been a cigarette butt on the tiles and three more in a tight little knot by the side of the pool, swirling in the current near one of the outlet vents.

Four cigarettes. How long did it take to smoke four cigarettes? How long had he been sprawled out in the cold on the lawn chair, watching the house? Before she went to bed at night, especially if Tyler was working late and she was alone, she often stripped naked and went over to the window and looked out at the lights of the ships in the harbor, and the city. It was almost a ritual. Usually she turned off the bedroom lights, but sometimes she didn't.

What had he seen?

And why hadn't she told Tyler about the chair, the cigarettes?

Maybe because she knew he'd call the cops again and she didn't want Detective Spears back in her living room, cataloguing the silverware. Or maybe it was something else.

She wondered where he was, what he was doing. If he had thought about her, as he had sat in the chair by the pool, the way she was thinking about him now . . .

Her pubic hair glistened in the light. She trailed the tips of her fingers languidly down her belly, touched herself the way she wished Tyler would learn to touch her, and allowed herself a small cry of pleasure.

13

The preliminary report from CLEU as well as Christy Kirk-patrick's fat autopsy report were waiting for Willows when he got back to 312 Main. There was also a thick pile of pink slips — telephone messages — cluttering his desk. He went through the messages first. He'd had five calls from his real estate agent and three calls from Dr Yang. There were more than a dozen calls from the local radio and television stations, all of which he'd pass on to Constable Fisher, who handled public relations.

Willows dragged the file from CLEU across his desk, flipped it open.

The lab hadn't been able to find any fingerprints or physical evidence of any kind on the ransom note. But the extortionist had made a mistake when he'd sealed the envelope and licked the uncancelled stamp.

Willows knew that blood wasn't the only body fluid that could be typed. About eighty percent of the general population are *secretors*, individuals who have ABO blood grouping substances present in certain body fluids, such as saliva.

Whoever had licked the stamp had been a secretor. His blood type was AB. The frequency of occurrence of AB types in the general population was a relatively small four and a half percent.

Of course, this information was useless until Willows and Parker had a suspect in custody, and obtained a court order enabling them to extract samples of whole blood and saliva from said suspect. And even then it would be impossible to determine absolute guilt, since approximately one person in twenty has type AB blood.

But as corroborative evidence — the kind of evidence that might sway an indecisive jury — the determination of blood type was *potentially* invaluable.

His phone rang. He picked up. A mistake. It was Celia Cambridge, his real estate agent. He could hear traffic in the background. She told him she was phoning from her car, the white Mercedes.

Eddy Orwell jogged into the squadroom. He'd been down in the weight room and was still wearing his baggy gray sweats.

Celia Cambridge said, "Jack, I've really been pushing it, and I'm getting nowhere. I've shown your house to five different families since I last talked to you, and I haven't even got a nibble. In today's market, that can only mean one thing."

Willows glanced over his shoulder, hoping to spot Bradley. If the Inspector caught Eddy wearing sweats in the squadroom, he'd shout his ears off.

Celia Cambridge said, "What it means is that your price is too high."

Farley Spears sat hunched over his desk writing a report. Willows and several other detectives watched, fascinated, as Orwell snuck behind Spears and put his massive sweaty arms around him and lifted him, chair and all, high over his head. Most of the detectives were in shirtsleeves and they were all wearing red suspenders — the latest fad to hit the squadroom. "Lemme go!" yelled Spears. That got a laugh. Spears rolled up the report he'd been writing and started hitting Orwell on the head.

"Are you there, Jack?"

"Yeah, sure."

Celia Cambridge said, "I think we should drop at least ten thousand."

When Willows originally listed the house, Cambridge suggested he use the Multiple Listing service, which meant guaranteed advertising in catalogues shared by all the local real estate agencies. It also meant that when she sold the house her commission would be a fat seven and a half percent. Willows had vetoed that particular idea.

He punched a few buttons on his calculator. A ten thousand reduction in price would cost Celia Cambridge exactly two hundred and fifty dollars in lost commission. He'd eat the balance.

He said, "I'll think about it."

"Sure, but remember, the longer your house is on the market, the harder it gets to sell."

"I'll bear that in mind."

"Why don't I give you a call this evening, say about eight?"

Orwell'd had all the laughs he was going to get. He lowered the chair until Farley Spears was once again back on firm ground.

Spears threw a pencil at him, and missed.

"Tell you what," said Willows, "I'll call you." He hung up. The telephone started ringing before he could take his hand off the receiver. He picked up, identified himself. It was a detective named Warner, from the Asian Crimes Squad. He wanted to know if Willows thought any of the Chinese or Vietnamese or Latin youth gangs might be mixed up in Kenny Lee's murder.

Willows told Warner he didn't have the slightest idea.

Warner said he had a case load that was breaking his back, and he'd be happy as a clam if Willows were to go so far as to state categorically that he had no reason to believe any of the youth gangs were in any way involved in the Kenny Lee case.

Willows said, "I wish I could do that for you, but I can't. Not right now. Anything new comes in, you'll be the first to hear about it."

Warner thanked him, and hung up.

Willows went back to the CLEU file. The words and phrases used in the ransom note had been cut out of local newspapers and a month-old issue of a glossy magazine called *Western Living*. The magazine cost two dollars if you bought it at the store, but he never did, because it was delivered free in the city's better neighborhoods, and every month without fail a copy appeared on his front porch.

The envelope was a cheap, common brand that could be bought at almost any stationery outlet.

Ditto for the single sheet of paper the cut-out words and phrases had been glued on.

The stamp, of course, could have been bought at any post office in the land.

Willows leaned back in his chair, scrubbed at his face with the palms of his hands.

He smelled stale sweat, glanced behind him.

"Hi," said Orwell.

"You try and pick me up, Eddy, I'll tell everybody about the time you made a grab for me in the locker room."

Orwell held up both hands palm outwards in a gesture of mock surrender. His hair was still damp from his workout. He said, "Anything happening on the Kenny Lee case?"

"Not that I know about. How about you, Eddy? You can't find something to do? Maybe I should let Bradley know you're free, he can find a spot for you. Traffic, probably."

Orwell chuckled. He rested a slim hip on Willows' desk. "You decide what to get me and Judith for a wedding present?"

"That still on?"

"We can hardly wait."

The wedding was set for mid-April, three months down the road. But Orwell had been soliciting presents since he'd first popped the question, way back in November. He reminded Willows that he had him down for a Moulinex food processor, reminded him what model he wanted.

Willows closed his eyes.

Orwell said, "I checked around. The Bay downtown has the best price."

Willows looked up at him, smiled. "I've been thinking about it, Eddy, and I've decided the best I can do is a toaster."

"We already got one, works real good."

"Not the kind of toaster I have in mind."

"Oh yeah, what kind of toaster is that?"

"An absolute bottom of the line, generic el cheapo two slicer. The kind that automatically turns bread into charcoal."

Orwell frowned. "What're you talking about?"

"I remember the toaster we had when I was a kid. It was heavy chrome, fancy as hell. With a thick, black and white cord."

"You wanna buy me and Judith an antique toaster? I don't think she'd like that, Jack."

"The sides dropped down," said Willows. "They were on hinges. You put the bread in and toasted one side and then had to turn the toast around and do the other side. It was so simple. Be perfect for you. The only problem I had with it, if you got started reading the comics or something and forgot what you were doing, that toaster was very unforgiving. It'd send up a column of smoke so foul you had to run for your life. Raisin bread was the worst.

There was no room for error. If you didn't hit it just right, you went to school with an empty stomach."

"School?" said Orwell, frowning.

"I don't know if you can still buy a toaster like that," Willows said. "But it's exactly what I want to get for you. And you know something else, Eddy?"

"What?"

Willows smiled. "It's exactly what you deserve."

"April fifteenth," said Orwell. "Bring the Moulinex or don't even bother to show up." He shifted so he had a little more hip on the desk. "I hear you're selling your house, right?"

"Who told you that?"

"Ask me who didn't," said Orwell. "It's a shorter list. How much you asking?"

"More than you can afford."

"Yeah?"

"Go take a shower, Eddy."

"I just took a shower. Hey, I'm serious about the house. Judith's parents are gonna loan us fifty grand for a down-payment. Last couple of weekends, we've been looking in the Coquitlam area."

"Nice," said Willows. Coquitlam was about thirty miles out of town, easily an hour's commute. Very few policemen with a family owned a home in the city, or even close in. On a cop's salary, it simply couldn't be done.

"So tell me, what're you asking?"

Willows slipped his wallet out of the breast pocket of his jacket. He opened it and withdrew Celia Cambridge's card.

"You're interested, give her a call."

"An agent? Get rid of her, we can both save a couple of bucks."

"Beat it, Eddy."

"You got an open house scheduled? Sunday afternoon be okay?"

"What's the plan, Eddy? You and Judith going to case the joint, steal all my household appliances?"

Willows turned to the coroner's report. The file was full of surprises. Kenny Lee had died of asphyxia — he'd suffocated on his own vomit.

An examination of Lee's eyes and eyelids determined the presence of petechiae in the conjunctivae — tiny hemorrhages in the form of dark specks seen on the mucous membrane lining the inner surface of the eyelids; a clear indication of asphyxia.

"Jack."

Willows glanced up. Bradley was standing in the open doorway to his office, the stub of an unlit cigar jutting from the corner of his mouth. He said, "Come and see me when Parker checks in, will you?"

Willows nodded. Bradley disappeared back inside his office and shut the door.

Kenny Lee was fifty-seven years old when he died. His height was five feet eight inches. His weight was one hundred and fifty-six pounds. He was in excellent physical condition. Muscular development was average for a man of his age and occupation. He had no scars or tattoos. His teeth were in good shape. There were no abnormalities or deformities of the body. Neither was there any evidence of fractures.

Willows studied the photographs of the body. He noted the deep abrasions and bruising the pathologist had found in the area of Lee's wrists and ankles. Those on the wrists were deeper. During his dying convulsions, Lee had apparently struggled against his copper wire bonds. Microscopic wood fibers had been found in the area of his shoulders. This suggested he'd been tied up, possibly to a chair. There was, however, no evidence of bruising around his stomach or ribcage.

Willows wondered if he had been naked during the entire period of his incarceration — the two and a half weeks that had passed between the time he disappeared and the discovery of his body.

The internal investigation had determined that prior to his death, Lee had suffered a subarachnoid hemorrhage due to a spontaneous rupture of a small aneurysm in the brain. In layman's terms, a minor artery had ruptured. The resulting hemorrhage had been slow. It was possible that Lee had remained conscious up until the very moment of his death, but that the hemorrhage had caused him to suddenly become disturbed or assaultive.

If the hemorrhage had resulted in assaultive conduct — and it was a typical result — it would explain the laceration and bruising around Lee's wrists.

Marks on his left hand and left wrist indicated he wore a watch and wedding ring. This had been confirmed by his widow.

Willows checked his notes. Lee had not been wearing any jewelry when he'd been pulled from the pond. The missing persons report originally filed by his wife said he wore a wedding band with a single small diamond, and a gold-colored Lorus watch on a gold expansion band. The watch had been presented to him a year earlier, by his employees, on the anniversary of the seventeenth year of publication of the *Chinese Times*.

Neither the watch nor the ring had been found when they'd drained the pond.

Willows made a note to check the city's pawn shops.

The pathologist was of the opinion that the damage to Kenny Lee's wrists had occurred just prior to death. Marks on the ankles were less recent.

He was also of the opinion that Lee had died three days before his body had been dumped in the gardens and that — based on body temperature and the amount of water sprayed on the body — he had been there approximately six to ten hours before he was discovered by Dr Yang.

It was impossible to determine if the aneurysm had occurred as a consequence of fear, unrelieved stress or a frantic attempt Lee might have made to free himself of his bonds.

Cause of death was homicide — a neutral term that did not attach blame but merely indicated Kenny Lee had not died of natural causes.

Lee's stomach was empty except for fluids. He had not eaten solid food in at least five days.

Willows turned back to the pictures. He wasn't looking for anything in particular — his intent was to burn into his brain an image of the victim. Keep it personal, in a way.

He closed the file and locked it in the gray metal cabinet adjacent to his desk.

Farley Spears said, "Hey, Jack."

Willows looked up.

Spears said, "You got any Pepto Bismol, or a pack of Tums?"

"Yeah, sure." Willows sorted through the top drawer of his desk and came up with an unopened pack of Tums. He tossed the pack underhand to Spears.

"Thanks."

"Stomach bothering you, Farley?"

"Must've been something I ate."

Spears looked pale. As he ripped open the foil on the pack of Tums, Willows saw that his hands were trembling.

Willows hesitated, and then said, "You going to be okay?"

"It's Orwell. He gets to me, sometimes." Spears popped several Tums into his mouth and chewed slowly. "Monday morning, we took a call, woman claims she was downtown and a couple of kids jump in her car, force her to drive 'em up Kingsway a couple of miles. Complainant lives on Point Grey Road, one of those big houses on the water. Me 'n Eddy go out and have a talk with her. She's really worried. One of the kids took her checkbook and she figures maybe they'll drop by and pay her a visit. Orwell don't take her seriously. He's so busy checking out her legs he hardly hears a word she says." Spears ate another Tums. "Couple of hours later we get a call from her old man. He's a stockbroker. Connected. We catch some flak. Orwell invites her down to take a peek at the pictures. Fine. Except why didn't he do it when we first talked to her?" Spears rolled his shoulders. "I dunno what it is about the guy. He just *grates* on me, know what I mean?" He ate another mint, tossed what was left of the pack back to Willows, pushed away from his desk. "Anybody wants me, I'm in the can." He grinned. "Back by quitting time, if I'm lucky."

Willows slid open a drawer. He thumped the yellow pages down on his desk and searched through the listings until he found pawnbrokers. He picked up the telephone and dialled the first number. Busy. He disconnected.

The phone rang. He picked up.

"Detective Willows."

"This is Dr Yang."

"What can I do for you, Doctor?"

Yang said, "I simply wished to know if there has been any progress on the case. A television crew was here again this morning, asking me questions and harassing my staff. As you may well imagine, their presence is most inconvenient."

"We're doing everything we can," said Willows. "Next time, refer them to our public relations department and let them handle it."

"You have not made an arrest, I take it?"

"Not yet," said Willows.

Yang sighed into the telephone. Willows picked up a pencil, turned it over and over in his hand. Finally Yang said, "You'll let me know if there are any new developments?"

"Yes, of course."

Yang sighed again; an ill wind that blew nobody any good.

Willows hung up. He began to redial the pawnshop number. Parker walked into the squadroom. He cradled the phone. "How'd it go at the morgue?"

"Great place to visit, but I wouldn't want to die there."

"Mrs Lee hold up okay?"

"About what you'd expect."

Willows said, "The inspector wants to see us. You ready for that, or you want to grab a coffee first?"

"Let's get it over with."

"Always a good idea."

"I had it first, and I'm saving it for my epitaph."

Bradley had his feet up on his desk. His heavy black lace-ups were shiny as glass. His hair was combed in a new style, straight back from his forehead. The crease in his dark blue pants was immaculate and his shirt was crisp and white as new-fallen snow. The silver buttons on his epaulets gleamed brightly. He waved at the two plain wooden chairs lined up against the far wall. "Have a seat. Make yourself at home."

He smiled at Parker. "You were at the morgue this morning, with Mrs Lee?"

"Just got back."

"How'd she take it?"

"Broke down and cried."

"Didn't confess, though, huh?"

"Not yet," said Parker.

Bradley turned to Willows. "You got Kirkpatrick's report?"

"Lee popped an artery. Experienced convulsions and died of asphyxiation."

"Doesn't matter. We're still looking at kidnapping and forcible confinement. Extortion. In all likelihood a second-degree murder rap."

Bradley swung his gleaming shoes off the desk. He leaned

forward. His chair squeaked. He flipped open the lid of his carved cedar humidor and selected a cigar. "First degree'd be a lot better, but it's probably still worth trying to nail the guy who did it. Lee's wife know how he died?"

"Not yet," said Willows.

"Let's keep it that way, for now. Anything else?"

"Maybe Fisher could toss Yang a pacifier."

Bradley nodded. He turned the cigar in his fingers, examining it from every angle. "CLEU?"

"Not much. No prints on the envelope. The paper and envelope were garden-variety stuff. The cut-out words and letters came from the local papers and *Western Living* magazine."

Bradley fished in his pocket for his clippers. He snipped at the end of his cigar.

"There was a stamp on the envelope," said Willows. "Whoever licked it is a secretor — type AB blood."

Bradley put the clippers back in his pocket.

Willows said, "Lee was wearing a gold Lorus watch and a wedding ring when he disappeared. They're missing."

"Pawn shops?"

"I'm working on it."

"Nothing from any of the people who worked for him, his friends?"

"Not yet."

"When was the last time he made a trip to Vegas?"

"Late August."

"Maybe you ought to make a long-distance call. See if the Vegas cops have got anything on him."

Willows nodded. "Melinda's very protective of her brother. I thought I'd phone Boston, see if we can trace his movements during the weekend of the murder."

"He a suspect?"

"No, I just think it's kind of odd he hasn't made it into town yet."

Bradley struck one of his big wooden kitchen matches against the side of his desk. He worked the flame around the cigar, blew a cloud of Cuban smoke at the ceiling.

It was his way of saying the meeting was over.

14

Garret, sucked in by the sexy blonde starlet on the cover, was reading a magazine. *Newsweek*, or maybe it was *People*. Billy always had a hard time telling the two apart. He drank some beer and watched Garret's eyes scan back and forth, up and down. He was the only guy Billy'd ever met who moved his lips looking at pictures.

Garret's boots were up on the coffee table. Billy kicked him in the ankle. "Whatcha readin'?"

"Thing on Burt Reynolds. Does he wear a rug, or what?"

"Hair by Dupont," said Billy. "He don't comb it, he *vacuums* it."

"Think so?" Garret turned the magazine upside down, trying for a different angle. "Looks pretty real to me."

"Sinatra, he wears a hairpiece, right? I mean, it's a fact. But you couldn't tell by looking at him. What it boils down to is how much you got to spend."

"Those guys got a lot," said Garret. "Millionaires, both of 'em."

"We could be that rich," said Billy.

"Sure thing, Billy."

"Almost," said Billy defensively.

Garret turned to the next page. "I thought Madonna had gone and died or something, but look, there she is."

"I got a real good idea," said Billy.

"She'd never go for it."

"I'm talking about an idea for making a whole lot of money."

"How much is it gonna be this time?"

Billy's intention had been to make Garret wait a minute, build the suspense. But he lost his cool and blurted it out. "Maybe half a million."

Garret rolled his eyes, as if Billy was out of his mind. He said, "Okay, that's more like it. Back at McDonald's it was a couple million. Now you're being reasonable."

Billy said, "I was thinking about robbing an armored car."

Garret thought that was pretty funny. Garret sure got a laugh out of that one.

Billy lit a cigarette. He waited until Garret had calmed down and then said, "I wanna show you something," and clomped out of the living room, his back stiff and angry.

Garret didn't know what he was supposed to do — go after him or wait where he was, or what. He said, "Hey, Billy?"

Billy came back into the living room. The stub of his cigarette drooped from the corner of his mouth. He stopped on the far side of the coffee table, the Colt Python held loosely in his right hand.

"Maybe robbing an armored car ain't such a bad idea after all," said Garret.

The tendons on Billy's wrist stood out as he pulled back the hammer. The Python made a sharp double click.

"That thing loaded?"

Billy crouched, brought up his arm. His voice low and throaty, he said, "Get ready to die, mothafucka!"

"Quit foolin' around," whispered Garret, staring into the black hole of the muzzle.

Billy pulled the trigger. A tongue of orange and yellow flame leapt at Garret's empty face. The sound of the shot seemed to explode inside his head, reverberate endlessly through the house.

Garret shrieked in pain, slapped at his face with his hands. "Jesus Christ, Billy!"

Billy had put the .357 Magnum round in a vice, pried out the wadcutter. A home-made blank. What he hadn't counted on was the burning powder fragments that peppered Garret's face.

"Lighten up," said Billy. "It was only a blank." He laughed. "Still kicked like a mule, though. No wonder cops always act so tough. You got one of these babies riding on your hip, you *are* tough."

"I don't want nothin' to do with any armored car," said Garret, his voice hardly more than a whisper.

"Why the fuck not? You're walking out of a liquor store pushing a dolly loaded down with a bunch of bags full of cash, you think you'd of had time to go for your piece?" He shook his head. "No way, man. Hands up or you're dead meat."

"Think about it, Billy. Those guys have got guns. You won't catch 'em sitting on the couch trying to look down Madonna's neckline. They're professionals. We mess with them, they'll blow our heads off."

"No way," said Billy firmly. He stuck the Python in his waistband, went into the kitchen and got a couple of cold cans of Moosehead beer out of the fridge, came back into the living room and tossed a can to Garret, slumped back down in his chair. Garret popped the tab and drank thirstily.

Billy said, "We'd be wearing masks. Ski masks. You know the kind I mean, made like a big sock that you pull right over your head. Couple of holes cut in 'em so you can see out?"

"Got it all figured, do you?"

"Wanna spend the rest of your life stealing radios, Garret?"

Garret shrugged.

"Have you even bothered to think about it?"

Garret licked some foam off the top of his beer can. "I'm only eighteen years old, Billy. Jesus, I'm still a fuckin' teenager. So tell me, what's the rush?"

For a moment, Billy's face was solemn and still. He said, "It's now or never, Garret."

"Why's that, exactly?"

"Because as people get older, they get worn out by life, afraid of things. Afraid to take chances. You and me, we might think we're different. But if we don't do something now, take advantage . . . "

"What?" said Garret.

"We're gonna end up just the same as everybody else, tight-ass and broke."

"Speak for yourself. *I'm* doing okay."

"Oh yeah, sure. Cleaning out car ashtrays, wiping down the hubcaps. Big deal." Billy stared at Garret, gave him that refrigerator look he did so well. Garret stared back for a minute and then caved in, ducked down behind his beer.

"C'mere," said Billy, "I got something else I wanna show you."

"What, another gun barrel? Gonna take another shot at me, is that it?"

Garret followed Billy out of the living room and down a narrow grungy hall into Billy's bedroom. Billy shut the door and locked it. On the wall he'd taped a number of *Playboy* pin-ups, and a new thing — a map of the city. He said, "Take a look at this, tell me what you see."

Garret studied the map, but Billy ran out of patience before he could figure it out. He thrust a finger at the intersection of two thin blue lines. "See the little red cross?"

"Yeah, right." There were crosses all over the map, fifteen or twenty of them, drawn in red ink. The lines were very straight. Billy must've used a ruler.

"Liquor store," said Billy. "That one's at Broadway and Maple. There's also a Safeway and a gardening supply store. Lots of parking."

"Convenient," said Garret.

Billy went over to his bed, lifted the mattress and hauled out a twelve-gauge Remington pump. He worked the slide and pointed the weapon at Garret and squeezed the trigger. The gun made a sharp clicking sound. Garret's body flinched even though his brain knew what was coming.

"Too late," said Billy. "If it'd been loaded, your brains would be splattered all over the wall. A bad day for you, Garret, when you come right down to it. I mean, you been shot twice and killed both times."

"What's the fuckin' point?"

"Point is, you didn't have time to react. You saw me reach under the bed and haul out the gun, point it at you and pull the trigger. And what did you do? Stood there like a dummy."

"It wasn't loaded."

"Yeah, but you didn't know that, did you?"

"I knew you wouldn't shoot me."

Billy grinned. "You did, huh?"

"If you'd wanted to shoot me, you'd of done it with the pistol."

"You're right," said Billy. "Not as messy." He tossed the shotgun to Garret. "For you. A present."

"Where'd you get it?"

"Stole it. Know how many handgun permits are given out in this city every year, Garret? About five hundred. Know how many handguns get stolen out of people's houses every year? Almost three hundred."

"So why didn't you steal a pistol, if it's so easy?"

"Because I was shopping for you, and I wanted a piece you didn't have to be a deadeye dick with, to hit what you were pointing at. Scatterguns, they call 'em. The pellets fly out all over the place. Also, a shotgun's a lot scarier looking. The average citizen, from watching so much TV, he *knows* a twelve-gauge can cut him in half."

"Got any ammo?"

"A whole box," said Billy.

"Lemme see."

Billy jabbed a finger at the red cross he'd drawn at the intersection of Broadway and Maple. "I stood in a lineup there last Friday night and they had four cash registers working. The one I was watching did almost two hundred dollars' worth of business in less than seven minutes. I worked it out, and you know what it adds up to? Almost two grand an hour. That's *one* cash register, and they had four of them in there."

"What time was this?"

"Nine, a little after."

"Friday night, nine o'clock. That'd probably be the busiest time, they wouldn't usually be that crowded."

Billy looked a little startled. For a split second his face was like the Python exploding, all angry and red. Then he said, "Jesus, you think I don't know that? All I'm saying is that we're talking about a hell of a lot of cash, is all."

"How often does the armored car come around to pick the money up?"

"I don't know. It's one of the things we got to find out."

"How're we gonna do that, Billy?"

"Like I said, the liquor store's right next to a big supermarket, a Safeway. Parking lot must hold a couple of hundred cars. Plus you got a gas station and 7-Eleven on the other side of Maple. So there's always people coming and going, to pick up a quart of milk or whatever. Kids hanging around, playing the video games or hoping to score some beer. We can park at the far end of the lot, sit there and smoke and listen to the radio. Couple of days, we'll know how often the armored car guys come around."

"What if somebody spots us?"

"Don't worry about it. Can't happen. Like I told you, the place is a goddamn beehive."

Garret considered the bleak prospect of spending two long days with Billy in his rusty Pinto, slowly freezing to death because the heater was busted. Billy toying with his pistol, taking a bead on the shopping carts as they went by. He tried to imagine pointing the Remington at a two-hundred-pound combat-trained male adult. He'd had better luck fantasizing about Madonna.

Still, it was what he wanted, more or less. A grab at the brass ring, serious money. And Billy was right. They offed the guards, just walked up and shot them and scooped the cash, chances were real good they'd get away with it.

Billy, watching Garret, saw every syllable drift through his brain as clearly as if there was a billboard mounted on his acned forehead.

He said, "Maybe you'd rather spend the rest of your life licking BMW's clean with your tongue."

"Not really."

Billy smiled. He gave Garret a carefully weighted punch on the meaty part of the shoulder; a blow that was both a bashful display of macho intimacy and a lurking threat of future violence, brutal and intimidating.

"Wanna take a ride?"

"Where?"

"No place in particular. Out and around. Get some fresh air, grab something to eat."

"I was gonna go home for dinner tonight. Told my mom I'd be in by six."

"So you lied."

It took them almost forty-five minutes to make the trip from Billy's house to the liquor store at Broadway and Maple. The sky was dark, low, solid-looking black clouds from horizon to horizon. It had stopped snowing. The air smelled damp. There was slush in the gutters, but the roads were clear. During the ride Garret kept twisting in his seat, glancing back down the road.

"Something bothering you?"

"Why this particular store, Billy, instead of one a little closer to home?"

"This is the West Side. People around here buy a case of Scotch instead of a six-pack of beer. More cash in our pockets." The car in front of them, a white Honda driven by a blonde with shoulder-length hair, indicated a left turn. Billy switched lanes, shot past her. "See that? This neighborhood, you take the trouble to signal when you're gonna make a turn. Somebody in a crosswalk, you hit the brakes instead of the pedestrian. What's the word I'm looking for? *Polite.*"

Billy lit a cigarette, tossed the empty pack out the window.

"Notice the houses? Big, well taken care of. The people look better fed, the cars they drive are shiny and new. Except for guys like us, nobody litters. The West Side, Garret, where the fat cats live."

"Fat cats, huh," said Garret.

"Thing is," said Billy, "the crime rate over here is a hell of a lot lower. Which means there are less patrol cars cruising around. And that's why it's worth driving all the way over here."

"Because there aren't as many cops."

"Right."

"But if there isn't as much crime, the cops don't have as much to do. So if they get a call says a couple of guys have knocked over an armored car, they'll probably respond to it."

"Don't matter where you are," said Billy, "*everybody* responds to an armored car robbery. It's the kind of stuff cops live for."

"Terrific."

"Hey, let's go in with both eyes open."

They drove past the liquor store. It was set well back from the street on the far side of the parking lot. The shopping market and 7-Eleven were right where Billy had said they'd be. Billy drove to the far end of the block, turned left on Arbutus and drove another block and made another left. Now they were heading east on Tenth Avenue. They bounced over a set of railroad tracks and Billy made another left, into the parking lot. They cruised slowly past the liquor store. There was a lot of foot traffic, people coming out carrying cases of beer and brown paper bags full of wine or maybe hard liquor, vodka, rum. You name it.

Billy was right, the place had four cash registers and they were all clicking away, making music.

"Check out the redhead at the end," said Billy. "You ever see jeans that tight? She farts, she's gonna spray denim all over the block."

Garret laughed, some of his tension easing. There was a shaggy-looking black guy banging away on a guitar outside the liquor store's double glass doors. Garret craned his neck to see how much money he had in his hat. He patted himself down, frowned. "Got a smoke?"

"All out." Billy waited until a dark gray Camaro got out of his way and then slid into a parking slot. He turned off the engine and climbed out of the car.

"Where you going?" Garret opened his door but didn't get out of the car.

"Thought you wanted some cigarettes." Billy started across Maple to the 7-Eleven.

Garret trailed along behind. "Yeah, but I'm broke."

Billy kept walking. "What happened to the money we got for last week's radios, for Chrissake?"

"I spent some of it, gave the rest to my mother."

"What the hell for?"

"Because she needs it."

Billy reached for the 7-Eleven door, but didn't open it, forcing Garret to break stride. "And now your wallet's flapping in the wind. Real smart." He pushed open the door, and, as he went inside, turned and looked back across the street at the bright plate-glass windows of the liquor store. He thought about the cute clerk in the skin-tight jeans, how her big green eyes would widen in amazement if she knew what they'd been talking about, what he was about to do.

The 7-Eleven was crowded, people buying gas, kids loaded down with six-packs of Coke or Pepsi, more kinds of junk food than you could even think about. A video game at the back was making puffy explosive sounds. Billy and Garret wandered down the aisle, past banks of a million different kinds and flavors of chewing gum and candy bars.

The video game was called *Rambo*. The kid playing the game dropped a quarter. An animated helicopter thundered onscreen, hovered and dropped a soldier wearing green jungle fatigues and a red headband. He was armed with a knife about three inches long, and an automatic rifle. The chopper thundered offscreen. The soldier started towards the forest and was immediately attacked.

The kid started hitting a red button, punching it with his thumb. Rambo's automatic rifle erupted, and the slaughter began.

Billy went over to the rank of glass-doored coolers that lined two walls of the store. He swung open a door and grabbed a Coke.

"Want one?"

Garret shook his head. They headed back towards the cash register. Billy slammed the can of Coke down on the counter. The clerk, a short, fat kid wearing an ugly 7-Eleven jacket that was about two sizes too small for him, gave him a hard look.

Billy said, "What kind of smokes you want, Garret?"

"Players Filter."

"You heard him," said Billy.

The clerk reached up and fumbled in an overhead rack. His armpits were stained with sweat. He dropped the pack of cigarettes on the counter next to the Coke and turned to the cash register.

Billy, his voice low, said, "Don't bother to ring it up."

The clerk paused, staring at him.

Billy unzipped his jacket, let him get a quick peek at the Python.

"Your treat, right?"

The clerk swallowed. He nodded his head up and down very slowly, and then said, "Yeah, sure. Whatever you say."

"One more thing," said Billy. "Since we're such good friends, think you could loan us a few bucks?"

The clerk hit the cash register. The drawer popped open.

"Just the folding money. Might as well put it in a bag, along with the Coke and smokes."

The clerk shut the cash drawer, reached for a plastic bag. Billy kept his hand on the gun as the clerk stuffed everything into the bag, handed it across the counter.

Billy turned to Garret. "Take it, dummy."

Garret grabbed the bag.

"Thank you," said Billy.

"Have a nice day," said the clerk, and then realized what he'd said, and flushed red.

Garret followed Billy as he walked slowly around the back of the building. Billy took the money and Coke and smokes out of the bag and threw the bag away.

Garret said, "Whyn't you tell me you were gonna rob the place?"

"Didn't plan to do it."

They came out at the front of the building, but on the opposite side from the entrance, by the self-serve gas pumps. Garret followed Billy as he ambled slowly past the pumps to the sidewalk. Inside the 7-Eleven, a crowd of customers surrounded the clerk, who was waving his arms in the air. At the pumps, a man in a tweed overcoat finished filling his Volvo and racked the hose and started towards the store. He paused when he saw what was going on inside, then spun on his heel and got in his car and drove away.

"See that?"

"Yeah."

Billy poked him in the ribs. "A goddamn full tank of premium. Guy probably made more than us."

There were sirens in the distance, but Billy didn't seem to be in much of a hurry. The traffic cleared and they crossed Maple and strolled across the parking lot. Nobody in the area of the liquor store seemed to know an armed robbery had just gone down on the other side of the street. They climbed into the Pinto. Billy popped open his Coke and tossed Garret the pack of cigarettes. "Light me one."

Garret fumbled for his matches. Billy got the Pinto started and drove slowly out of the lot.

There were three patrol cars parked at an angle in front of the 7-Eleven, roof lights flashing red and blue. Another patrol car bounced over the curb, skidded to a stop by the pumps.

Billy chugged some Coke, burped loudly. He took the roll of bills out of his pocket and counted it twice. A hundred and twenty-seven dollars. He said, "See how fuckin' *easy* it is, Garret?"

When they were out of sight of the 7-Eleven, Billy vigorously shook his can of Coke, sprayed the interior of the car with sticky brown foam. When Garret finally stopped yelling, Billy said, "Next time, it's gonna be champagne. I *guarantee* it!"

15

Every cop has at least one snitch — somebody with an ear to the cesspool who's willing to trade information for money.

Willows' favorite was a guy named Bobby Chow. Once upon a time Bobby had been a high profile drug lawyer, but he'd made a serious mistake — sold his services for a kilo of cocaine in lieu of cash. When the case went to court, Bobby lost. And his client, looking to settle the score and maybe knock a few years off his sentence, had sold Bobby down the river.

Suddenly Bobby Chow had almost ten thousand a month in overhead, and zero income. He'd bought himself a good lawyer, but the lawyer hadn't been good enough. Bobby'd been disbarred, naturally, but during the pre-sentencing hearing had given up a few names. Downtown guys. He wasn't the only lawyer who worked the barter system, and by then he was sweating a river, ready to spill every bean in his pot.

Willows had been working the drug squad when Bobby had fallen; he'd been instrumental in seeing that he was on parole forever but didn't do any hard time.

So, although Bobby had lost his licence to practise, and all of his three-piece friends, he still had Jack Willows.

And Willows still owned Bobby.

He kept Bobby's telephone number filed away in his memory instead of the Rolodex, where anybody could look it up. He grabbed the phone, began to dial.

Parker, hovering, said, "Coffee?"

Willows nodded, not looking up.

The phone rang eleven times. When Bobby finally answered, his voice was thick and congested, as if he'd been in the middle of drinking a cup of sand. "Jack, it's you. What a treat. Qué pasa?" Bobby sniffed into the phone. Sinus problems. Willows doubted he had a cold.

"In the mood for lunch, Bobby?"

"Haven't had breakfast yet, tell you the truth. But then, I rarely do. How about the Hotel Vancouver?"

Willows said, "I'm on a limited budget. You want to spend my money on a ten-dollar sandwich, it's fine with me."

"Maybe that ain't such a hot idea after all," said Bobby quickly. He coughed into the telephone. "How about Cassidy's? You know it?"

"By reputation," said Willows. The place was a beer joint, live bands and strippers.

"Never been there?"

"Not lately."

"I was just looking at the ad in the paper. Happens to be Well Endowed week, should be a real eye-opener."

"When can you be there, Bobby?"

There was a pause. "Uh, I dunno. What time is it now?"

"Quarter to twelve."

"Couple hours, say around two?"

Willows didn't say anything, let the pressure build.

Bobby said, "I gotta take a bath, dig up a clean pair of socks, maybe iron a shirt . . . "

"Two o'clock, Bobby. Want to write it down?"

Bobby giggled. "Yeah, sure. Got a pen?"

Willows hung up. Bobby had a never-ending problem with his cash flow. If he was straight enough to make it, he'd be there. Willows flipped open his notebook and jotted down the date and time and location of the meeting, using Bobby's first name only.

Parker had been talking with Farley Spears down at the far end of the squadroom. Spears said something and Parker laughed and then made her way back to Willows' desk carrying two styrofoam cups of coffee.

Willows accepted a cup. "Thanks. Farley in a good mood, is he?"

"Told me the one about the hooker and the chicken farmer," said Parker. The joke had been doing the rounds at 312 Main for weeks, but because Spears had put in so much sick time, he'd only heard it that morning.

"Why'd you laugh? You didn't think it was funny the first time you heard it."

"If I hadn't laughed, he would've thought I didn't get it, and told it all over again, but slowly." Parker sipped from her cup. "Get in touch with Bobby?"

Willows nodded.

"Set up a meet?"

"I hope so."

"When?"

"This afternoon, two o'clock."

"Where?"

"Joint called Cassidy's. You ever heard of it?"

"Well Endowed week. They should run a shuttle. End of shift, the place is full of cops." Parker almost added that some of them were even married, but held her tongue.

Willows said, "Been in touch with Asian Crimes?"

"They're doing what they can. But they're kind of vague about exactly what that amounts to."

"You going to talk to Mrs Lee again?"

"In about an hour. Want some lunch?"

"Thanks, but I think I'll hold off until I see my snitch."

Parker hesitated, and then nodded and said, "Okay, I'll talk to you later."

For his date with Bobby Chow, Willows changed into a pair of black Reeboks, faded Levis and a black leather bomber jacket. He signed an unmarked car out of the pool and drove across town to Cassidy's. There was a parking lot behind the building, and an automatic ticket machine. Willows dropped a dollar's worth of quarters, tossed the ticket on the dashboard and locked the car. As he walked across the asphalt towards the back door of the bar, he could hear the percussive thump of drums, heavy and very loud.

He went up a short flight of concrete steps. There was a small landing by the door. A puddle of congealed vomit drooled down the cement wall.

Willows yanked open the door. The noise grabbed him by the lapels and tried to shove him back outside. The door banged shut behind him. He smelled stale beer and fresh sweat. The bar was horseshoe-shaped, with a raised platform for strippers in the middle. Mirror balls and multicolored strips of neon light pulsed through the haze of smoke and music. A naked woman, her pubic hair dyed in bands of red and blue and green, snapped her fingers as she wandered aimlessly around the stage. A drunk in jeans and a T-shirt waved his beer at Willows and said, "You the taxi?" Willows ignored him. He couldn't see Bobby Chow anywhere.

The drunk lurched to his feet. "Hey, I'm *talkin'* to you, fella! You the taxi, or what?"

"Taxi's on its way," said Willows. To his left there was a kind of amphitheatre, rows of long narrow tables and stools arranged in a half-circle facing a raised stage.

Gynecology Row, a cop had called it. Willows moved off to his right, towards a row of high-backed booths.

The stripper was rolling languidly around on a white shag rug cut in the shape of a polar bear skin. Someone threw a handful of coins that glittered silver in the light.

Bobby Chow was slumped in the booth farthest from the roar of the music. His dark blue pinstripe suit was freshly pressed. His button-down shirt looked brand new and his bright red tie was nothing but silk. Willows picked up his drink, sniffed. A single-malt.

"Nice place, Bobby."

Bobby reached out and snagged a passing waiter. He drained his glass and thumped it down on the tray. "The same, better make it a double. And gimme a cheeseburger double bacon, side of fries and extra ketchup. Something for you, Jack?"

"A draft."

Bobby grinned. "Drinking on duty, shame on you."

"Am I on duty, Bobby?"

Bobby's grin faded. "What d'you mean?"

"You here to talk business, or just soak up a free lunch?"

"Don't gimme a hard time, Jack. Please. I thought we were buddies." Bobby leaned back, closed his eyes. "Things haven't been going all that wonderful, lately, it's a fact."

Willows ran his fingers across the glossy black surface of the table. Some kind of composite. Hard as rock. He'd known Bobby a long time, since before the fall. Bobby looked too good to be true — better than he had any right to be. He was a little on the thin side but his eyes were clear and he was freshly shaved and if Willows was any judge of haircuts, Bobby'd dropped a fifty. And there was something else — the diamond Bobby used to wear in his left ear but had been a long time gone was back again and bigger than ever.

"You look pretty good, Bobby, for somebody who feels so bad."

Bobby opened his eyes. "Things are pickin' up, kind of. In a way. I'm working again."

The waiter dropped Bobby's Scotch and Willows' pint of draft on the table. Bobby drained half his glass, licked his lips and gave Willows a twisted grin.

Willows waited. Bobby's problem — or one of them, anyway — had always been that he didn't need two people to hold a conversation. His loose mouth had ended up costing him a fat six-figure income and his membership in the bar. A man like Bobby, Willows doubted he'd changed all that much. Or ever would.

Bobby said, "This is just between you and me, Jack."

"Sure," said Willows, wondering how many times Bobby had used that phrase.

"I'm doing legal work for a guy sells lottery tickets by mail. Grosses about five million a month. No lie. Millions. Got a couple of computer geniuses working for him, you know the type. Idiot savants. Some kind of software deal. Mailing lists. He's got customers all over the States. They choose their own numbers, as many numbers as they want. He buys the tickets and they pay in advance, in American currency. That's fifteen percent pure cream right there. Also, he charges them a fee for doing all the footwork. The computers keep track of the numbers. Some dope actually picks a winner, we send him a certified check."

"How long you had the job?"

"Couple of months, somewhere in there."

"Had any winners?"

"Sure, lots of 'em."

"Anything big?"

"First one I know about was last week. Some guy in Seattle. Don't get me wrong, it was nothing huge."

"How much?"

Bobby's glass was empty. He glanced around, looking for the

waiter. "He hit five numbers out of six. Payout was a hundred and fifteen thousand dollars, somewhere in there."

"And you sent the guy a check, just like that. No problem."

"Right, right." There was a long, slow drum roll from the stage. Bobby sat up straight so he could get a better look.

Willows said, "That's your end, the paperwork?"

"More or less."

"I guess it can take quite a while, sometimes, to get that paperwork done?"

Bobby rubbed his hands together, grinned. He was at the point where he'd talked enough to satisfy that inner need that kept grinding away at him, and now he wished he'd kept his mouth shut. But he never would.

Willows said, "So what happens, you tread water until you're sure the ticket-holder doesn't know he's a winner, then forget about it?"

Bobby smiled. "No way, Jack. The bowl's so full of milk, nobody needs to squeeze the teat any harder."

The waiter arrived with the food and another round of drinks. Bobby said, "I like a man who thinks ahead." He peeled a pair of crisp new twenties from a roll thick enough to choke a whore, dropped the money on the tray. Bobby'd slurred his words a little, and his eyes had taken on a slightly glassy look. Willows sipped at his pint, making it last. Bobby used his teeth to rip open a foil packet of ketchup. There was another drum roll from the stage, but this time he didn't bother to look up.

"So where've you been the past couple of months, Jack? I hear from you, then I don't hear from you. Naturally I wonder what's going on."

"Just the usual, Bobby."

"Crime, huh. It's a growing commodity. How's the wife and kids?"

"Fine, just fine."

"You got a boy and a girl, right? One of each. The boy, he's what, about twelve?"

"Somewhere in there."

Bobby nodded, picked a sliver of bacon off the table and popped it in his mouth. He kept his head down as he chewed. "Kids still in school?"

Willows nodded.

"Your wife, she okay?"

Willows said, "Let's not talk about my family, Bobby. Since you don't have one, it doesn't seem fair."

On the stage, the stripper lay down on the mock polar bear rug and turned herself into a pretzel.

Willows said, "Hear about the body that turned up in the Sun Yat-Sen Gardens a few days ago?"

"Guy drowned, or was it froze to death? Step right up, ladies and gentlemen, and take a look at the famous human popsicle."

Willows drank some more beer, just a taste.

"Or should I be thinking about somebody else?" said Bobby.

"No, you've got the right one. Kenny Lee. But he didn't drown, and he didn't freeze to death."

"No shit, a scoop."

"He was snatched, Bobby."

"Yeah?"

"His family got a ransom note. But on the telephone, the one call he was allowed to make, Lee told them not to pay."

"Advice they gladly followed, no doubt."

Willows gave him a look.

Bobby said, "The Chinese Benevolent Society put up a reward, yes?"

"Ten thousand," said Willows. "I hear they're going to bump it to fifteen at the end of the week."

"Big pile of money."

"Heard anything, Bobby?"

Bobby nervously stroked his diamond. "Just 'cause I'm Chinese, it doesn't mean I got inside info on everybody who gets bumped off in Chinatown."

"How much they pay you, this new job of yours?"

"Why?"

"What'd that suit cost you, about a grand?"

"You think *I* knocked the guy off?"

"Relax, Bobby. I'm not trying to drop this on you."

"That supposed to be an apology?"

"If you need one."

Bobby shoved the last of his cheeseburger into his mouth,

began talking with his mouth full. His idea of revenge. "What do I know . . . Let's see . . . " He glanced up, grinning. "I know for a fact that I could use another drink."

"Ever do any work for Lee?"

Bobby shook his head. "I went after him, when I first opened an office. Trying to hustle new clients, right? Told him whatever he was paying, I'd knock thirty percent off the hourly rate. He wasn't interested. I left him a card, but he never got back to me."

"When was that?"

"Must be ten years ago, Jack." Bobby used the tip of his finger to scrape the last of the ketchup from his plate, licked the finger clean. Willows wondered how much his manicure had cost him.

"And that was it, you didn't push?"

"Wouldn't have looked good, Jack. Loss of face for all concerned."

Bobby was talking to Willows, but his eye was on the waiter. He lifted his empty glass high above his head, turned it upside down. A few drops of Scotch fell to the table. Bobby said, "Where'd the people who run this dump do their hiring, the intensive care ward?"

"You don't know anybody might've been interested in Lee?"

"Not a soul."

"Souls don't have anything to do with it, Bobby. You sure you haven't heard anything?"

"Not a word, Jack. And I've been listening, believe me. Soon as I heard Lee'd been iced, I started trying to figure out how I could make a buck out of it."

Willows nodded. "Dumping him in the pond, is that something you'd expect, if the people who put him there were Chinese?"

"Seems like a pretty good idea to me. How much they ask for, the ransom?"

"They started at two hundred and fifty, worked their way down."

"How far down?"

"Bottomed out at a hundred grand."

Bobby tried to look impressed. It didn't quite come off.

The waiter arrived with Bobby's drink. He tried to sell Willows another pint of beer, and failed.

"The way I see it," said Bobby, "when they saw they were going to come up empty, they decided to cut their losses. Dumping him in the pond guaranteed a hell of a lot of publicity. They go after somebody else in the community, the family of whoever gets snatched is going to know they mean business."

Willows pulled two twenties and a ten from his wallet. He pushed the money across the table. Bobby Chow snatched it up, stuffed it in his pants pocket.

"Money for nothing, Bobby. You hear anything, you know how to get in touch."

"When the reward goes to fifteen, something might come up."

Willows pushed away from the table, stood up. He put his hand on Bobby's shoulder, leaned towards him, letting him feel the weight. "I find out you got something and you're sitting on it, I'll sit on you, Bobby."

"No, I'm clean. Really."

Willows leaned a little closer. "Know what I think?"

Bobby smiled nervously. "No way, never."

"I think you figured out a way to mess around with the computer records. I think you bounced some numbers and dates. I think you paid for your new clothes and your fifty-dollar haircut and manicure with the hundred and fifteen grand that was supposed to have gone to Seattle. And you know something else? If I figured it out this fast, your boss isn't going to be too far behind."

Bobby's shoulders slumped. He put his drink down on the table and covered his face with his hands and began to cry.

Willows said, "How much you spend?"

After a moment Bobby wiped his eyes and nose with his red silk tie, got himself under control. "All of it. Close enough, anyway." He stared into his glass for a moment and then knocked back the rest of the Scotch.

Willows stood there, waiting for whatever might come next.

Bobby pointed at Willows' beer. He said, "Mind if I finish that, since you're leaving?"

Outside, it had begun to snow again. Willows stood by his car, keys in hand, watching the soft white flakes drift slowly down. He thought about how nice it would be if it snowed forever, never stopped, buried the city and everyone in it. Then he unlocked the car and got inside and drove back to whatever was waiting for him at 312 Main.

16

Billy eased shut the door, turned on the light by the bed. He shrugged out of his black leather jacket and went over to the window and pulled the raggedy curtains. Light from the window illuminated a rectangle of falling snow.

Billy placed the palm of his hand against the glass, felt the chill.

He pulled his T-shirt over his head, balled it up and threw it in a corner. No fat on Billy. He unbuckled his belt, played with the zipper of his Levis.

A gust of wind rattled the window and made the snow jump and swirl.

He stepped out of the jeans. Now he was naked except for his red bikini shorts. He wondered if she was there, if she was watching.

Yeah, she was watching, all right.

He *knew* she was watching.

He stepped out of the shorts. They lay at his feet like a crumpled pool of blood.

He looked down at himself.

Nothing.

He couldn't stop thinking about Nancy Crown.

It was five minutes past midnight. Probably she'd be in bed by now. Asleep and dreaming. He'd done more than a few B&E's in his life, and he knew how to case a joint. He was pretty sure he'd figured out where Nancy's bedroom was — top floor, right. He remembered that the back wall was mirrored.

He imagined a bed so big it'd take you all morning to climb out of it. Silk sheets, slippery and smooth.

Five minutes past midnight. Not all that late, really. Was it possible she and her husband were making love? A thunderbolt of rage swept through Billy. His heart pounded in his chest. His body shook. His knees felt weak. He yanked shut the curtains and sat down on the bed and lit a cigarette, sucked the smoke deep into his lungs. He couldn't stop himself. He kept creating scenarios, situations.

He pictured Nancy and her fatass husband cuddled up on the wall-to-wall in front of the fireplace, maybe having a nightcap, talking about the day and how it went.

He remembered the way her hair had looked, her eyes and the shape of her mouth.

He thought about her lying there in that great big bed, her body smooth as silk. Her husband climbing in next to her, reaching out.

A woman like that, in a house like that. How did it happen? Guy was probably twice her age. Fat, balding.

He inhaled the sweet memory of her perfume.

And he tortured himself, thinking about them lying there together between those slippery sheets, the whole goddamn city laid out in front of them on the other side of the plate-glass windows, lights softened by the snow. He knew what it would be like in that big house. Warm, quiet. *Peaceful.* The carpet soft and thick. Expensive furniture. White-painted walls. A built-in stereo. Everything brand-new, shiny and clean.

He wanted her. He wanted to teach her all the things she knew nothing about.

He thought about the way she'd stared at him as he'd tossed her the keys to her shiny black car. Nobody had ever looked at him like that before. So directly. As if she could see right into the heart of him.

And he knew in his heart that even though she might not admit it, she wanted him just as badly as he wanted her.

He lit another cigarette, smoked it down to the filter, checked his watch.

Twenty-three minutes to one.

He rolled out of bed, slipped on a pair of black jeans and a black sweater, black sneakers. He retrieved the Python from the closet, grabbed his black leather jacket. Made sure he had the keys to the Pinto.

All he was gonna do was check out the neighborhood. Cruise

by the house. See what he could see. If he was in the mood, maybe sit by the pool for awhile.

Or, if the lights were out, he might crack open the sliding glass door and take a quick look inside.

17

Parker said, "You hear what happened to Farley yesterday?"

"No, what?"

"He collapsed at his desk, just after lunch. Stood up clutching his chest, said something nobody caught and then dropped like a stone. Last I heard he was in the emergency ward at St Paul's."

Willows said, "You here when it happened?"

Parker shook her head. "No, it was about an hour before I got back from Mrs Lee's. By then, you'd gone home."

Willows nodded. After his date with Bobby Chow, he'd spent the afternoon at his local bar, Cullpepper's. But he wasn't about to admit it to Parker. He said, "Anybody at the hospital with him?"

"Inspector Bradley."

"Somebody called Farley's wife, I hope."

"Orwell."

"Yeah?" Willows rubbed his jaw. "He gave Farley kind of a rough ride yesterday morning. I wonder if that's what he's worried about." Willows opened a desk drawer, slid it shut. "How'd it go with the Lee family?"

Parker shrugged. "Nothing new. Mrs Lee's still under sedation. Peter's due in about ten tonight. He phoned while I was there. Has to make a connecting flight from Seattle."

"You talked to him?"

"Briefly. Apparently he was out of town for the past few days."

"On a ski trip," said Willows. "Nobody could get in touch with him until late yesterday afternoon."

"You phoned Boston?"

"Talked to his roommate. Skiing is Peter's favorite thing. He's often gone for three or four days at a time. He usually goes with friends, but not always."

Parker said, "He told me he was with friends the weekend his father died."

"He volunteer the information, or you have to ask him?"

"I didn't ask him anything, Jack. I mean, I'm talking to him with his mother and sister standing there, listening to every word."

"He give you any names?"

"Said he'd be glad to provide them when he arrived. Tell me, how was your afternoon of wild debauchery with Bobby Chow?"

"You should've been there."

"I doubt it."

The telephone rang. Willows picked up. He listened for a moment and then reached for a pen and said, "What's the address?"

The pen moved across a piece of scrap paper. Parker peered over his shoulder. 12–1572 Alexander.

Willows said, "Yeah, ten minutes." He slammed down the telephone.

"What?" said Parker.

Willows grabbed his leather jacket from the back of his chair. "A guy named Tod Kidner rented some space in a warehouse on Alexander. Month to month. The owner's name is Chang. When he dropped by to pick up the rent nobody answered the door. So he unlocked it and walked in."

Parker followed Willows as he walked briskly down the beige-carpeted hall towards the elevator. A couple of uniformed patrolmen strolled past. One of them winked at Parker. She ignored him. Willows hit the button with his thumb. The elevator droned towards them. The doors slid open and they stepped inside. In the harsh glare of the fluorescents, Willows' skin was taut and pale.

"This guy Kidner said he needed the warehouse for some short-term storage space for a shipment of mountain bikes he was importing from Taiwan. The end of the month rolled around. Kidner hadn't been in touch and the rent was due. When Chang went in, the first thing he saw was a wooden chair, some rope, and a pile of clothes."

The elevator stopped and the doors slid open. They hurried across the slush-filled lane, chunks of rock salt grating under their feet.

"Then he took a closer look," Willows continued, "and saw a car battery stuck under the chair, electrical wires and alligator clips, a pool of dried blood."

"And dialled nine-eleven."

"That's right," said Willows, "and by now I'll bet he wishes he hadn't."

William Chang's silver Mercedes was parked in a tow-away zone at the far end of the block from the warehouse. Willows tapped the unmarked Ford's horn as he pulled in behind him. Chang's head came up. He stared into his rearview mirror as Willows and Parker got out of the car.

Chang was clearly a very nervous man. He'd rolled up the Mercedes' windows and locked all four doors. The cellular phone he'd used to dial 911 was in his lap.

Willows flashed his tin. Chang hit a button and his window slid down.

Willows introduced himself and Parker. He said, "Has anybody approached the warehouse since you called, Mr Chang?"

"No one." Chang glanced nervously up and down the street. "You are alone?"

"We have units stationed at both ends of the block. You can't see them, but they're there."

"May I go now?"

"Did you lock the warehouse when you left?"

"No, the door is open."

"And you're sure no one was hiding inside?"

"Impossible. It's a large room, but empty. Only four walls, nothing more."

"One moment, please."

Willows used the Ford's radio to call in the squad cars. He told a cop named Frank Wainwright to accompany Chang back to 312 Main and keep him happy until he and Parker got back.

Wainwright said, "Jeez, how long is that gonna take?"

"It's going to take as long as it takes, Frank."

"What if he decides to take a walk?"

"Remind him that he's a material witness in a murder case, and tell him, politely, all about the penalty for obstruction of justice."

The warehouse was big, three stories high. Peeling gray paint on clapboard. Plastic sheeting stapled over the windows. The low wooden steps had the consistency of cheese beneath their feet. Chang had left the door open, but there was no need for him to worry about the utility bill because the building was unheated.

Directly above the plain wooden chair in which Kenny Lee had died, a naked bulb hung from a beam, casting the chair in a pool of jaundiced yellow light.

Willows squatted down on his haunches. The battery had a Sears label. The punch-out adhesive guarantee strip indicated the battery had been bought during the previous month — December. The electrical wires were ordinary jumper cables. A car radio and a pair of cheap speakers stood on a small wooden box a few feet behind the chair. Small-gauge wires led from the radio to the battery, but weren't connected.

In the yellow light, the pools and scattered drops of dried blood looked like shiny blobs of black wax.

There was more blood on the sprung copper clamps of the jumper cables, and what looked on first examination like bits of flesh.

Willows said, "We're going to need a photographer. Dutton, if he's available. Lights. Forensics. Enough men to canvass and search the area."

Parker started towards the door. Willows said, "And get me a flashlight, will you?"

Kenny Lee's clothes were in a pile in the far corner of the warehouse. On the day he was snatched he'd been wearing a dark blue London Fog raincoat, a pair of black dress shoes, a gray off-the-rack suit with a Woodward's label, a white short-sleeved shirt, dark blue socks and pale blue boxer shorts. Everything was there. A uniform held the flashlight steady while Willows methodically tagged and marked and wrapped each article of clothing in a separate paper bag for shipment to the lab. Everything was carefully examined for visible trace evidence. He found several long black hairs on the shoulders of Lee's coat. These were placed in an evidence envelope to avoid the possibility of loss during transit. He heard footsteps and looked up to see Bradley hurrying towards him.

"Whatcha got?"

"Too soon to say, Inspector."

Bradley glanced at the cop, who needed a haircut. The cop cleared his throat. "I should get back to my unit. Want me to leave the flash?"

"Yeah, thanks." Willows took the flashlight, stood up. The cop marched briskly towards the door and then stepped aside to let Parker and Dutton and the forensics team enter the building.

Bradley said, "The parties I hate the most is where everybody shows up at once." He stuck a cigar in his mouth, fished a match out of his pocket. Willows gave him a look. *Don't mess up my crime scene*. Bradley scowled and put the match away.

Willows said, "How's Farley?"

"If he was a horse, I wouldn't bet on him." Bradley rubbed his leather-gloved hands together. "Why couldn't the perp have tied Lee up in a suite at the Hilton? God, but it's cold in here."

Parker helped set up the lights. Mel Dutton shot three rolls of film. A scene-of-crime cop named Julian Walsh fingerprinted every available surface. The whine of a vacuum cleaner echoed off the bare wooden walls and high, shadowy ceiling. The dried blood was scraped off the floor and emptied into glassine evidence envelopes. A wooden tongue depressor was used to clean the bits of flesh off the clamp and into another evidence bag.

Willows found the plastic bucket that had served Kenny Lee as a toilet in a corner beneath a scrap of rotting canvas tarpaulin. It would explain why Lee's ankles had been untied, how he'd been able to assume the lotus position before he died.

Walsh said, "You want me to bother dusting this? I mean, would you touch it if you weren't wearing gloves?"

"I wouldn't touch it even if I was wearing gloves," said his partner.

Parker said, "Just be glad it isn't the middle of August, Julian."

"Twenty pounds of frozen shit. Who do I know that's having a birthday?"

Willows touched the jumper cables together. There was a loud *crack* and a shower of sparks.

Julian, hunched over the bucket with his brush and powder, got a laugh when he yelled, "Knock it off, Jack! Christ, I almost dived in!"

Willows attached the wires from the car radio to the battery terminals. Cops moved in and out of the lights, black distorted shadows dancing across the walls. An old Hank Snow tune flowed from the speakers and a voice from the darkness said, "Mood music for horses. Ain't that sweet." Willows didn't bother to look up. The radio was tuned to 1420FM, a local country and western station.

The radio had a shiny black facing. The casing was sheet metal. There were traces of white fingerprint powder on the dials, black on the metal, but no visible prints. Willows picked the radio up and turned it over. A tiny jagged chunk of brown plastic clung to a mounting screw.

Parker knelt beside Willows. "What've you got?"

Willows pointed at the piece of plastic. "This look to you like it might've been ripped out of a car?"

"Theft from auto," said Parker. "What brand is it?"

Willows turned the radio rightside up. "Kenwood."

Parker considered the stats. On average, there were about fifty reported cases of theft from auto per day. Not all of the calls involved stolen tape decks. Call it thirty a day. That worked out to roughly nine hundred a month. What percentage would be Kenwood products? How far back would they have to go to find the owner of this particular radio, and where was the information likely to lead?

Willows wrapped the trailing wires around the radio and put it in a large brown paper bag.

Julian Walsh snapped shut his aluminum briefcase. He glanced at Willows and shrugged. "Nothing. Take your choice—either the perp wore gloves or he didn't have any fingers."

"Thanks, Julian."

"For nothing. What's the word on Spears?"

"All I know is he might've had a heart attack and that they took him to emergency."

"How old is he?"

"Early fifties, somewhere in there."

Walsh nodded. He'd celebrated his forty-ninth three weeks ago.

The vacuum bag was sealed in a larger plastic bag. Forensics would pore over the contents with a magnifying glass. There were gaps between the floorboards. Maybe they'd come up with something.

Willows used the palm of his hand to brush Walsh's fingerprint powder from the seat and back of the chair. He sat down. Parker looked at him. Willows said, "Turn the kleig lights off."

Parker pulled the plug. Now the only light in the warehouse came from the bulb dangling five feet above the chair. Willows sat motionless in the chair while the lights were packed up and removed. When there were only the two of them left he said, "I'll meet you back at the station, okay?"

"Yeah, sure."

Parker turned and took a quick look behind her as she shut the door.

Willows sat erect in the chair, his hands in his lap, staring straight ahead. His eyes were in deep shadow. With each breath he took, a small cloud of vapor drifted up into the pool of yellow light, and vanished.

Parker shut the door.

The warehouse was silent for a moment, and then a car or a truck drove past, and Willows heard the muffled hiss of tires on wet asphalt. He sat up a little straighter.

It was impossible to guess what thoughts had passed through Lee's mind as he'd sat there in the cold, naked and defenseless, waiting for his torturer to return.

Willows unzipped his leather jacket and tossed it on the floor. The wool sweater came next, then his shirt.

The cold jumped at him. He sat down, willed himself not to move. His skin pebbled. He began to shake. How much longer could it go on getting worse? He could feel the cold seeping into his bones. He remembered the icy water of the Sun Yat-Sen Gardens. This was just as bad.

He wondered if it was cold enough to eventually have an effect on his ability to think, reason.

Maybe that's why the killer had needed the battery; to inflict pain as a stimulant. Hot jolts of electricity to warm the icy brain.

They'd gone over every square inch of the warehouse. There was no telephone and no wall jack. Lee's call to his family had been made from a different location or had been pre-recorded.

Willows pulled on his shirt. He didn't take the time to button it up before he wriggled into his sweater. The zipper of the jacket was too much for his stiff fingers. He blew on his hands, then stepped up on the chair and warmed himself with the faint heat of the bulb.

He was looking for somebody who knew how to steal a radio out of a car. Maybe Chang would find the guy in one of the mug books, make a positive identification. Nail the killer with type AB blood who had a preference for cowboy music and torture. The battery was a solid lead. Maybe the killer had bought it with a credit card. Willows wondered how many Sears outlets existed in the city and surrounding suburbs. Maybe there was a store code somewhere on the battery that would narrow things down.

He started towards the door. He was still aching from the cold, shivering uncontrollably. How long had Kenny Lee lasted, in that chair? There was fingerprint powder on the light switch. Willows stepped outside and shut the door.

Parker was double-parked in front of the building. The Ford's engine was running; a plume of hot gases from the exhaust soured the air. She took one look at Willows and said, "Get in the car, Jack."

"Got to seal the door."

"I'll do it, okay?"

"Sure," said Willows, and climbed into the Ford. The heater was going full blast. He held his hands up to the vent.

When Parker got back in the car he said, "Any word on Farley?" Parker shook her head. "Want to go see him?"

"First things first," said Willows.

William Chang was waiting for them in the squad room, sitting on a chair beneath a bulletin board covered with police-related articles from the local papers. Willows offered him a cup of coffee from the pot the detectives kept on a counter at the end of the room.

Chang wasn't interested in coffee. Neither was he tempted by the chocolate-frosted donut Parker offered him. He made a show of checking his watch. The cops had kept him waiting almost two hours. All he wanted was to get the hell out of there.

Willows led him over to his desk, offered him a seat. Parker pulled up another chair. Willows said, "You're aware that a prominent member of the Chinese community, Kenny Lee, was found murdered last weekend."

Chang nodded his head vigorously. "Yes, of course."

"What you may not realize is that Mr Lee was missing for a lengthy period of time before his body was found."

"You think he was in my warehouse?"

"We're certain of it. For one thing, the clothes left in the warehouse exactly match the clothes Mr Lee was wearing when he disappeared."

Parker said, "That's why we've kept you waiting all this time, Mr Chang."

Chang glanced anxiously from Willows to Parker and back again. "You believe I am involved in this crime?"

"Definitely not," said Parker.

"But you are a witness," said Willows. "The only one we've got. Naturally there are a few questions we'd like to ask you."

"I think I would like to talk to my lawyer."

Willows hid his anger behind a smile. "Believe me, there's no need for that."

"I have the right to make a call, is this not so? Otherwise, I refuse to cooperate."

Willows pulled the phone across his desk, cleared a line and handed the receiver to Chang.

Parker said, "The thing is, if you feel you require a lawyer, we have no choice but to report that fact to the press."

Chang's finger hovered over the dial.

"Crooks need lawyers," said Parker. "Honest citizens usually don't."

"And most people know that," Willows said. "When they read in the newspapers that you are involved in Lee's murder and felt it necessary to . . . "

Chang slowly lowered the receiver into the cradle.

"On the other hand," said Parker, "there's no real need to mention your name at all."

Chang thought it over. To Willows, he said, "What guarantees can you offer?"

"I don't see any problems. In fact, keeping your name out of the papers might work to our advantage as well."

"The killer would not know that you had moved closer to him."

"Exactly."

"If he knew I had spoken to you, my life might be in danger."

"That's very unlikely."

"But . . . " Chang trailed off. He stared down at the telephone, considering possibilities.

Willows and Parker exchanged a quick glance. Willows said, "The man who called himself Tod Kidner. What did he look like?"

"Well, that's just it. It is difficult to say. We met at the warehouse, in the evening. It was very dark."

"What time?"

Chang hesitated. "About eight."

"What kind of car did Kidner have?"

"I don't know. He was waiting on the sidewalk when I arrived."

"And when you left?"

"He stayed behind."

"Why?"

"I didn't ask."

"You rented the warehouse to him on the spot?"

"Yes."

"How did he pay?"

"With cash. One month in advance. If he was to need the warehouse a second month, he was to call me by the middle of the month, January fifteenth."

Parker said, "What was the rent? How much did Kidner pay?"

Again, Chang hesitated. Then he shrugged and said, "One thousand dollars."

Willows said, "For an unheated warehouse? Isn't that a little steep?"

"It was the figure I suggested, and it was accepted without argument."

"The transaction took place in the warehouse?"

"Yes."

"He had that much money on him?"

"I don't take checks. Never." Chang blinked like an owl. "Checks can have a life of their own. They bounce. Cash is different. It does not move until you choose to move it."

"You're a philosopher, Mr Chang."

"A businessman. A realist."

"What denomination were the bills?"

"Twenties. Fifty of them."

155

"Did you give him a receipt?"

"It was not necessary."

"Why not?"

"Because he didn't ask."

"Where is the money now?"

"It . . . went into general accounts. Petty cash."

Willows leaned forward in his chair. "Now, I want you to think back, Mr Chang, and tell us everything you can remember about Tod Kidner."

"He was a young man. Maybe twenty years old. Thin. Tall, about six feet. And there is something else I remember about him. His smile. He smiled often and he had a very nice smile."

"What color were his eyes?"

Chang thought about it. Willows and Parker watched him thinking. After a moment he said, "Brown, perhaps. But I'm not sure."

"Was he wearing glasses?"

"No."

"What about his hair?"

"It was red, I think. He wore a hat."

"What kind of hat?"

"A cowboy hat. Black." Chang brought his hands together, a soft clap of delight. "Yes, and he had on a pair of heavy boots. Cowboy boots. They made a very loud sound as he walked across the floor."

"Was he wearing a coat or jacket?"

"A jacket. Leather. Black, or dark brown. It was short, it came to his waist. He had the collar turned up."

"Did you notice any scars on his face or hands?"

"No, none."

"Can you remember anything else about him?"

"He wore jeans. Blue jeans. They were tucked into the tops of his boots."

"When he spoke, did he have an accent?"

"No."

"Was his speech . . . educated?"

"I would say no. He swore a lot. A habit, I would say. Not because he was angry. His language was very coarse."

The phone rang. Willows picked up. He listened for a moment

and then said, "Yeah, a couple of minutes. You ready for us? Good." He hung up and turned to Chang. "We need just a little more of your time, Mr Chang. I'd like you to spend a few minutes with a police artist. With your help, I'm sure he'll be able to come up with a good likeness of the killer."

Chang glanced at his watch. "I have an appointment. May I use your phone?"

"As long as it isn't to call your lawyer," Willows said, and smiled to soften the unspoken threat.

Bailey switched the eraser to his left hand, sketched a few quick lines.

Chang said. "A little thicker. Yes. Good."

Kenny Lee's killer had an oval face, a prominent jaw, a broad forehead and heavy eyebrows. His nose was small, but straight. Pinched nostrils.

Willows wondered how accurate the composite drawing would turn out to be. Chang hadn't hesitated when he'd described the clothes the killer had worn, but he'd been unusually vague about his physical description. Was his sudden ability to remember details genuine, or the result of a decision to get the police off his back?

Willows said, "I'll need about thirty copies. ASAP."

Bailey tossed his pencil and drawing pad on his desk. "You got it, Jack."

Parker said, "Okay, Mr Chang. Let's go take a look at the mugbooks."

Chang nodded, but remained seated in his chair.

"Something wrong?"

"May I use the phone again?"

"Yeah, sure."

"And one other thing." Chang cleared his throat. "Perhaps I'll have that donut after all."

18

Nancy gave the sterling silver pitcher of Smirnov vodka martinis a final shake, poured a couple of doubles and added a twist of lemon to each glass. Turning her back to the living room, she glanced furtively out the window. Beyond the brightly-lit patio and steamy pool and the spidery shadows of shrubbery etched in snow, the unseen harbor was so dark and empty that it was almost as if she was living at the very end of the earth. The cliff-top fence, made of glass panels and designed not to be an encumbrance to the million-dollar view, worked very well in the daytime but at night acted as a mirror, reflecting the lights of the house. The low wall of reflected light served to emphasize the darkness beyond. Staring out the window, it was easy for her to believe that there was nothing out there, nothing there at all.

Fanciful.

She placed the drinks and two pale gray paper napkins on a tray. Pale gray was Tyler's favorite color. Bland, unexciting. The lights in the backyard were a security measure. His idea. Tyler didn't want her *worrying* about things. Clouds of steam rose from the pool and were quickly swallowed by the icy winter air. Nancy wondered, in a vague, unformed sort of way, what her car thief was up to.

She went through the kitchen and into the living room. Tyler had taken off his suit jacket and loosened his tie. He was sprawled out on the cream-colored Italian leather sofa, reading. The *Wall Street Journal*, what else. She put his napkin and drink down in front of him on the marble coffee table. He grunted his thanks and turned the page.

Nancy sat down on the other sofa, tucked her legs under her and drank about an inch of martini. The flames in the gas fireplace were pale blue at the bottom, light orange on top.

Anemic. She remembered fires from her childhood; walking hand in hand to the garage with her father to watch him split kindling — a silvery blur and then the meaty thump of the hatchet. The lovely, solid weight of the birch logs in her arms as she carried them into the house. Curling white strips of bark. The soft rustle of balled-up newspaper and the harsh scratch of the match across the tiles. The pungent smell of burning forests. Small explosions and sparks that jumped out at her and hit the brass screen and fell back. And for a moment Nancy was lost in childhood dreams of birchbark canoes gliding through dark waters, roaring fires among the shadows, bright-painted, wildly dancing men. Tongues of orange flame, the heat warming her body.

Tyler turned another page. He picked up his glass, sipped. Nancy looked at him. He was oblivious.

What did he think? Was it good? Was it terrific? Or was it the worst damn vodka martini he'd ever had in his life? She'd never know. But she was sure of one thing — her glass was empty and she was going to go get herself a refill.

She swung her legs off the sofa and headed for the kitchen. Tyler, immersed in his newspaper, didn't say a word.

It had started snowing again, the kind of fat and excessively fluffy flakes that didn't last. Everything was covered in a thin layer of snow. Everything except the swimming pool. The pool looked kind of slushy around the edges, but that was about it, the hot water heater was doing its job. She poured herself another double and wandered over to the sliding glass doors. Off to her right, the city was a haze of lights, all blurred into one another. She pressed her nose against the glass and could feel the cold even through the double-glazing.

She blew on the glass, used the tips of her fingers to draw a heart in the gray fog of condensation. The lines of the deck chairs were softened by the snow. All the color had been drained out of the world. Nancy reached out and flicked off the row of light switches, plunging the backyard into darkness. She counted to ten and turned the lights back on. No doubt about it, he definitely wasn't out there.

She drained her glass, went over to the counter and filled the glass up again and went back into the living room, dropped heavily on to the sofa. Tyler glanced up from his paper, gave her an enquiring look. She balanced the martini glass on her stomach. She felt lazy, half-asleep, sexy.

Tyler turned another page. Any minute now, he was going to light his goddamn stinking pipe and hold out his glass and ask her for a refill. And she knew he wouldn't even look at her, trouble to take his eyes off the page. She picked a bit of lint off her sweater. Why was it that black cashmere and lint had such an attraction for one another? And why did she keep thinking about that handsome, dangerous boy?

Tyler held out his glass. "Could I have a refill, honey?"

Nancy uncoiled her legs, padded across the carpet and took the glass out of his hand. Their fingers touched. But it was an accident, rather than by design.

Tyler said, "Hold the lemon."

Everything in the kitchen — everything in the whole damn house — was brand new, gleaming. And at the same time, dull. *Boring*.

Drift of steam from the pool, and parallel to the lip of the pool, thin dark lines of shadow.

She poured Tyler the world's biggest martini ever and put it down on the coffee table in easy reach and went back into the kitchen and unlocked the sliding glass door and pushed it open and stepped outside in her cotton slacks and thin black cashmere and bare feet. It was cold, a lot colder than she'd expected and much colder than the city they called Lotusland had any right to be, even if it was the end of January.

She walked across the balcony and down the steps and into the yard, over to the pool. Her feet stung from the cold, but she wasn't bored, not any longer.

Somebody had recently jumped the fence and walked all around the pool. Falling snow had blurred the definition of the footsteps. *His* footsteps. She knew it. She knelt and blew the fresh snow away. What a clever trick. Where in the world had she learned to do that? She blew a little harder. He must have rocked back and forth — she could see the imprint of his shoe from heel to toe. No, not shoe. Boot. The outline was crisp and clear, the depression in shadow, defined by the lights. He'd stayed long enough to smoke a cigarette right down to the filter. She picked up the butt and sniffed. The scent was faint and took her a moment to identify.

Menthol.

She walked down the length of the yard to the waist-high wall of safety glass, flicked the cigarette butt out into the falling snow. It was a fifty-foot drop to the beach. Fifty feet, straight down. Death. You couldn't see it, but it was there.

Nancy started back towards the house. Her feet were numb. So was the rest of her, come to think of it. She slid open the glass door and stepped inside and slid the door shut and turned off the outside lights.

Tyler had finally lost interest in his goddamn paper.

Tyler was sound asleep.

19

Garret raised his voice a little, pressing home the point that he knew the law, how it worked. The way he saw it, the time they'd spent learning how to break into a BMW or Porsche or fucking Volvo didn't have an awful lot to do with cracking an armored car. It was too big a bite, too many things could go wrong. If they got caught they'd do a quarter century, no chance of parole. He didn't *ever* want to be thirty years old, never mind blow out his candles in a fucking maximum security prison.

They were at Billy's house, smoking dope and getting wasted, Billy working hard to sell Garret on what a great idea it was to risk a couple of counts of first degree murder for a sackful of cash.

Garret kept pretending he wasn't interested. In the joint, the cons'd be all over them like flies on honey. Doing dirty things to them. So forget it, Billy. No way was he going to rob an armored car.

Billy kept hammering away at him. Threatening him, making jokes. Trying everything he could think of to get a handle on Garret's fear and put it to rest.

Over and over again, Garret kept saying no. Billy didn't hear a word he said. He was like a hungry wasp at summer's last picnic. Circling around Garret, buzzing him.

Finally, Billy said let's at least go take a look, and Garret caved in.

They spent all that afternoon in the Safeway parking lot, staring at the liquor store and the people that went in and out. A fat old guy in a yellow raincoat stood by the door, endlessly playing the same three-chord tune on a battered guitar, hustling for nickels and dimes. After a while, just to pass the time, Garret started keeping track of the percentage of people who tossed money into the musician's open guitar case, trying to work out how much the guy was making. Not a hell of a lot, but more than Garret and Billy. At ten to eleven a clerk locked the doors and a few minutes later the last customer was gone and shortly afterwards the lights went out.

Garret said, "We could bust 'em at closing time."

Billy shook his head. "They got a safe. And you can bet your ass there's a direct line to the cops. All we'd get is the money in the till."

"Could be three, maybe four thousand dollars, Billy."

"Big fuckin' deal. Know what your problem is? You got no fuckin' ambition. Three grand. Jesus, we might as well bust a gumball machine."

Billy turned the ignition key. The Pinto's engine caught and held. Billy'd dropped a new set of plugs in the car and stolen a heavy-duty battery out of a brand-new Econoline parked in a lot on Kingsway. The Pinto looked like shit but it was a beater; he knew it wouldn't let him down.

The next morning, they were back in the parking lot by ten, parked close enough to the liquor store to watch the manager fumble through his keys and unlock the door.

Billy had bought a couple of cheap sleeping bags at the Army & Navy down on Hastings, but the Pinto was cold as the inside of a meatlocker, you could spit icicles. Garret stomped his feet on the rusty floorboards, trying to keep warm, wondering for maybe the millionth time if he was making a mistake. Could Billy keep his act together long enough for Garret to do *his* tough guy thing? He dragged the toe of his boot across the rubber mat. Lee's wallet a little cancerous bump down there, nothing you'd notice unless you were looking for it. Well, the homicide cops would be looking soon enough, if things worked out the way he'd planned.

A bottle blonde in a white fur coat came out of the liquor store, pushing a shopping cart full of booze.

"Party time," said Billy. "Bet she spent five hundred bucks and drinks it all herself."

"Why don't we rob her, go home and get drunk? Be a lot more fun than sitting here freezing our asses off."

It was so cold inside the Pinto that whenever either of them said anything, little puffs of vapor shot out of their mouths. Garret hated every minute of it. By now they'd spent enough time in the car to develop certain routines; they took turns scraping frost off the inside of the windshield and, every hour or so, trotting across the packed ice and snow to the 7-Eleven for coffee.

Billy had made the first trip, on the flip of a coin. The clerk they'd robbed hadn't been there. Probably he'd been fired.

Billy looked at his watch. It was twenty past six, and the light was starting to fail. The liquor store was open from ten in the morning to eleven at night. Almost five more hours to go.

"Hungry?"

Garret ducked his head. "Yeah, a little."

"Wanna make a run over to the 7-Eleven, get something to eat?"

Garret shrugged. The sleeping bag slipped off his shoulders. He pulled it back up.

"Warm in the store," Billy reminded him.

"What about you, you hungry?"

"I wouldn't mind a coffee, maybe a cheeseburger."

"I couldn't eat another one of those goddamn burgers if it was the last food on earth," said Garret.

"Hit the Safeway, the deli counter. Get 'em to make you a ham and cheese, whatever you want."

"Something hot."

"Hotdog and a coffee," suggested Billy, even though he knew damn well that Garret never drank anything but Coke. Except booze, of course, but there was no alcohol on board because Billy figured it was pretty goddamn important, considering they were getting ready to do some robbing and shooting, that they stay sober for a change, keep a clear head.

Garret shifted in his seat. "Got any money?"

"What happened to that ten I gave you?"

"Spent it."

Billy dropped the Colt Python on the car seat and dug deep in his jeans, came up with a crumpled twenty. He tossed the bill on the dashboard. Garret scooped it up, yanked open his door. Billy grabbed his arm. "Better leave the piece here, Garret."

"What? Oh, yeah, right." Garret gave Billy a dopy grin and shoved the Remington pump to one side. Billy made sure the safety was on and covered the shotgun with a corner of his sleeping bag. Garret climbed out of the Pinto and slammed the door shut behind him. Hands stuffed in his pockets and shoulders hunched, he trudged through the snow and parked cars towards the Safeway.

Billy turned the key in the ignition. The Pinto's engine caught, faltered, held steady. He brought the revs up and turned on the heater. A gust of lukewarm air swept across his knees. He lit a cigarette. The store's automatic door flipped open and Garret shot through like he was a human pinball, swivelled to stare at a checkout girl and bounced off a metal revolving rack of paperback books. What a fuckin' clown. Billy watched him stroll over to the magazine stand. Girls or hot cars, that was about all he was interested in. For Garret, heaven was a bikini flopped across the hood of a Corvette.

Billy cradled the Python on his lap. He ran his hand along the polished walnut stock of the shotgun.

He started thinking about Nancy Crown again. Watched wide-eyed as she reached up to loosen the clasp that held her hair in place, her breasts moving under her sweater, that long, glossy blonde hair shimmering as it tumbled across her naked shoulders, that pale skin.

She was beautiful, and the more he thought about her, the more beautiful she became.

He'd been to her house three times now, slipping like a thief through the darkness. Each time, he'd sniffed around the doors and windows and then stood by the pool, snow falling all around him, silence. At four o'clock on a cold winter's morning there was no traffic and no birdsong. Only a gradually thickening silence.

The last time he'd visited her, he'd turned his back to the house to light a smoke, not wanting to risk the bright flare of the lighter. A shaft of moonlight had slipped through the clouds and he'd suddenly become aware of the ocean, the fact that it was right there, at the end of the yard, fifty feet below him. A faint rustling sound came from the beach, cold black water massaging the shore. He got his cigarette going and blew smoke at the moon. Flakes of snow drifted into the ocean and vanished.

Billy flicked cigarette ash to the dirty, crumbling floor of the Pinto. The heater was working better now. He held his hands out to the flow of warm air.

There were always lights on in the house. Even when she went to bed, there were lights on. In the kitchen and living room, where he figured the downstairs bathroom was, the den. The whole main floor of the house was awash with light. Even upstairs, there were lights on in the hall and several of the rooms. As far as he could tell, only the bedroom was in darkness. Standing in the backyard, he couldn't tell if she left the bedroom door open or not. But the door must be shut because after she turned the light out the room was in total darkness, he couldn't see a goddamn thing.

That's when his imagination went into overdrive, when he was blind. Noises. He heard noises. Faint at first, vague and indistinct. But familiar, and rapidly becoming louder. The soft rustle of sheets; the sound of her body moving in the bed and the shape of her body beneath silk. Her body rising and falling and turning and turning. He pictured her lying on her back and then rolling over on her side, the curve of hip as she moved to face him.

He heard the sound of her breathing. A soft moan of pain or tiny cry of pleasure. A long, drawn-out sigh.

The soundtrack to her dreams.

And then there would be a gust of wind and rattle of branches or maybe a car would shoot by, and he couldn't be sure what he'd heard, if he'd actually heard anything at all.

More silence, the weight of it pressing down on him as he leaned into the night.

Heavy black cloud drifting across the blank white face of the moon.

Darkness.

Billy turned his back and hunched his shoulders to light another cigarette, cupped his hands around the flame.

And then he heard the voice of her husband, distant, muttered words he couldn't quite catch. Soft whispers. Entreaties, demands. Would she do this and would she do that. More rustling of sheets.

Billy paced the length of the pool, prowling and sneering. He spat in the steaming water, kicked a deck chair into the deep end. The crisp and brittle snow crunched beneath his heels. What was real and what was not? He had no idea, no way of knowing. In his rage and impotence he wanted to smash the whole goddamn world, kick it to pieces. His ears burned.

Would she do this, would she do that?

A bitter wind snapped at him. A storm of snow filled the car. Garret slammed the door shut. The plastic bag he was carrying leaked good smells.

Billy cleared his throat. An after-image of Nancy Crown lying naked on a bed flickered in his brain. He said, "Where the fuck you been, all this time?"

"They were real busy, you shoulda seen the lineup." Garret briskly rubbed his hands together, blew on them. "Nobody eats at home anymore. Or if they do, it's takeout."

Billy rooted through the food. He popped open a foam container, peeked inside.

"What the fuck is this?"

"Potato salad."

"*Potato salad?*"

"It's good. The girl at the counter, she let me have a taste."

"She did, huh?" Billy tossed the container back in the bag, tried another. Some kind of meat that looked like little runty sausages, in a thick brown sauce that was steaming hot. He grabbed one between his finger and thumb. Hot. He stuck it in his mouth, chewed.

"What else you got?"

"Buffalo wings."

Billy gave Garret his dead-fish look.

"Chicken," explained Garret. "Spicy, you'll like 'em."

Billy ate another sausage.

Garret had a plastic fork. He filled his mouth with potato salad.

Billy said, "You're a weird guy, Garret. It's five below zero, we're in the middle of a fuckin' snowstorm, and you got a fever for potato salad. What is it, your brain froze solid?"

"Potato salad and sausages."

"You can't have any fuckin' sausages. I'm gonna eat 'em all."

"That ain't fair!"

Billy gave Garret a look of sheer disbelief. He ate another sausage, glanced up and saw the big, silvery-gray bulk of the Loomis armored car parked in front of the liquor store.

"*Jesus Christ!*"

"What?" mumbled Garret, a big goop of potato salad falling out of his mouth.

Billy spilled hot brown sauce all over his sleeping bag. He stuck the half-empty container on the dashboard, and reached for the shotgun.

Garret stared at him, bug-eyed with fear. Had Billy somehow peered inside his brain, found out what he was planning?

Billy's legs were all tangled up in the sleeping bag. He kicked free. The shotgun was across his lap, pointing at Garret's belly. He worked the pump. Garret snatched up the Python. He thumbed back the hammer and pointed the revolver at Billy's face, the barrel so close to his nose Billy could smell the gun oil.

"Garret, fuck off!"

Garret held the gun steady, in both hands. His arms were bent at the elbow. He squinted down the barrel, one eye squeezed tight. "Drop it!" he yelled in a tone of voice Billy had never heard before.

It seeped into Billy's mind at last what Garret had said to him, what he must have been thinking when Billy grabbed the pump. He took his hand off the Remington and rubbed the windshield clean, pointed.

Garret saw the armored car. He saw the liquor store door open wide and the guy standing out there in the cold playing numb-finger guitar step back. Saw the two Loomis guys in their gray uniforms, one of them pushing a dolly loaded down with canvas sacks, the other staying a few steps behind him, his hand on the butt of his holstered weapon.

The guy with the gun unlocked the back door of the armored car. The second guard began to throw bags of money into the car.

"Shit," said Billy.

Garret carefully lowered the Python's hammer.

"Shit," said Billy again.

The guard picked up the dolly and pushed it inside the car. He climbed in and then the guy with the gun took one last quick look around and went in after him. The door swung shut and the truck pulled smoothly away from the liquor store.

The guy with the guitar went back to playing.

Billy worked the Remington's slide, ejected the shell from the breech. Brass, plastic. A half-ounce of powder and a couple ounces of double-ought lead. A load that would blow a hole the size of a baseball right through a man, chop him down, kill him so goddamn fast. The shell hit the door panel with a dull thud. Billy picked it up off the floor and stuck it in his jacket pocket.

"I thought you were gonna shoot me," said Garret.

Billy said, "Well, you got it all wrong. We're gonna shoot *them*, remember?"

A guy in a black trenchcoat came out of the liquor store. The guitar player broke off his tune to hold the door open. The guy in the trenchcoat didn't even look at him, just walked right by. Billy couldn't blame him; the musician couldn't even hit a clean chord. The guitar was mainly for show, a prop. All the guy was, really, was a doorman. The trenchcoat hurried through the snow to a cream Mercedes.

"Bet he's got a Blaupunkt," said Garret. "Thousand dollar stereo system in that car."

"And we'd get fifty bucks for it," said Billy.

The trenchcoat got into his eighty-thousand-dollar car. He hadn't even bothered to lock it. The Merc's headlights flared, cutting twin paths of sparkling light through the falling snow.

Nancy would know people like that, rich people who drove expensive cars and had doors opened for them all the time and didn't even notice. Billy glanced at his watch. Five minutes to eleven. He wondered what she was doing. Saturday night, she wouldn't be in bed, not yet. Watching television, maybe. Or out somewhere, at an art gallery opening, a play. All Billy had to go on was movies he'd seen. He'd never been to a play, inside an art gallery, attended a symphony.

He rolled down his window, flicked his cigarette into the cold night air, rolled the window back up and lit a fresh cigarette.

"Now what?" said Garret.

Billy checked the gas gauge. He still had a quarter tank. He could drive down to Nancy's; her house was only a few miles away, a ten-minute drive. Make Garret wait in the Pinto while he checked out the house. But he'd have to park a block or so away, or Garret would find out where she lived, and he didn't want that. Also, Garret would start asking questions. Watching TV, you got up to take a piss, Garret had to know where you were going and when you'd be back. Billy didn't want any questions because, more and more often lately, he'd found himself wanting to talk about her. Tell somebody about the way she held herself, the smooth, gliding way she walked, how nicely she dressed, the big, brightly-lit house she lived in. And he wanted to tell somebody about the warmth and exquisite loneliness he felt as he stood by the steaming pool, darkness all around him, silence.

He said, "You ever been in love, Garret?"

Garret laughed. "Sure, hundreds of times. And I said so, too. Hey, baby, I think I'm in love . . . "

"No," said Billy. "I mean . . . the real thing. Where you really love someone and want to do something for her. Even if she doesn't love you."

Garret lifted his nose and sniffed the air. "Got a leaky exhaust? Your brain full of carbon monoxide, is that your problem?"

"Forget it."

Garret made a grab for the foam carton full of little sausages. Billy didn't try to stop him. Garret chewed and swallowed. "No, I never been in love. Except I love my mom, if that's what you mean."

Billy said, "I always figured there was something between the two of you."

"Fuck off." Garret licked thick brown sauce from his fingers, went after another sausage. He said, "Slippery little bastards, aren't they?"

Billy said, "I mean, you're both ugly as a shoe box full of shit, so I guess it figures."

"Fuck *right* off," said Garret. He popped a sausage in his mouth and dug energetically around in the sauce. "How many sausages you eat?"

Billy shrugged. "Five, maybe six."

"I only had three."

"Want me to stick my finger down my throat, see what I can come up with?" A clerk unlocked the door of the liquor store to let the last of the customers out. There were still a dozen or more cars in the parking lot — the Safeway was open until midnight. Billy leaned forward to release the emergency brake.

"Hold it a minute," said Garret.

"What?"

"I'm feeling lonely. Thought I'd see if Sandy's in the mood for a little romance."

"Who?"

"Sandy. At the deli."

"Delicious Sandy."

"Yeah." Defensively, Garret said, "She gave me a real nice smile."

Billy checked the sticker on the sausage container's plastic lid. Three dollars and fifty cents. Sandy had given Garret a big smile and a spoonful of free potato salad, and maybe fifty-two cents worth of sausages and three bucks worth of sauce.

Garret said, "Thought I'd ask her if she wants a ride home after work."

"In my car."

"I'd do it for you."

Billy slapped him on the shoulder. "Go for it, big guy."

Garret got out of the car and started towards the Safeway, his boots scuffing up the snow. Billy wrapped the shotgun and pistol in a sleeping bag, went around to the back of the car and stuck everything in the trunk.

Garret was gone five minutes max, came back with his hands in his pockets. He wasn't smiling. Billy crouched down low. Garret finally noticed that the car was empty, looked around. Billy waited patiently until his back was turned and then stood up and took his shot. Garret's head exploded in a white froth. He dropped to one knee.

Billy fired again, missed. Garret swore and scooped a double handful of snow off the roof of a Pontiac. Billy aimed at his crotch and hit him a good one in the knee. Garret cursed again and wound up and threw hard, caught Billy in the chest. They chased each other around the parking lot until Garret's hands were numb and he held them up in mock surrender. Billy popped him again, from point-blank range. Wet and shivering, the two would-be armored car robbers climbed back into the idling Pinto.

"What'd she say, where is she?"

Garret shrugged. "Said she needed time to think about it. Told me to come back when they close. She's gotta put away the fish and meat, clean the counters. Be finished about quarter after twelve."

"Fuck that." Billy put the Pinto in gear.

"We could drive around," said Garret. "Go find a pool hall and play for awhile and come back."

Billy shook his head. "I'm gonna go home, take a shower and crawl into bed. You're so crazy about her, stick around."

"And then what, she's got a headache and I take the fucking bus all the way across town? Forget it."

Billy let out the clutch. The Pinto crawled across the lot, tires slithering on the soft, fresh snow.

"Rob an armored car," said Garret. "Get rich and be happy for the rest of your life. You made it sound so easy."

"It is," said Billy. "Wait and see."

"Maybe," said Garret, rattling Billy's chain, "maybe we oughtta try something a little smaller, work up to the big stuff."

"Climb that ladder rung by rung?"

"We didn't do so good tonight, did we?"

"You got a free dinner, Garret. What the fuck else you want out of me?"

"I just think we're in over our head, that's all."

"Next week," said Billy. "Tuesday or Wednesday, that's when they'll be back."

"You said Saturday was best, when they'd have the most money."

Billy drove past the 7-Eleven. There were a bunch of kids slouching around by the gas pumps, smoking dope and hoping the place would blow up, probably. He said, "You wanna wait until Saturday? Okay, we'll wait."

"I wanna steal some radios, that's what I want to do. Fuck, Billy. I'm broke."

"Stay broke," said Billy. "Then you got a motive you can understand."

Garret rolled down the window and threw the plastic Safeway bag and the foam containers and coffee cups out on the street.

"Knock it off," said Billy.

Garret rolled the window back up.

Billy said, "This's a nice part of town, people just don't do that kind of shit over here."

Garret said, "Lemme get this straight. We're gonna blow away a couple of guys and steal maybe a quarter of a million bucks, and you're worried about littering?"

"We got a job to do. That don't mean you got a right to turn the neighborhood into your own personal garbage can."

"Good point," said Garret, working hard to keep his face straight.

20

Inspector Homer Bradley went over to the window and got up on his tippy-toes and looked across the roof of the neighboring building, at the harbor and mountains. It was still snowing. The water was a dull, murky gray and the mountains had lost their definition, reduced by distance and the falling snow to vague, hulking shapes.

Bradley rocked on his heels, went over to his desk. He tossed the remains of his lunch — a takeout ham on rye from a nearby restaurant called the Meat Market — into his wastebasket.

His office door was wide open. A cop, Dan Oikawa, sauntered down the length of the squadroom carrying a handful of files. Oikawa was one of several homicide detectives working on the unsolved murders of fourteen of the city's female prostitutes. He'd recently grown a Fu Manchu moustache, and was wearing dark gray slacks and a white shirt with thick, dark blue stripes, a pair of bright red suspenders. The red suspender fad had been going strong for a couple of weeks now. What was next, Bradley wondered — pork pie hats? Orwell, also wearing red suspenders, limped past Bradley's door. Now what in hell was wrong with *him*? Bradley said, "Hey, Eddy."

Orwell stopped dead in his tracks, turned to face the open door. He had a full mug of coffee in his hand. A trickle of coffee splashed over the rim and across his wrist, but he pretended not to notice.

Bradley said, "Seen Jack, or Claire?"

Orwell shook his head.

Bradley said, "You limping?"

Orwell adjusted his suspenders. "I just bought a new pair of shoes."

Bradley glanced down at Orwell's feet. The shoes looked new, all right. Maybe not brand-new, but close. Orwell had a thing about clothes; whatever he happened to be wearing always looked as if it had been made to measure. How he did it on a cop's salary, Bradley had no idea. But he knew one thing for sure, and that was if the rumor about Judith's pregnancy was true, Orwell was going to have to cut back on his wardrobe.

"Get the door, will you, Eddy?"

"Yeah, sure." Orwell spilled a little more coffee as he lurched forward.

Bradley leaned back in his chair, shut his eyes. The fluorescents hissed and crackled. He stared at the stack of paperwork waiting for him. Tonight, he was going to have to go shopping, find something for Orwell's wedding. Eddy wanted a Moulinex food processor, whatever the hell that was. He'd even given Bradley a list of stores that carried the model he wanted.

Bradley flipped open the lid of the carved cedar humidor his wife had given him as a parting gift the day their divorce had come through. He chose a cigar, stuck it in his mouth but didn't light it, glowered at his Timex. Willows was due in less than five minutes.

Bradley was worried about Willows. During the past few years he'd been involved in three fatal shootings. A little over a year ago, he and Parker and Dan Oikawa had shot and killed a young woman named Tracy Peel. It was a clear case of self-defense; Peel had been armed with a .45 and had killed a man during the brief course of the shoot-out. But she'd also been a single parent with an infant child, a girl named Rebecca. Willows had turned Rebecca into an orphan.

Bradley had insisted on psychological counselling, despite Willows' objections. Bradley understood and sympathized with his position. Cops were a macho bunch of guys. Willows' sessions with the shrink would be noted on his permanent record.

And now his wife had left him, gone to Toronto, two thousand five hundred miles away. Walked off and taken the children with her. Bradley'd heard a rumor Willows was selling his house. He had also heard that he and Parker had a relationship that was more than strictly professional. For the past couple of months, Bradley had weighed the pros and cons of breaking up the partnership.

Then the Lee case had hit the papers, putting all his plans on hold.

The case was going downhill fast. A local paper had somehow managed to get a picture of Lee's corpse and printed it on the front page, right next to the police composite of the man who'd rented Chang's warehouse. The Chinese community was outraged.

The last thing Jack needed was more pressure. But in a few more minutes, pressure was what Bradley was going to have to apply.

He struck one of his big wooden kitchen matches, lit the cigar. He'd long ago given up on the idea that he had a will of iron. Things got better and things got worse, and he, like everyone else, reacted to stress in essentially predictable ways. But a couple of months ago he'd managed to cut his ration of tobacco down to two cigars a day, and he was holding steady and a little bit proud of himself. Bad time to light up, though, with Willows and Parker just around the corner. Jack was a born-again non-smoker and his bad attitude had rubbed off on Parker. But an Inspector was an Inspector was an Inspector, whereas a Detective was just another cop who happened by the grace of God and his superiors to be temporarily out of uniform. So nothing was ever said out loud about Bradley's smoking. But Willows had a knack for speaking his mind without bothering to open his mouth that Bradley found immensely irritating.

The pebbled glass panel in his door rattled, and the door swung open. Willows and Parker. Bradley waved them inside. He flicked ash at his wastebasket. Missed. He said, "What've you got for me, kids?"

Willows said, "Forensics is still working on the stuff we vacuumed out of the warehouse. It doesn't look promising. The outdoor search yielded absolutely zilch. No trace evidence at all."

"The snow didn't help," said Parker.

Bradley tried a smoke ring. No dice.

"The owner of the warehouse, William Chang, wants the scene released," said Willows. "Says he's losing a ton of money, threatened to sue."

"What'd you tell him?"

Parker said, "That we'd do what we could."

"Let's leave it at that, for the time being. What about the canvass?"

Willows flipped open his notebook. "There are three skid-row hotels on the block, all of them on the far side of the street. Two more hotels and a couple of small businesses and several restaurants on the other side of the alley. We've written up fifty-seven questionnaires, so far. No witnesses. There are a couple of dozen area residents we haven't been able to get in touch with yet."

"How long's the recanvass going to take?"

"With four teams working on it, at least a full day."

Bradley said, "This goddamn investigation's taking too much time. CKVU did a half-hour special on the case last night. You see it?"

Willows nodded. Somebody had videotaped the program and he and Parker watched it on the color television in the detectives' lounge.

"That show didn't do a hell of a lot for our image," Bradley said. "The Chief'd like to see this one wrapped up, and so would I." He leaned back in his chair. "The key, the one you found when you drained the pond. It fits the padlock on the warehouse door but it's a dead-end, right? I mean, as far as you know, you can't do anything with it."

Parker said, "That's right, Inspector."

"Good. We can feed it to the press. Maybe they'll choke to death on the damn thing." He flicked another quarter-inch of cigar ash at the wastebasket. A direct hit. Maybe even an omen. "I'm going to assign Oikawa and Jeff Norton to the case. Either of you got any problems with that?"

Parker glanced at Willows, who said, "Sounds like a good idea to me." Oikawa had been a detective less than three years. Norton had only been wearing a suit for a couple of months. Willows was still the supervising detective. And he had to admit that Bradley was right; he needed all the manpower he could get.

"Keep in touch." Distorted ringlets of smoke hung in the air as Bradley waved his cigar — a magician's gesture of dismissal.

Willows' phone started ringing as he walked towards his desk, almost as if it had been waiting for him and seen him coming. He picked up. "Willows."

"It's Bobby." A pause. "Bobby Chow."

"What's up, Bobby?"

"I quit my job."

"Smart move."

"Couple of days too late," Bobby said. "They smashed my Benz all to shit, Jack."

"Come on down and lay a charge."

Willows held the phone away from his ear, letting the harsh, sardonic cackle of Bobby's laughter leak out of the receiver.

Bobby, whispering, said, "Jack, *I got something for you.* I'm in a brown Ford in the A&W lot at Twenty-sixth and Fraser. Think you can find it?"

"You straight, Bobby?"

"Kinda ripped, Jack. How long it gonna take you to get here?"

"Depends on the traffic. Twenty minutes, maybe half an hour."

"Brown Ford," said Bobby. "A four-door. Hertz sticker on the back bumper. I mention they beat the shit out of my Benz?"

"Yeah, Bobby. I think you did."

"With sledge-hammers." Another burst of that scary, twisted laughter. "Ever been inside a car while a couple of animals pound on it with ten-pound hammers? Lemme tell you, I squeezed the steering wheel so fuckin' hard that after they left I had to pry myself loose with my teeth."

"Got a watch, Bobby?"

"Yeah, sure."

"What time is it?"

"Uh . . . quarter past twelve?"

"Close enough. Stay put, okay? Half an hour."

"Shit," said Bobby, and disconnected.

This time out, the car pool gave Willows and Parker a baby-blue Chevrolet Celebrity. Willows started the car and turned on the heater and put the gearshift in reverse and backed out of the slot, spun the wheel and headed up the ramp towards the exit.

Parker said, "It's the house, isn't it?"

"What?"

"Selling the house, that's what's bothering you, got you down. The real estate agent still after you to drop your price?"

"Yeah."

"Don't do it," said Parker. "You wait long enough, you'll get every dime you're asking."

Willows nodded, not wanting to talk about it. His wife, Sheila, had telephoned twice during the week. Her parents had loaned her thirty thousand dollars to make a down payment on a condo. She wanted Willows to sell the house and she wanted it done as quickly as possible.

He braked at the mouth of the alley. A bright orange city dumptruck loaded with salt raced down Hastings, ran a yellow light. He waited for an elderly Chinese with a cane to clear the alley and then turned right, worked his way over to the far lane and signalled a left turn.

"I've lived in this city since I was a kid," Parker said. "This is the coldest winter I can remember. What happened to the greenhouse effect, now that we need it?"

"Repressed," said Willows. "It's a plot to keep the price of cucumbers high." The light changed. He made his turn and they accelerated up Hastings.

Bobby's rented Ford was parked in the A&W lot at the far end of a row of ten slots. Willows pulled in next to him, tapped the horn. Bobby's head came up. He glanced vaguely around, and then his head fell back and he shut his eyes.

Parker said, "Who is this guy?"

"Rip van Winkle. Hungry?"

"You bet."

"Order something for me." Willows opened his door. "I'll see if I can wake him up."

Willows got out of the car. A girl in a mud-brown A&W uniform hurried towards him. He paused, waiting. The girl said, "We think he's a drug addict. The police are on their way."

Willows flashed his badge. He turned his back on the girl and yanked open the passenger-side door of Bobby's Ford. Bobby struggled upright, yawned hugely. His eyes popped open. He glanced wildly around.

Willows said, "You on the nod, Bobby?"

Bobby Chow's eyes settled down. He blinked three times, slowly as an owl. "Nah . . . Got a little wired, is all. Tight. Felt like I had handcuffs on my brain . . . Ate a couple too many downers." He smiled. A trickle of saliva worked its way down his chin. He said, "I called you, right?" He took a furtive look over his shoulder. "There's a payphone on the corner . . . Yeah, there it is, see it?" He wiped his chin, smiled. "Appreciate you dropping by on such short notice, Jack."

Willows said, "Where'd you get the car?"

"Hertz?"

"Let's see the rental slip, Bobby."

"Got it here somewhere . . . " Bobby Chow patted himself down, opened the glove box, shrugged.

There was a big T-shaped plastic console next to the parking slot. Parker studied the menu, rolled down her window and pressed a button. The voice that came through the intercom was more incomprehensible than anything she'd ever heard at an airport. She ordered two "Teenburgers" with fries, a cup of coffee and a pot of tea.

There was another burst of static. Hoping for the best, she asked for ketchup.

A black and white pulled into the lot. Parker tapped the horn. She caught the driver's eye, waved him away.

In the Ford, Bobby Chow was talking a mile a minute, while Willows listened patiently.

The food arrived on a plastic tray that hooked on to the window. The tab was eight dollars and fifty cents.

Parker paid with a ten. She opened her door and got out of the car, opened the back door of Bobby's Ford and unhooked the tray, got into the Ford with it balanced in her hands. She put the tray down on the seat beside her and shut the door. Bobby said, "If somebody complained about the service, it sure as hell wasn't me."

Parker handed Willows his food and a white porcelain mug of coffee.

Bobby Chow said, "How'd you know what I wanted?"

Willows put the food on the dashboard.

"A *Teenburger*," said Bobby. "Every time I knock back one of these babies I feel ten years younger."

Bobby Chow ate his hamburger in five large bites. He licked mayonnaise from the gold foil wrapper, balled up the wrapper with trembling hands, tossed it on the floor of the car. "Sugar?"

Parker handed him three small white envelopes. Bobby sweetened his coffee, added cream. He said, "You Jack's partner?"

Parker sipped her coffee. She'd had better, but she'd had worse.

"Silent partner, huh?" Bobby grabbed a handful of french fries.

Willows said, "What've you got for us, Bobby?"

Bobby shrugged. "Not much, really. I was all doped up when I phoned. My mind's a lot clearer now. Sorry I wasted your time."

Willows opened his door. "Let's go, Bobby."

Bobby grabbed the steering wheel with both hands. "No way. I got to finish my lunch."

Willows scooped up a handful of ketchup-smeared french fries and stuffed them in the breast pocket of Bobby's suit. "Take it with you."

Bobby licked his lips, studying the look in Willows' eyes. After a moment he said, "Good idea, Jack."

Mountain View cemetery contains one hundred and six acres of gently rolling, well tended lawn, thousands of graves and a crematorium. It's the only cemetery inside the city limits, and the main gate is five blocks from the A&W. Willows and Parker, with Bobby slouched in the Celebrity's backseat, drove slowly down a narrow road of cracked and faded asphalt.

After a few minutes, Willows stopped the car. "Out, Bobby."

"Now?"

Willows climbed out of the car. After a moment's hesitation, Parker followed him. Willows yanked open the back door.

"What?" said Bobby.

"We're going to take a walk." Willows grabbed Chow by the arm and hauled him out of the car.

"Leggo, you're hurting me!"

"Not yet, but soon."

"Jack . . ." said Parker.

Willows ignored her.

The grass was gray with frost, and crisp as breakfast cereal beneath their feet. Willows walked Bobby into the forest of tombstones and pointed at a rectangle of pink granite.

"Sit."

Bobby sat.

"Grand theft auto, Bobby. Your probation officer's gonna laugh his head off."

"The key was in the fuckin' ignition. The fuckin' door wasn't locked! So I fucked up the paperwork. Jeez, it was a simple mistake. Error of judgement. Could've happened to anybody! Long as I pay, Hertz don't give a shit. I wanna see my lawyer!"

Willows said, "Why don't you take a walk, Claire."

Parker didn't move.

Bobby said, "She wants to be with you. Hey, maybe it's love."

Willows knocked him off the tombstone and face down into the brittle, frozen grass.

Bobby started crying.

Parker said, "That's enough, Jack."

"I don't think so."

"It's more than enough," said Parker.

Willows nudged Chow in the ribs with the toe of his brogue. He said, "Is she right, Bobby? Or do you want some more?"

Bobby got up on his hands and knees. He wiped the tears from his face. "Knock it off! You can't do this, you're a cop!"

"And you're a snitch. Don't forget it."

Bobby looked wildly around. On the far side of the cemetery, an old woman was laying a wreath on a grave. Bobby started screaming for help.

Willows waited until he ran out of air and then punched him in the kidneys.

"Jesus Christ!"

"He can't hear you either. And neither can Kenny Lee. But I can, and I'm listening."

"When I called you I was wired, half-asleep . . . Jack, I didn't know what I was saying!"

"Kenny Lee had a wife, two kids. He's on his way over here, Bobby. The day after tomorrow, they're going to bury him right here in this cemetery."

Willows felt a hand on his shoulder. Parker. He spun away, grabbed a fistful of Bobby's lapel and dragged him across the grass, smashed his face into a sagging granite tombstone. Bobby spat blood.

Parker said, "Hit him again and I'll file a report. I mean it, Jack."

Willows turned his back on her and strode across the manicured lawn towards the unmarked car.

Bobby, still on his hands and knees, said, "I asked around. Lee was no high stakes gambler. He didn't owe anybody a goddamn penny." He wiped his nose. "You hear what I said, lady?"

Parker said, "Bobby, don't even think about laying a complaint. Understand?"

"Yeah, sure."

"Look at me."

Bobby blinked away his tears.

"He's my partner. You lay a complaint, we'll find a way to put you away for the rest of your miserable life."

Parker leaned forward. Bobby flinched. She ruffled his greasy hair and then stood up and strode briskly across the frozen grass to the car. Willows was in the passenger seat, staring straight ahead. She got behind the wheel and put the car in gear.

Willows said, "Drop me off somewhere, will you. I think I'll call it a day."

"Drop you off where?"

"Eddy's. I could use a drink."

"You don't need a drink, Jack. What you need is a whole new outlook on life."

Parker braked at the gates, waited for the traffic to clear and turned right on Fraser.

"Bobby rolled over."

"Yeah?" Willows didn't sound surprised.

"Melinda was right. Despite his trips to Vegas, her father wasn't a gambler."

Willows thought about it. He said, "We ought to call Vegas again. Lee must've been in *some* kind of trouble. He had a reason for flying all the way down there, right? Maybe the Vegas cops have got a sheet on him."

Parker said, "It's worth a try. Still want me to drop you off?"

"Let's go back to work."

"You keep hitting people, Jack, you're going to lose your badge."

"Not as long as I keep hitting people like Bobby, I won't."

Parker said, "Why don't you arrange to take a few days off, go see your kids."

"I've been thinking about it."

"They miss you, too, Jack."

"Yeah, I know."

A chair had been drawn up next to Willows' desk. The woman sprawled in it was wearing heavy black boots, a pair of skintight black leather pants and a fuzzy pink angora sweater. Her hair was the color of radishes and she sported a diamond in her left nostril. As Willows and Parker made their way across the squadroom towards her, she stood up, tugged at the pink sweater. "You're Detectives Willows and Parker?"

Willows nodded.

She offered a hand decorated with a tattoo of a red and blue butterfly. "I'm Beverly." She sat back down in the chair, unfolded a scrap of newspaper and smoothed it out on her black leather thigh. "I work the late shift at a restaurant down on Pender. This guy?" She pointed at the police artist's composite sketch of the man who'd rented William Chang's warehouse. "He came in for a cup of coffee the night before they found this other one, the Chinese guy who froze to death."

"You're sure it's him?"

"Yeah, positive. A redhead, like me, except natural. Real smart-ass. Asked me if it hurt when I sneezed." She touched her nose. "Talking about my diamond, and I didn't like it, not one bit."

She hadn't liked the way he'd stood her up, either, but there was no point in telling the cops about *that*.

"Did you get a name . . . "

"Wouldn't tell me. But I was leaning way over the counter when he paid for his coffee. Cup of coffee and a slice of apple pie, that's what he had. Two dollars and thirty cents. No tip. When he opened his wallet, I got a peek at his driver's licence."

"Was it local?"

"Yeah, sure." Beverly smiled. The diamond twinkled; a star to be wished upon. "His name was Garret."

Parker said, "Is that a first or a last name?"

"I don't know, I only got a quick look. A guy opens his wallet, you don't want him to catch you staring."

"Right," said Parker, nodding.

Willows started asking questions. Half an hour later, he

184

knew — or hoped he knew — Garret's approximate height and weight, the color of his eyes, that he had no discernible speech pattern or accent, and that on the night in question he'd worn jeans and a black leather jacket, a pair of fancy cowboy boots and a black cowboy hat.

"You mind if I talk to my partner for a minute?" He drew Parker aside. "Anything else?"

"She's a shallow pond, Jack. I think we've drained her dry."

Beverly said, "So, what're you gonna do now?"

"Run the name through the computer, see what we come up with." Parker smiled. "We get lucky and come up with something, you mind looking at some pictures?"

"I can't, I gotta go to work."

"Not now. Maybe tomorrow, though. Would you do that for us?"

"Yeah, sure. Tell you the truth, I'd like to go to the trial, watch him squirm."

Parker moved closer, stepped between Beverly and Jack Willows. Speaking very softly, almost whispering, she said, "Did he *do* something to you?"

"Stood me up," Beverly said, blurting it out. She blushed, her skin taking on a shade somewhere between the pink of her sweater and the fire-engine red of her hair.

"If it does go to trial," said Parker, "you'll know all about it, don't worry."

Eddy Orwell came out of a witness interrogation room as Parker, still murmuring words of sympathy, walked Beverly to the elevator. He kept his eyes on the black leather until it disappeared from view and then turned to Willows and said, "Hear about Farley?"

"Only that they operated on him, nothing since."

Parker sat back down at her desk. Orwell, looming over her, said, "You hear about Farley?"

Parker glared up at him. "Back off, Eddy. Give me some breathing room." She made a note on a pad. "Jack, we should give some thought to how Beverly's going to look in court."

"Maybe somebody could give her a hand with her wardrobe. Angora and leather, it can't be all she owns."

"I wouldn't bet on it."

"Me either," said Orwell, "the way she walked out of here, she sure owes me. Anyhow, about Farley. It was touch and go. I been spending all my spare time with him, night and day."

"That's really terrific. What a wonderful guy."

"So if Judith calls, would you mind telling her where I was?"

Parker said, "Know something, Eddy?"

"No, what?"

"You're disgusting."

"Jack?" said Eddy.

"Really disgusting, Eddy." Willows dialled the long distance operator, got Las Vegas and asked for the number of the Vegas police. He disconnected, dialled again.

Orwell said, "How it happened, they were playing that game, you wet the top of a beer glass and stretch a paper napkin over it, drop some coins on the napkin and take turns burning cigarette holes in it. Last person to burn a hole before the coins fall through has to pay for the next round. Farley and the morgue guys, that's what they were up to. Farley kept losing and he cut his losses by eating the money. Ever heard of anything like it? He must've been smashed out of his mind."

Willows said, "Fascinating story, Eddy. But the way I heard it, Farley had a heart attack and he's going to be just fine."

Parker opened the thick black plastic ring binder containing the Lee file. There it was, on page 113. Melinda Lee's emphatic statement that her father was at most a recreational gambler.

Willows spoke briefly into the phone, hung up.

Parker said, "They got anything?"

"Going to call back."

Parker began to write her daily report. Half an hour crawled past.

Willows' phone rang and he snatched it up.

The Vegas police department knew Kenny Lee very well. During the past two years he'd flown into town on three separate occasions. The first time had been to pay a five figure bill at the Sands Hotel. An overdrawn Visa card issued in Lee's name but in the possession of his son, Peter, had been used to cover a suite at the Sands, as well as several cash advances lost at the tables. Lee's other two trips to Vegas had been for the express purpose of posting bail for the kid. The charges weren't serious — a gross indecency and a drunk and disorderly. Willows asked about the first charge and was told the Lee kid had been caught pissing on a Lincoln parked in front of the Flamingo. At high noon.

Willows thanked the Vegas desk sergeant and hung up. Parker lifted an interrogative eyebrow.

Willows said, "Claire, did Lee's son say who he took his ski trip with?"

"I didn't ask him."

"When you questioned him, how did he react?"

"He was tense, naturally. I assumed it was due to the circumstances of his father's death. Why, what did you find out?"

"Kenny Lee made those trips to Vegas to wipe up the mess his son made. The kid racked up some serious losses at the Sands. Daddy had to bail him out. What do you know about the terms of Lee's will?"

"Everything went to his wife. But the Chinese live in a male-dominated society, Jack. Maybe the kid figured he could take over the paper, eventually sell out for a bundle."

"Head back to Nevada and make his fortune," Willows said thoughtfully. "Be nice to tie him and this Garret kid together."

He pictured the naked body of Kenny Lee sitting bolt upright in the full-lotus position on the frozen surface of the artfully designed pond in the Sun Yat-Sen Gardens. The corpse encased in a shroud of cloudy ice.

Those frosty, blinded eyes.

21

Nancy lay on her side, facing the big glass wall and the lights of West Vancouver. Her husband was asleep on his stomach, sprawled across the middle of the bed. His mouth was wide open. He was snoring. Nancy could smell the wine. When had it become so predictable? Tyler was like an elevator. Up. Down. Off we go. A machine would be more fun, because a machine would do exactly what she wanted, whereas poor dull Tyler labored under the misapprehension that he knew what she wanted, and she . . .

She'd lost it somewhere along the line, the ability to talk to him. Be blunt without hurting him. She didn't think she could do it any more, talk to him the way they used to talk. Always giving as well as taking. Too many little things had gone wrong. They'd moved too far away from each other — shouting wouldn't span the gap. And besides, she didn't know how Tyler would react if she told him what was on her mind, how she felt their life had deteriorated. The way Tyler was now, she was afraid he might blow a gasket, explode. Say things she'd never be able to forgive. And then where would she be? Out on her ass. Life taken from a brown paper bag wasn't an appealing prospect. Too many of her friends had been savaged by the courts, and Tyler could certainly be ruthless, she knew that much about him. No, sitting down for a heart-to-heart talk about their sex life was out of the question. She wasn't willing to risk it.

So a couple of times a week, if things were going well at the office, Tyler did his elevator trick and she got what she could out of it, and that was that.

There had to be something else out there, but what was it? Something unpredictable, wild.

A police car or ambulance or maybe a fire truck — she knew

they had different sirens but had never learned to tell the difference — wailed past on its way to some kind of tragedy, an accident.

Tyler's snoring faltered. He rolled towards her, and she felt herself tense up. His breathing steadied, grew deeper.

She slowly relaxed, the stiffness seeping out of her body.

He was her husband, for God's sake. In all the years they'd been together, he'd hardly raised his voice to her. What was the big problem?

She was dying of boredom, that was the problem.

Nancy lay on her side, watching the steady red glow of the numerals on the digital alarm clock, counting off the seconds, letting another five minutes drift by, just to be sure.

At 11:43, she eased out of bed and went over to the window, her bare feet silent on the thick carpet.

The pool was a perfect rectangle of aquamarine. Snow, hard and crystalline, glittered and sparkled under the security lights. The branches of the small birch copse next to the fence cast a spiderweb of shadows on the pale ground. The harbor was a patch of black cloth hemmed with tiny orange lights. She moved a little to her left, so she could see the lights of the downtown core.

Nothing moved.

He was out there, somewhere in the city. She wondered what he was doing, if he was thinking of her.

Maybe he was on his way over right this minute.

She was wearing a rose-colored silk nightdress with spaghetti straps. She eased one strap over her shoulder, and then the other. The silk pooled at her feet. She stood there for a moment, one leg cocked.

Nothing moved.

She turned her back on the plate glass, late-night still life, and went into the bathroom and carefully shut the door. The floods and heat lamps and fan switched on automatically. She turned on the shower, adjusted the water temperature and stepped into the stall, slid shut the glass door.

The water drummed down on her breasts, stiffened her nipples.

She imagined him forcing a window, a door. Striding boldly up the stairs. Pushing open the bedroom door. Tyler had vanished; he simply wasn't there. He heard the shower and walked into the bathroom. Nancy watched him strip off his black leather jacket, those tight, faded jeans. His socks. Underpants. She wondered what kind of underpants he wore. She pictured him in bikini-style briefs, skimpy and bulging. His body was hard, flat and angular.

She leaned weakly against the black-tiled wall of the shower. The spray pounded against the back of her neck. Her heart pounded against her ribs. Her very bones and all the strength that was in her dissolved in the billowing steam.

She clenched her teeth, trying not to scream. God, *what* was the matter with her? She turned off the water and stepped out of the glass cubicle. Wrapped a towel around her hair.

The infrareds shone down on her, bathing her in a warm red glow.

Nancy took another towel from the rack and patted herself dry, went back into the bedroom.

Tyler had rolled over on his back. He'd never been what you might call handsome; it was his *intensity* she'd first been attracted to. As he lay there, sleeping, his eyes shut and his face slack, she couldn't find a lot in him that was admirable.

Nancy went back over to the window, looked down. He was there and then he wasn't there — and never had been. A winter mirage.

She slipped back into the bed. The electric blanket had kept the sheets warm for her. She stared at the bright red numerals of the alarm clock. When the minute changed, she closed her eyes and counted slowly to sixty, then opened her eyes and watched it change again. Once again, she remembered the way he had leaned towards her in the car, the smell of his body.

Her fear, excitement. Finally acknowledging it, she admitted to herself that she had wanted him just as badly then as she wanted him now.

22

At eight o'clock in the morning the cheap plastic alarm clock Billy'd shoplifted from London Drugs made a horrible metallic gargling sound, like a wind-up Jiminy Cricket being squeezed to death. Billy snatched at the Python, sat bolt upright with his eyes wide open. He stared at the shrieking clock for a moment, then brought the heavy barrel of the revolver down hard, putting the cricket out of its misery.

The time was now 8:01 and for that particular clock, time had stopped forever.

Easy enough to steal a new one.

The house was silent. It was so cold he could see his breath. He eased out of bed, dressed in a pair of jeans and sweatshirt, pulled on his cowboy boots and black leather jacket.

The thermostat was turned down to sixty. His goddamn mother, always looking to save a dime. He cranked it up to eighty. In the basement, the furnace clicked on. He went into the kitchen and filled the kettle and put it on the stove, rinsed out a cup. His mother had forgotten to buy coffee. Shit. Angrily, he stomped into the bathroom, urinated and then stood in front of the mirror, examining himself. His hair was a mess. He combed it carefully, getting it just right. There was a dark stubble on his chin. He decided against shaving. Two or three days' growth made him look older, tougher. He brushed his teeth, smiled, and then let the smile fade and his green eyes get cold and distant. The killer look he'd been practising.

The living room was a shambles, the air heavy with stale cigarette smoke. He dug out the telephone and dialled Garret's number.

Garret answered on the first ring, his voice thick with sleep.

Billy said, "You get the wheels?"

"No problem."

"Something with a heater, I hope."

"Caddy," said Garret. "Figured if I was going to steal a car, might as well be something with a little class." Garret had taken a midnight ride out to the airport, prowled the long-term lot and found the Caddy, black with a sunroof, tinted windows. He'd hot-wired the car, paid twenty-two bucks in parking fees to a sleepy attendant, driven into town and parked a block from his house.

"A Cadillac," said Billy, the words laced with envy. "No shit."

Garret smiled into the receiver. It was the kind of cowboy thing Billy liked to do; steal a luxury automobile and cruise around town, put himself at risk just for the hell of it. But Garret had told him no, *he* was gonna choose the wheels, and that was that. Billy gave him one of his ice-cube looks, but let it go. Just as well. Now that they were getting down to it, Garret was running on a short fuse. That time Billy'd peppered his face with the Colt, he was ready to kill him just for the pleasure of watching him die.

And the feeling hadn't entirely gone away.

"Nine thirty," said Billy. "Be there, understand."

"Whatever you say," said Garret, and hung up.

At twenty past nine Billy parked his Pinto on Tenth Avenue, two blocks from the liquor store. Garret pulled in behind him five minutes later. At nine thirty sharp, they drove the Caddy into the Safeway lot. Garret parked in a slot facing the liquor store. The sky was clear and the sun was up. Everything was dripping, the world was turning to slush. Meltdown. They were about fifty feet from the liquor store's glass doors, close enough to see what was going on inside. Not much. The clerks getting ready for the first rush of boozers.

Garret fished a pair of black knitted ski masks out of an Eatons bag. One mask had red trim around the eye and mouth holes. The trim on the other mask was blue. Billy went for the red but Garret snatched it away. He tossed the blue-trimmed mask to Billy. The price tag was still attached. Eleven dollars and ninety-five cents.

Garret said, "You can pay for yours out of your end. And the taxi ride I had to take out to the airport, the twenty-five bucks I paid in parking fees. Call it sixty, altogether."

"Got to spend money to steal money," said Billy, grinning.

Garret checked the load in the Remington pump. The shotgun held two shells in the magazine, another in the chamber. He had twelve more rounds, six in each of his jacket pockets.

Billy eased back the Python's hammer and spun the cylinder. He'd practised dry-firing at home, sighted in on Arsenio Hall or whoever's head happened to fill the television screen, squeezed the trigger and shot them between the eyes. But this was a whole different thing altogether. Loaded, the gun was much heavier. He'd played with it as if it was a toy, but it didn't feel like a toy now. All the fun had gone out of it. Loaded, the Python was a deadly weapon.

He wondered what it was going to be like, dropping the hammer on a man, instead of the brighter-than-life electronic image of a talk-show host.

His hands were damp with sweat. He wiped them on the coarse material of the ski mask.

Garret said, "Nervous?"

"No way." Billy pointed. "Where'd you get the watch?"

"That ain't a watch, it's a fuckin' chronometer." Garret fondly tapped the crystal of his new toy; a black plastic digital Casio with bright green and yellow and red plastic buttons sticking out of it.

"Don't wanna be late for dinner, that it?"

"It's a sports model. For joggers. When we get out of the car, I push the red button."

"Right," said Billy. "Good idea. Then what, we run like hell?"

"The red button's the stopwatch function. What we're gonna do is the same as robbing a bank, Billy. Except we don't go inside. I figure we got three minutes max. A hundred eighty seconds."

"Then what?"

"The cops are rolling and we're outta here. We're history."

Billy lit a cigarette, rolled down the window a crack and tossed the smoking match on to the asphalt. "*Tickety tickety tick!* Shoot the guards! Grab the cash! *Tickety tickety tick!* Split second precision. I like it. Real fuckin' professional."

Garret studied his new watch. 9:49:07. Eight, nine, ten . . . He pushed open his door.

"Where you goin'?"

"For coffee."

193

"Two creams, hold the sugar," said Billy. "Everybody tells me I'm sweet enough as it is."

Garret slammed shut the door.

The parking lot was starting to fill up. It was astounding, the number of people who decided to buy their groceries at ten o'clock on a Tuesday morning. Why choose that particular time? Probably because there was nothing to watch on television. A gold-colored Volvo station wagon pulled in parallel to him, three slots away. The cheap model, a 240 DL. A woman got out of the car. She was in her early twenties, wearing black cords and a hip-length red leather jacket with hugely padded shoulders, dopey black rubber boots with red soles. Her hair was short and brown. She opened the back door of the car and hauled out a baby in a pink snow suit. Her eyes caught Billy's. He smiled at her and waved at the kid. She turned her back on him. Carrying the baby in her arms, she walked stiffly through the slush towards the Safeway.

Billy went over it in his mind. The armored car pulled up. It stopped in front of the liquor store. The driver took a quick look around. Something he'd done a thousand times before. Routine. The rear door swung open and the two armed guards jumped out. They went into the liquor store and stayed inside anywhere from three to five minutes. When they came out, it was the second guy who had the money. The first guy led the way towards the armored car, his hand resting on the butt of his gun. They'd wait until he reached out to open the door for his buddy, and then Billy'd be on top of him. The Python coming out from under his jacket.

The way they'd planned it, Billy was supposed to shoot first. Instead of killing the guard, he'd pop him in the back of the leg, through the kneecap. Disable the sucker, instead of blowing him away.

A split second later, Garret was going to do the same thing to the guy with the money. Shotgun him in the leg.

Then the easy part. Billy's job was to grab the canvas bags full of cash while Garret used the Remington for crowd control.

As Billy wheeled the Caddy out of the parking lot and into the home stretch, Garret would take a few shots at the armored car. The driver was protected by about an inch of bulletproof glass;

the idea wasn't to waste him, just encourage him to keep his head down.

They'd lose the Caddy on Tenth Avenue, switch to the cold car, the Pinto. Time the cops figured it out, they'd be long gone.

Nothing to it, Billy kept telling himself.

The Caddy's door swung open. Garret climbed inside, shut the door, handed Billy a styrofoam coffee cup and a bag of nachos. It was seven minutes past ten.

At quarter to eleven, the woman with the baby pushed a rusty shopping cart up to the gold Volvo, unloaded the pink snow suit and a couple of hundred dollars' worth of food. Billy tried to catch her eye, but she was having none of it. He wondered what the red leather jacket had cost. She got into the car and slowly drove away.

At one thirty, Garret risked another quick trip to the 7-Eleven for more coffee and a couple of hamburgers.

At a few minutes past three, Billy trotted over to the convenience store to use the bathroom.

By four o'clock, it was starting to get dark.

At ten minutes past four, a man in jeans and a ski jacket set up shop by the liquor store doors and began to play a trombone. Billy listened for a moment and then turned up the volume on the Caddy's radio.

At twenty-three minutes to five, a patrol car cruised slowly into the parking lot and stopped in front of the trombone player. The two cops in the car got out. The musician didn't miss a note.

Billy slouched a little lower in the seat. Garret studied the rearview mirror. They waited.

The cops stood with their hands on their hips. The trombone said something and then slapped his forehead and bent to grab his hatful of change. A clerk watching from inside the liquor store clapped his hands. The trombone jay-walked across Maple Street and the cops climbed back in the squad car and drove away.

Garret turned the radio down.

Billy had to go to the bathroom again. Garret gave him a look, but didn't say anything.

By ten thirty, they had been sitting in the Caddy almost thirteen hours, and they were stiff and tired and hungry, ready to call it a night and go home.

At ten thirty-seven, the Loomis armored car eased into the parking lot, its silver-painted body gleaming under the sodium-vapor lights.

Garret said, "You awake, Billy?"

Billy nodded. His throat was dry.

The rear door swung open. The two Loomis guys jumped out. It was their last shift ever, but they didn't know it, not yet. One of them had a small metal dolly. His partner shut the armored car's thick metal door. Billy rolled down his window. The dolly had rubber wheels, but he could still hear the sound of it rolling across the shiny wet asphalt.

The two men entered the liquor store. Billy lost them, but he knew where they were going. To the left, towards the glassed-in manager's office, the safe.

Garret was studying his watch.

10:39:17

Billy lit a cigarette. His hands were steady. He held the burning match out in front of him, so Garret could see how strong he was.

Garret kept staring at his watch.

In the armored car, the driver saw the small bright flame appear behind the Caddy's windshield. The flame held steady for five, maybe ten seconds. He spoke into the microphone pinned to his uniform collar.

"Fourteen Alpha."

The answer came immediately. "Fourteen Alpha clear."

The flame had disappeared. It was probably nothing, the driver thought, but at least he'd look alert, they'd know he was doing his job. He cleared his throat. "I got an eighty-eight Cadillac, black, tag number Andrew Niner Bike three zero four."

"Check."

In the Caddy, Billy turned his cold green eyes on Garret. "Don't fuck this up."

Garret thought about it for a couple of seconds and then decided, what the hell, why not tell him. No harm in it now, nothing Billy could do. He said, "Listen up, Billy. There's something you should know about me."

Billy's head came around. Garret had never talked to him like that before, each word hard as a brick, slamming down on him.

Garret said, "Remember that guy they found in the Chinese

196

gardens? On the pond, frozen solid? We saw it on the late night news?"

"Yeah, sure. What about it?"

"That was me did him."

"Bullshit."

"Five grand up front. His kid paid me. Met him at work, waxed his BMW for him. We got to talking and one thing led to another."

Well, that wasn't *exactly* how it had gone down. But Billy was paying attention for once, so Garret kept up the monologue.

"Kid's gonna inherit the family business. The five's only a down payment, but he don't know it yet. Soon as he gets his hands on the money I'm gonna start squeezin'. Blackmail, you ever heard of it?"

Billy said, "What'd you do with the money?"

"Spent it on the Mustang. Leather seats, rolled and tufted. *Ten* coats candy-apple red lacquer. Car's gonna be ready in a couple more weeks."

"Bullshit," said Billy again, but there was a look in his eyes that Garret had never seen before. Respect, tinged with fear. He was staring at a brand-new Garret; his buddy the hard-nosed killer. Garret stared back at him, watched the wheels slowly turning. He'd told Billy about the murder to keep him in line. In a few more minutes it wouldn't matter anyway. Because no matter how much money they came away with, it was only going to be about half of what Garret needed.

The homicide cops, investigating Billy's death, would find Kenny Lee's wallet under the rubber floormat of the Pinto, Lee's ring and gold Lorus watch hidden in the trunk. It'd give the cops everything they needed to wrap the case. And even if they did come after him, he had a bulletproof alibi. A guy he knew, dude who boosted *whole cars*, and not just the radios, but had a clean sheet, no record, was going to cover him for a piece of the action.

As for Billy, well . . . The kid was only seventeen, but this was it. He wasn't going to get any older.

Garret stepped out of the car, the shotgun held tight against his leg. He said, "Let's do it, kid."

Billy found himself hurrying across the parking lot, trying to catch up. He saw the liquor store door swing open. A short, fat man carrying a case of beer in both hands walked directly towards him. The man gave Garret an odd look, stopped dead in his tracks.

The liquor store door swung open again. Billy looked at Garret and saw that he was wearing his black ski mask under his cowboy hat. Billy's mask was on the front seat of the Caddy. And Garret had murdered the Chinese guy and never said a word. How about that. Suddenly Billy felt like that poor dope on the Letterman show, the one without the remote control transmitter, the dummy.

Too late for that, too.

Garret brought the shotgun up. Billy unzipped his jacket.

The fat man yelled something.

Billy drew his Python and fired from the hip, hitting the man in the chest and knocking him down.

Inside the armored car, the radio crackled briefly. "Fourteen Alpha, that car's hot."

"Shots fired!" yelled the driver. "We got a robbery in progress! It's goin' down right this fuckin' minute! Shots fired! Shots fired!"

The shotgun exploded. Garret worked the slide. The spent shell bounced off Billy's left arm. The fat man was on his knees and he was still yelling, his chest a mass of blood. Billy thought, *it ain't over until you stop singing*, and shot at him again, and missed by twenty feet. The Remington exploded a second and then a third time. Both guards were down. It was amazing, how fast it had all happened. Black liquid flowed across the slushy asphalt.

The wail of a siren filled the air. Billy glanced wildly around. The sound was coming from the armored car. A rotating red light on top of the cab threw a fine spray of blood into the air. Billy could see a profile of the driver, his face up against the glass. He started towards the money, hesitated.

Garret hit him in the small of the back with the flat of his hand.

"C'mon, hurry up! What the fuck are you waiting for! Grab the fucking cash!"

Billy staggered forward. He pointed his gun at the fallen guards, and then saw that Garret's marksmanship, if he'd aimed at their legs, hadn't been all that good. Both men had been shot in the head.

Billy fell to his knees and threw up. The shotgun went off again. The red emergency light shattered but the siren kept screaming and the fat man wouldn't stop yelling.

Billy wiped his mouth. Garret was standing over him, shoving double-ought loads into the Remington. He grabbed a handful of Billy's jacket and hauled him to his feet.

Billy grabbed a canvas bag. Too heavy. Coins. He dropped the bag and grabbed another one and then another one. He switched both bags to his left hand and started running towards the car. Garret fired another round and Billy heard the load of buckshot slam into the metal flank of the armored car.

Garret yanked open the Caddy's door. He threw the shotgun in the backseat, climbed in, slammed the door, flicked on the car's brights.

In the sudden wash of light, he saw Billy standing about twenty feet away, the big canvas bags of money in his left hand, the Python in his right hand aimed at a fat guy in a black raincoat trying to hide behind a case of beer.

Garret leaned on the horn. Billy turned to stare at him, his face white, blank.

Garret put the Caddy in gear. It was hard to think straight. There were people screaming, running around all over the place. So much noise. He hit the gas and the car jumped forward. Do the kid now, or do him later? Billy fired at a guy who was down on his knees in front of the liquor store. A bolt of dirty orange lightning stabbed from the Python's barrel. Garret slammed on the brakes and leaned over and opened the door.

"Get in the fuckin' car, Billy!"

Billy laughed. His mouth was all teeth. He yelled, "It ain't over until the fat man stops singing!" and popped another cap. Garret leaned out, one hand on the wheel. He grabbed a moneybag and pulled hard. Billy followed the bag into the car. Garret punched it. The Caddy leapt forward.

The armored car driver's face was right up against the heavily-tinted glass. If he left the safety of the car, chances were fairly good that he'd be shot at and excellent that he'd lose his job.

But his two buddies were down, and the way they'd dropped, he was pretty sure they weren't gonna collect their pensions, body armor or not.

He swung the passenger-side door open an inch, and waited. The black Caddy sped towards him. He took one last sweeping look at his field of fire. The parking lot was deserted. If there was anyone out there, they were staying low. All the noise and action was behind him, outside the liquor store and Safeway.

The Caddy was going to pass within ten feet of him, heading towards the Maple Street exit. He checked the shotgun's safety and then the Caddy was right there and it was time to kick the heavy door open and blast away. One two three. The barrel jumped. He was deafened by the explosions and blinded by the muzzle blast.

The Caddy shot past, trailing a spoor of glass and chrome trim on the asphalt. The gleaming black car accelerated across Maple and the 7-Eleven's parking lot and buried itself in the building's cinder-block wall.

The driver climbed stiffly out of the armored car. He ached all over, was exhausted, felt as if he'd just finished a hundred-mile run.

He forced himself to walk around to the rear of the car. His buddies had both taken head shots. There were still three bags of money piled on the dolly, splattered with blood and fragments of bone and bits of human flesh. You'd have to be fucking Bela Lugosi to make a grab for that kind of loot.

Even so . . .

He picked up the dolly and tossed it inside the armored car, locked the door.

Then he reloaded his weapon and began to walk slowly and purposefully towards the smoking wreckage of the Cadillac.

23

There were five mug shots. Beverly stared at the one in the middle. "No, not that one."

Willows said, "You sure?"

"Positive."

"Good, because he's a cop."

"Really?"

"Yeah, really."

Beverly said, "You'd never guess. What about this one?"

"You tell me."

"I think he's the one. In fact, I'm positive."

Willows turned the photograph over. He handed her a pen. "Would you mind signing the back, please."

"Yeah, sure. How'd I do?"

"Not bad," said Parker. "Not bad at all."

"When a guy stands you up, it makes it kind of hard to forget him. I mean, it's such an unusual thing."

Willows said, "Yeah, I'm sure it is."

"Not that I wanted to go out with him all that much in the first place." She smiled warmly at Willows. "The fact is, I generally prefer older men."

Parker said, "I think she kind of liked you."

Willows signalled, turned on to Thirty-third. "What makes you say that?"

"I don't know. Maybe the way she kept pulling at her sweater. Or didn't you notice?"

Willows smiled. "Oh, I noticed, all right." He drove slowly down the block, parked the unmarked Ford in front of the Lee house.

The street was silent, empty except for a covey of starlings that chopped at the frozen grass further down the boulevard. Chunky granules of rock salt lay on the curving pink sidewalk leading to Lee's house. They climbed the steps and Willows rang the bell. The rapidly darkening sky was the color of brushed aluminum; a flawless, silvery gray. Parker watched the starlings swagger back and forth across the distant lawn. After a moment she said, "Maybe nobody's home."

Willows nodded, pushed the bell again. He turned as the door swung open without warning. Melinda Lee stared up at him as if she'd never seen him before.

Parker said, "We'd like to talk to your brother for a moment, if he's home."

"No, he's out. I don't know where."

Willows said, "It wasn't important." He slipped a photograph from his coat pocket. "Have you ever seen this man?"

Melinda Lee stared at Garret's smirking face.

Parker said, "We believe he may have been involved in your father's murder. Tell us, Melinda, have you ever seen him before?"

The child nodded. Her eyes filled with tears.

Parker said, "When?"

"During Christmas vacation."

"Your brother didn't come home for Christmas, did he?"

"No." She pointed at the mug shot. "That man, did he kill my father?"

"It's a possibility. We think . . . " Parker glanced at Willows. "Tell me, where did you see him? What were the circumstances?"

"He was in a car, a shiny red car. Mother had sent me to the store. He drove along beside me, very close to the sidewalk. He was wearing a cowboy hat. He took it off and waved it at me, asked me if I wanted a ride . . ."

"Was he alone?"

"Yes."

"Did you ever see him again?"

"No, never."

Willows showed her a second photograph — a mug shot of Billy. "What about him?"

Melinda shook her head.

202

"This one is Billy. The other one's name is Garret. A couple of cowboys. The best of friends."

"No, I don't know him."

Willows said, "Okay, fine. It doesn't matter." He put the photographs back in his pocket.

Melinda Lee said, "I'll tell Peter you wanted to talk to him."

"It's okay," said Willows. "Don't worry, it wasn't important."

Back in the car, Parker said, "Now what?"

"We wait." Willows started the Ford, drove to the far end of the block, made a U-turn, and parked behind a snow-covered van.

Parker said, "That poor kid."

"Nothing we can do about it."

Parker said, "Yeah, I know. That's what bothers me."

At ten seventeen, almost six hours after they'd set up the stakeout, Peter Lee strolled down the street and entered the house.

Parker called in a request for a backup, two cars. Willows stretched, easing out the kinks. They waited another five long minutes for the black and whites. Willows got out of the Ford and talked to the uniforms. He gave them Lee's description and told them he wanted one car stationed at each end of the block. They checked to make sure the walkie-talkies were working. Willows climbed back into the Ford and drove down the block. He gave the squad cars a few minutes to get into position and then he and Parker got out of the car.

Mrs Lee answered the door. Her eyes widened in surprise. Parker said, "We'd like to talk to Peter, Mrs Lee."

The woman nodded, and stepped aside. Willows and Parker entered the house.

"He's in the bathroom. I'll tell him you're here."

"Thank you." The two detectives followed her down a carpeted hall. She knocked softly on a cream-painted door.

"Peter?"

Willows unbuttoned his coat.

Mrs Lee tried the door. It was locked.

Willows stepped past her and hit the door with his fist. The woman gave him a frightened look.

Parker said, "Is there a key?"

203

"No, the lock is on the inside."

Parker took Mrs Lee by the arm and guided her to one side, out of the way.

Willows kicked hard, the heel of his shoe slamming into the door just below the lock. The door buckled, but held. He braced himself and lashed out again, putting all his weight behind the blow. The door crashed inward, knocked over a chair.

There was water running in the sink, but the room was empty.

Willows checked the window. It was shut tight, but wasn't locked. The backyard was a barren patch of snowy lawn. At the rear, there was a two-car garage.

"Where's the door to the backyard?"

"This way."

Mrs Lee led them into the kitchen. Willows said, "Stay in the house. Keep away from the window." Mrs Lee began to cry. She turned her back on him. Willows pushed open the door. He and Parker hurried down the porch steps. The garage's side door was shut. A single small window faced the house, but the glass was dark.

Willows trotted across the grass to a fence made of vertical cedar boards with a lattice top. The fence was six feet high — the maximum height allowed in the city. Willows swung open the gate. The wide metal door that provided access to the garage from the lane was shut tight. Willows went back into the yard, around to the window. He pressed his face against the dusty glass and saw the dim shapes of two cars; a BMW and a Buick station wagon. The wagon was parked at an odd angle, the front end of the car tight against the side wall of the garage.

Parker said, "The car there?"

Willows nodded. He scrubbed at the glass with the palm of his hand.

"Think he's inside?"

Willows put his ear to the window and heard a faint rumbling; the sound of a car motor. He drew his revolver — a snubnose Smith & Wesson. "He's in there, all right."

They hurried back through the gate. Parker snapped open her purse and drew her .38, moved twenty feet down the alley to the far side of the garage. There was no way of knowing which car Peter was in, or which way he'd turn when he came out of the garage. Willows pounded on the metal garage door. He holstered his gun and grabbed a handle in the door and yanked hard. It didn't move an inch.

Parker looked at him. "He isn't coming out, is he? Christ!"

They ran back into the yard. Willows' foot slammed repeatedly into the door. Wood splintered but the door held.

Willows remembered the station wagon, the way it was parked at an odd angle. He turned to Parker. "We're going to need an ambulance, Claire."

Parker pressed the transmit button on the walkie-talkie. The red battery light flickered and died. She dropped her gun in her purse and sprinted across the melting snow towards the house.

Willows stripped off his coat and wrapped it around his fist. The window was a single pane of glass in an aluminum frame. He shielded his eyes with his left arm and punched at the glass. It cracked and he punched it again. This time it shattered. The sharp stench of carbon monoxide filled his nostrils. His coat was in shreds.

It seemed to take forever to clear the jagged shards of glass away from the frame. He gripped the windowsill, got a leg up. His shoe scraped against stucco. A sliver of glass stabbed into his shoulder. He lost his balance and fell, rolled off the hood of the wagon and landed on his hands and knees on oil-stained cement. The foul and poisonous air burned in his lungs, brought tears to his eyes. The engines of both cars were racing, spewing out carbon monoxide. The boy must have used something to hold down the gas pedals. The station wagon was empty. He yanked at the door but it was locked. The BMW's windows were tinted, and in the fog of exhaust fumes he couldn't see inside. He tried the door. Locked. He leaned back against the flank of the wagon, kicked out. The side window exploded. He unlocked the door. Peter Lee was slumped behind the wheel. Willows grabbed his arm and pulled.

Lee had fastened his seatbelt. Willows fumbled with the buckle, got it free and dragged Lee's body across the seat, out of the car. He pulled the boy's limp body towards the rear of the garage, tripped and fell, crawled forward until his head banged into a wall.

Yelling. Somebody was yelling at him.

Claire.

Her voice seemed very far away.

He struggled to regain his feet. His groping hands found a smooth surface. The wall. He shuffled sideways. His fingers hit a switch and slid away. He couldn't stop coughing. His throat was tight, his eyes streaming with tears. His lungs were burning and he'd lost all sense of direction. His hands fluttered across the wall. The tips of his wide-spread fingers bumped into the switch. He pushed up. The switch didn't move. He felt the last of his strength draining out of him. The sensation was incredibly physical. It was as if his will to live was a crystal clear liquid, and his body had been breached and it was all pouring out of him, his life was draining out of him . . . fading.

The switch must have been installed incorrectly. The wiring . . . He pushed down instead of up.

There was a dull grinding as the electric motor began to reel in chain. After a moment, the door began to lift slowly from the ground.

A flock of starlings swirled like a ragged black cloud through Willows' oxygen-starved brain. He managed a single ponderous step towards the light, and then collapsed.

Parker caught him, held him upright. The garage door continued to inch upward. Willows had a death grip on Peter Lee's body. They fell into the lane.

24

Garret hadn't bothered to fasten his seatbelt, and neither had Billy. There was no time to react. Like synchronized would-be suicides, their helpless bodies tried to take a header through the fractured windshield and into the wreck of the store. But the Cadillac was equipped with all the options, including the latest in protective devices, the airbag. The windshield rushed at Billy and then the bag blossomed in front of him like a great big pillow, swallowed him up and saved his life. The bag was charged by a pressure cartridge. It had been designed to expand in only a few thousandths of a second, and then begin to collapse almost immediately, allowing the occupants of the car to escape.

The airbags functioned perfectly, but something was wrong with Garret; he wasn't moving. Billy yelled at him again, and then saw that a shotgun blast had ripped a chunk out of the top of the bench seat, messed up Garret's left shoulder pretty bad.

Billy wriggled and squirmed, struggled to escape the soft, pillowy clutches of the bag. He managed to get his door open, fell out of the car. The Colt lay on the asphalt. He snatched at it. His ears were ringing. Somebody in a uniform ran towards him. He snapped off three or four shots — under such trying circumstances, it was impossible to keep an accurate count.

The uniform went down, cut a groove through the slush and lay still.

Billy got his feet under him. The Caddy had knocked a pretty fair-sized hole in the wall of the 7-Eleven. There was room enough to walk inside. The interior of the store was a shambles. The big floor-to-ceiling glass display cases of milk and fruit juices and soft drinks had tumbled. Must be a million cans of Coke in there, and he was as thirsty as he'd ever been. He squeezed off another shot, not aiming at anything in particular. The bullet hit a gas pump. An old man who'd been tanking up his car was startled into dropping the hose. Premium gasoline splattered across the car's exhaust pipe, burst into flames. Billy stepped gingerly over a concrete building block, reached past the crumpled fender of the Caddy and grabbed an ice-cold can of Diet Coke.

The burning car's gas tank exploded. A jagged piece of shrapnel whizzed through the air and buried itself in the shaggy flank of a Collie tethered to a bike rack next to the front door of the 7-Eleven. The dog bared its fangs and started screaming. Billy had never heard such a nerve-racking sound. So *human*.

Enough was enough.

He started running.

Billy ran in a straight line, following his nose. He hurdled the sprawled-out body lying belly-up in a pool of blood in the middle of Maple Street, stumbled on the curb and bounced off the wall of the liquor store. The impact jolted him hard enough to start him thinking again. He glanced over his shoulder. The car and pumps in front of the 7-Eleven were on fire, bright flames shooting fifty feet into the air. The Caddy's brake lights glowed red and the horn blared endlessly, like a warning that had come far too late. Garret's slumped form was backlit in orange and red. He seemed to have lost interest in the situation, but Billy supposed that was fair enough, given his condition.

Billy sprinted up Maple to Tenth Avenue, turned right. He jogged past an armory, neatly parked rows of military vehicles. Across the railway tracks. Traffic on Arbutus was thick, and moving fast. Billy kept going. He heard the shriek of brakes, another horn. He didn't slow down.

The Pinto was right where he'd left it. He tossed the Python on the front seat and fumbled in his pockets for the keys, then remembered he'd hidden them under the seat.

He found the keys and started the car. The exhaust belched black smoke. Behind him, there was a lurid orange glow in the sky, a flickering light that jaundiced the low-hanging cloud. He could still hear the screaming of the wounded dog. No, sirens. A screaming that filled his head and made it impossible to think clearly. He put the Pinto in gear and floored it and drove straight into the rear end of a Ford pickup. The Pinto's headlights shattered and died.

Driving blind, Billy headed for the big house on Point Grey Road.

Nancy wanted to go to a movie, but Tyler wasn't in the mood. She cleaned up the kitchen and dining room while he read the evening paper, then shrugged into her coat and drove the BMW up to Broadway and rented a video — a French detective film called *Chou Pantin*. She hung her coat in the hall closet and paid a quick visit to the wine cellar in the basement, chose a dusty bottle of Napa Brothers beaujolais. Maybe a little red wine would start the blood moving through her husband's veins.

When she came back upstairs, Tyler was reading the sports section. He had no interest in baseball or hockey or football, but felt it necessary to stay abreast of the sporting news in order to function in casual office conversation.

Nancy used a gas-powered opener to pop the Napa Brothers cork. She took two glasses from the shelf above the refrigerator and placed the bottle and glasses and two soft-pink cloth napkins on a mahogany tray, carried the tray into the living room on her way to the stairs.

Tyler neatly folded the sports section and tossed it on the coffee table.

"What's going on, Nance?"

"I rented a movie. I'm going to watch it upstairs."

Tyler nodded. "Two glasses, huh. Thirsty?"

"I thought you might care to join me."

"What's the movie?"

Nancy told him. He frowned. "Is it . . . sexy?"

"It's a thriller."

"A sexy thriller?"

"Not that I know of, Tyler."

"Subtitles, or dubbed?"

Nancy gave him a look. She hated dubbed films, and Tyler knew it. It was one of the things they'd had in common, before they were married and Tyler got rich and she started feeling middle-aged and neglected.

Tyler said, "Be up in a minute." He scratched his stomach.

Nancy, climbing the thickly carpeted stairs, wondered why it was that as men got older, their pants got baggier and their shirts got tighter.

She went into the master bedroom, put the tray down on the nightstand on her side of the bed, walked across the room and slipped the video into the VCR. A tiny red light glowed brightly. The universal remote control was on top of the television. Tyler went into a rage if he had to go searching for it. In his life, there was a place for everything and he strongly believed everything should be kept in its place. Including his wife.

Nancy picked up the rectangle of black plastic and punched several buttons, careful of her fingernails. The Sony flicked into life and then the VCR made a nasty whining sound. She fast-forwarded to the FBI copyright warning and stabbed delicately at the PAUSE button. The screen held steady.

She poured herself a third of a glass of wine and drank it down and poured herself another.

The hall light went out and Tyler walked into the bedroom. He glanced at the screen and then at Nancy and then back at the screen. He said, "I'm going to take a quick shower."

Nancy said, "Okay," in a neutral tone of voice.

Tyler tilted his head and raised his eyebrows. He gave her a ridiculous, leering wink. "Care to join me?"

"I'll have to think about it."

Tyler grinned and said, "I'll soap you in all those special places you like so much but can't quite reach."

Nancy said, "Now I've *really* got some thinking to do."

Unbuttoning his shirt, Tyler went into the ensuite and shut the door softly behind him.

Billy couldn't stop thinking about Garret, if he was dead, and what *that* was like. At the time, scrambling to get free of the car, the shoulder wound had been a blur, a red smear. But now, in retrospect, he saw the wound with vivid clarity.

It was just amazing, how much time the two of them had spent joking and bitching and freezing their asses off in that parking lot, waiting. And then it was just amazing how fast it was all over.

Billy knew it was impossible, but he wanted a chance to do it over again, and get it right this time. Take charge, and not be manipulated. As he drove his Pinto due west towards the house on Point Grey Road, he replayed the botched holdup over and over again.

It never took more than a few seconds, and it always came out the same.

Billy had kept Garret on a short leash since the day they'd met, fucking *years* ago. But it was Garret who was first out of the Caddy. And it was Garret who goddamn *ran* at those uniforms, Garret who pulled the Remington's trigger and blew a man away and then swivelled his hips as he worked the pump and fired again. Explosions that rocked Billy's world.

They'd sat around in his living room, drinking beer and practising the techniques of murder, drawing down on talk-show hosts. Talking about *firepower*. What a gun could do to a man.

Billy'd never had the faintest idea.

Garret pushed aside the partially deflated airbag. He crawled out of the Caddy and stumbled across Maple Street, back to the liquor store parking lot. The armored car's emergency siren was still screaming. He stared blankly down at the two guards with their faces shot off and nothing there but hamburger. He glanced up, looked all around, and yelled, "Billy!"

The manager of the liquor store waited until Garret's back was turned and then crouched and scooped up a dead man's .38.

Garret heard the scrape of metal on asphalt. He turned and fired. The load of buckshot struck the man in the chest. Garret was shooting with one arm and was in a considerable amount of pain. It was a lucky hit and he'd have gladly admitted it, had anyone asked.

Predictably, no one did.

Garret lowered the shotgun until the muzzle touched the asphalt, braced the weapon between his knees and shoved two fresh shells into the chamber and worked the slide. People were running in all directions, scattering like rabbits. A wealth of targets, but the sucker he really wanted to puncture was long gone.

He had a pretty good idea he knew where to find him, though.

Nancy sipped a little more wine and then began to take off her clothes. She wasn't at all sure that she was in the mood, just yet.

But on the other hand, Tyler's invitations were far too infrequent to ignore.

Traffic on Point Grey Road slowed and then came to an abrupt stop. Billy wondered if some fool'd had an accident. Then he saw the black and white, and the cop with the flashlight. The car behind him was too close for him to back up. Not that he was much inclined to take a detour. He worked the Pinto's gearshift, making sure the car was in low gear, and cradled the Python in his lap. There was only one cop. As he inched closer, he kept the nose of the Pinto up against the rear bumper of the car in front of him, so the cop couldn't see the smashed headlights. He lit a cigarette, rolled down his window and cocked the Colt.

The cop glanced up, and then looked away. He waved his arm. The car in front of Billy moved forward. He hit the gas, and the Pinto bucked and lurched and all of a sudden he had his second rear-ender of the night.

The cop's flashlight lanced towards him. Squinting, Billy fired into the blinding white eye of the beam. The light skidded sideways, and down. Billy raised his arm to protect his night vision and pulled the trigger again, shot through the Pinto's windshield and right through the rear window of the car in front of him.

The car bolted down the street, tires screeching, and Billy gave chase. He was half a block away when he heard the wail of the siren. The lights of the black and white filled his mirror.

Billy shifted into second. Better. The car in front of him swerved sharply off the road, and rolled.

He heard a popping sound behind him, the dull *thwack* of a police wadcutter hitting metal. His faithful Pinto lurched as a tire blew out. There was an intersection just ahead. Waterloo Street. The name meant nothing to him. He yanked on the wheel. The Pinto drifted across the road and up on the boulevard. He pushed open the door and jumped, mowed snowy wet grass with his face, ended up on his hands and knees.

The crippled Pinto struggled up the boulevard. Billy scrambled to his feet. He jumped a fence and started running.

The cops would bring dogs to sniff him down. Pals of that goddamn Collie, probably. He needed something to spoil his scent. A sudden rainstorm, or a creek. Why was it that there was never a creek around when he needed one?

In the distance, someone shouted. A heartbeat later the night was splintered by a sound Billy had come to know all too well; the percussive thunder of a revolver fired at full speed.

Garret was dead. Bad enough, but now they'd got the Pinto, too.

Nancy waited until Tyler had finished showering and then turned the temperature up a little and let the water beat down on her. Tyler'd made a few moves on her and hadn't done too badly, all in all. But the truth was she had a hard time feeling sexy when he was wearing that goofy plastic shower cap.

She bent from the waist and ran a palm lightly up the calf of her leg. Her skin was soft and smooth. No need to use the razor. She counted to one hundred, as slowly as she knew how, then turned the water off and stepped out of the shower. She liked to keep Tyler waiting; it honed his appetite. But the timing had to be just right. If she left him too long, she'd come in and find him sound asleep. Dreaming of stocks and bonds, no doubt.

She towelled herself dry and brushed her hair, used her lipstick and pursed her lips and knelt to kiss away the excess on the end sheet of the fat roll of designer toilet paper. Now why in the world had she done that? Tyler probably wouldn't even notice, and if he did, he certainly wouldn't think it was very funny. Instead of laughing, he'd probably insist on trying to make sense of what she'd done, *analyze* her.

Nancy opened the bathroom door and switched off the light. Tyler was sitting up in bed, a glass of wine in his hand. He turned towards her and said, "Where's the goddamn remote, Nance? I can't find it anywhere."

Garret found a Volvo with a woman in it, crouched on the floor with her mouth full of purse. It took him a minute to work out that she was biting the purse to stop from screaming. He reached over with his left arm and patted her on the rump, wanting her to know how much he appreciated the peace and quiet.

Billy ran two blocks and then collapsed behind a low stone wall, his chest heaving. A black and white zipped past. He waited until he had his wind back and then lit a cigarette and crossed the street. The house was dark but the matching Mercedes were both in the garage, safely tucked away for the night. Billy climbed the fence and went around to the back of the house. He was on familiar ground now. The thought calmed him.

Somebody had folded up the deck chairs and leaned them against the side of the house. Mist rose from the pool, drifted into the black sky. He pressed his face against the sliding glass door and peered inside, then tried the door. It wasn't locked. He stepped inside. The house was silent. He slid the door shut behind him. There was a fire in the living room. He ambled over to it and warmed his hands.

Nancy turned off the bedside lamp and eased into Tyler's arms. The room was filled with a soft blue light from the freeze-frame FBI warning. Tyler hit the remote and the film started. His skin was still damp from the shower. The actors spoke their lines and the subtitles flashed across the bottom of the screen. Nancy lay with her head on her husband's chest and stared dreamily out across the black water at the constellation of lights that was West Vancouver.

Garret pried the purse out of the woman's mouth and turned it upside down and dumped the contents on the car seat. There was a lot of stuff in there that was new to him, that he was curious about. But no keys. He said, "Where's the fucking keys, lady?" and then saw that they were in the ignition.

He crouched low in the seat and reached up to adjust the rearview mirror so he could watch the action in front of the liquor store. Looked like every cop in the city had come to the party.

He said, "We're just gonna sit here until the dust settles, and then we're gonna go for a little ride and I'm gonna let you go. Okay?"

The woman started crying.

"That's the idea," said Garret. "Get it out of your system, you'll feel better."

It was cold in the car. He could feel the warmth leaking out of his body, a stiffening in his joints. The woman's sobbing had taken on an oddly soothing rhythm. The sodium-vapor lights that illuminated the parking lot flickered on and off. He wondered how the fire in front of the 7-Eleven had started. The parking lot slipped in and out of focus.

He leaned back and closed his eyes, knowing a little rest would do him good.

Someone upstairs was speaking in a foreign language. Billy went over to the landing at the bottom of the stairs, his boots silent on the carpet. He whispered, "Is that you, Nancy?" and reached out to lay a hand on the banister. Much to his surprise, he found he was still carrying the Python.

He didn't know quite what to do, how to handle the situation. He cocked his head, listening. He heard the soft hiss of the gas fireplace and distant mumble of voices. He started up the stairs, going slowly at first and then losing his patience, suddenly in a hurry, taking the steps two and three at a time.

An apparition danced in front of the lights. Nancy blinked. It was still there. A reflection. She rolled over on her side, heedless of Tyler. A kid in jeans and a black leather jacket stood there in the bedroom door, staring at her.

Tyler sat up. He said, "Who the hell are you?" And then he grabbed his bathrobe and said, "Get the hell out of here, or I'll call the police."

The kid ignored him. He only had eyes for Nancy.

Tyler shrugged into his bathrobe. He stood up. The kid showed him the gun.

Tyler hesitated.

Nancy said, "He's the one who . . . "

Billy said, "I'm in big trouble, Nancy. You have to help me."

Tyler tied a knot in the terrycloth belt of his robe. Nancy watched him, the way his hands moved, with so much purpose. As if he was giving himself time to work things out, make a decision. He had a way of tying the knot so the two ends of the belt hung straight down. He'd worked it out himself. Just one of those little details that made his life so full.

She said, "Tyler, be careful." The words sounded ridiculous, but she couldn't think of anything else to say.

Tyler moved around to the foot of the bed. Billy pointed the Python at him. Tyler said, "Get the hell out of my house, kid." Billy smiled as coldly as he knew how. He stuck the pistol in the waistband of his jeans. His hand hovered over the butt. He said, "Try me."

Nancy would never forget the savage, unflinching look in Tyler's eyes as he rushed at Billy, determined to bring him down.

Billy yanked the Python out of his jeans and pulled the trigger three times, just as fast as he could. The hammer fell on the spent casings and made a dull click that was about as ominous as some old geezer clacking his teeth while he waited for a bus.

Tyler snatched the empty, useless gun out of Billy's hand. He swung wildly and hit Billy flush on the nose and knocked him on his ass.

Billy ran. Tyler chased him down the hall. Billy jumped the banister and landed halfway down the stairs, tumbled head over heels to the bottom and regained his feet and hot-footed it through the living room and shiny kitchen and then, still picking up speed, right through the plate-glass door.

The glass exploded. Billy shrieked, and brought his hands up to his bloody face. His momentum carried him across the frosty yard towards the glass fence and killer drop to the beach. His boots hit the slush-covered slate flagstones surrounding the pool and he cartwheeled through the air as spectacularly as if he'd been thrown from a horse.

Tyler heard the dull thud as Billy's head smacked the unforgiving tiles, saw his body go limp. Billy slid into the steaming water.

Vanished in the mist.

Tyler put the Colt stainless down on the counter. He had kicked off his shoes when he was reading the paper in front of the fireplace. He slipped the shoes on his bare feet and crunched across the shattered glass towards the pool. Billy was lying face down in the water, a halo of pink around his head. Tyler watched him for what seemed like a very long time but was probably only a few minutes. He went back into the kitchen and dialled 911. The operator answered after nine rings. She made him repeat his name and address and asked him if it was an emergency call.

Tyler said yes. She asked him to please stay on the line until a patrol car arrived. He thanked her for her interest and hung up.

He climbed the stairs and paused just out of sight of the bedroom doorway. The kid seemed to know Nancy very well. He'd spoken as if they were close friends. Or something worse. Tyler wondered if there were any questions he should ask. He decided the answer was no, and went into the bedroom and took his wife in his arms and comforted her as best he could.

It didn't take the cops long to get there. When Tyler complimented them on the speed with which they'd arrived, one of them said they happened to be in the neighborhood.

Tyler smiled, not sure whether he was being kidded or not. He wanted to get back upstairs to his wife but hung around out in the yard because he didn't want to risk appearing disinterested in the body, callous.

Eddy Orwell shone his flashlight into the steaming pool. He ran the beam of light slowly down the length of Billy's body, across the black leather jacket, tight jeans and silver-studded boots. It was the cowboy from the liquor store shooting, not much doubt about it. The dirty bastard who'd blown away the armored car guys.

Tyler said, "Is he dead?"

"How long's he been in there?"

"About ten minutes."

"Yeah, he's dead, all right."

The way the detective was looking at him, it seemed to Tyler that an explanation would be in order. He said, "He broke into my home. And he threatened my wife with a gun."

"No rush, but have you got a pike pole, something like that, we can use to get him a little closer so I can pull him out?"

Tyler nodded, started to turn away.

Orwell sniffed the air. "Another thing, Mr Crown. It's none of my business, but have you thought about maybe using a little less chlorine?"

25

Willows had lost consciousness by the time the paramedics got to him. He lay on his back on the icy asphalt as they affirmed that he was breathing. His respiration was up — a bad sign. One of the paramedics measured him for the plastic tube that would carry oxygen down his throat and into his lungs. His partner yelled at Willows and shook him hard, applied what should have been a painful amount of pressure to the web of flesh between Willows' index finger and thumb.

No response.

They intubated him. The oxygen began to flow. A quick head-to-toe check confirmed that Willows had no other visible injuries.

Parker hovered anxiously in the background while they gently laid her partner on a gurney and lifted him inside the ambulance. He was hooked up to a cardiac monitor. Parker climbed inside. The doors slammed shut and they got underway, the siren clawed its way up the scale.

"No signs of arrythmia."

Willows' vital signs — blood pressure and pulse — were optimistic. A small flashlight was used to check his pupil reflexes. A few minutes later, he began to gag.

"Valium?"

"Don't think we need it. His oxygen level's climbing fast. Let's pull the tube."

Willows opened his eyes. He focused on Parker and then the intravenous line running into his wrist. "What the hell's that for?"

"In case we needed to administer drugs."

"Get rid of it." Willows' voice was thick, sluggish. He struggled to sit up.

"Take it easy, now. How're you feeling?"

"I could use an aspirin." Willows' centre of gravity shifted as the ambulance turned a corner. "Where we going?"

"Grace. Be there in a couple of minutes."

Willows glared at Parker. "What about Peter Lee?"

"He didn't make it, Jack."

"We gotta go back."

"First things first, fella." The paramedic smiled down at him. "We have to X-ray you, make sure we didn't do any damage to your lungs when we stuck that tube down your throat."

"Turn this thing around." Willows yanked at the tape holding the intravenous in place.

The paramedic laid a hand on his shoulder. "It's okay, I'll do it."

Up front, the radio crackled and the driver said, "Holy Christ."

Parker heard the phrase "shots fired". She said, "What's going on?"

"Couple of guys robbed an armored car at Maple and Broadway. There's four or maybe five people been shot, a gas station on fire, cars exploding all over the damn place."

The radio crackled again.

"Fuckin' Wild West shootout," shouted the paramedic. "They're wearing cowboy hats, high-heeled boots. Drove off in a black Cadillac."

"Hit it," said Willows. "Let's move."

It took them eighteen minutes to make the three-mile run through heavy traffic. The parking lot in front of the Safeway and liquor store was thick with police cars and fire trucks and ambulances. A temporary command post had been set up. The Emergency Response Team was in full warpaint and the dog squad was all bright-eyed and snarly. Reporters and photographers and mini-cam units from the local papers and radio and TV stations fought to interview or photograph anything that moved.

The gas pumps had been shut off and the fire at the 7-Eleven was under control, but still burning. The shrill screams of the wounded echoed across the street. Willows and Parker jumped out of the ambulance. Willows saw Bradley and a vice cop named Kearns standing by the armored car. He and Parker hurried across the lot.

"What's the situation, Inspector?"

"We've got five fatalities. Three Loomis people, a guy who worked at the liquor store, and an old guy who was in the wrong place when the pumps went up." Bradley had an unlit cigar in his mouth. He spat a shred of tobacco in the general direction of a mini-cam crew. "The perps both got away. No wonder, a mess like this."

A cop ran up with a message slip. Bradley read it and said, "Scratch one. They got him in a house on Point Grey Road."

Parker said, "How'd his partner get away?"

"On foot." Bradley scratched his nose. "In all this slush, the dogs couldn't track a can of Alpo."

Willows surveyed the parking lot. It was almost a block long. There was a gardening shop at the far end, surrounded by a high wooden fence. At a guess, there were probably a hundred and fifty or more cars in the lot.

"The Tenth Avenue exit secured?"

Bradley nodded. "We're waiting for the ERT guys to get their act together. In the meantime, we've got all these people want to go home and make dinner, watch themselves on the news."

Willows turned to Parker. "Let's take a walk."

Bradley said, "What's on your mind, Jack?"

"Nothing in particular. Just thought we'd take a look around."

"I don't think that's such a hot idea. A couple more minutes, we'll get organized."

Willows said, "We lost the Lee kid."

"Yeah, I heard."

"If we'd been a bit quicker, he'd still be alive and kicking."

"In a cell," Bradley pointed out, but Willows was already walking away.

Bradley searched his pockets until he found a match, fired up and lit the cigar. A kid in a black snowsuit tried to pet a police dog, and was snatched away by his mother. Better count your fingers, kid. Bradley blew out the match, pinched it between his fingers and dropped it in his pocket.

The parking slots were in a herringbone pattern; two double rows and one single. The yellow lines had been obliterated by the snow and slush, but for the most part the drivers had stuck to the pattern. Willows and Parker had each taken one double row, and were moving slowly towards the far end of the lot. Bradley saw a flash of light on Parker's badge as she bent to look in a window. Most of the cars were empty, but exhaust fumes trailed from half a dozen vehicles. Probably the people inside were listening to the radio and wondering when the hell they were going to get out of there.

Not until we've got your name, address and telephone number, thought Bradley, grinning malevolently.

At the far end of the lot, a pale blue Volvo station wagon was parked up against a fence. There was something about the car that was wrong; a jarring note. Willows moved a little closer. His head throbbed. Parker saw that something had caught his attention and ran towards him.

Willows said, "The Volvo. There's nobody inside, but the windows are fogged up."

Parker said, "Could be the family dog, Jack." She drew her revolver.

"Check the rearview mirror," said Willows.

The Volvo's interior was dark, but Parker saw that the rearview mirror had been turned at right-angles to the windshield, providing a view of the parking lot to anyone crouched down inside the car. She glanced over her shoulder. A hundred yards behind them, the ERT team and dog handlers were fanning out for a sweep of the parking lot. She waved, but no one looked up.

"Let's just hold our position, Jack. They'll be here soon enough."

"Maybe not."

Parker hurried to keep up as Willows walked briskly towards the Tenth Avenue exit. He said, "He can see out the side and he can see behind him, in the side mirror. But he's blind at the front."

"You hope."

They circled around to the front of the Volvo and then crouched and moved towards the car. Parker knelt by the front bumper, her left hand pressing up against the chrome grill with its distinctive diagonal bar.

Willows continued along the side of the car, staying low. He made it as far as the driver's door, reached up and got a firm grasp

221

on the door handle. He glanced behind him. Parker nodded. He yanked open the door.

The woman was down on her knees in the cramped space between the gas and brake pedals and the seat. Her upper body lay across the seat. Her head was turned towards Willows but her eyes were closed.

Garret was on the floor on the passenger side of the car. The sawed-off barrel of the shotgun was pointed straight at Willows' face. Garret's eyes were wide open. He looked dead, but he wasn't, not quite. Rivulets of dried blood, dark brown and glossy, trailed from his nostrils and open mouth, down his chin and chest and across the barrel and polished wooden stock of the gun.

Willows leaned into the car. He said, "Hi, Garret. We've been looking for you." He pressed the barrel of his .38 lightly against Garret's upper lip. The shotgun's safety catch was mounted in the trigger guard. Willows reached past the woman and flicked the safety on. He said, "Kenny Lee. You remember him?"

Garret blinked.

Willows pushed his revolver a little harder into Garret's face. "You tortured that poor old man to death, didn't you? Decided you liked killing people and making easy money, is that what happened? Five corpses back there, Garret. I hope you got enough of it to last a lifetime, because that's how long you'll be gone."

Willows helped the woman out of the car. She began to cry. Parker made soothing noises, but was careful not to touch her.

Willows said, "We need an ambulance, Claire."

But first he had to take care of that sharp thorn in every cop's side, section 10(b) of the Canadian Charter of Rights. He turned to Garret. "You're under arrest. You have the right to retain and instruct counsel without delay. If you can't afford a lawyer, legal aid will be made available."

The woman Garret had held hostage began screaming, a terrible, keening wail.

Willows said, "I'll tell you something. I wish to God that when I opened that car door, you'd tried to pull the trigger one more time. And I'll tell you something else. Six months from now, you're going to wish it too. Know why? Because you're going to be real popular in the joint. Those cons are going to love you to death, kid."

Garret blinked again.

Except for that single tiny movement, he was so still he might've been frozen solid.